The Sparrow's Path

Neal Ghosh

To Rachel and Leela

Saturday

"I don't know why Linda invited me to dinner on Thursday," Barbara pondered aloud. "That's the thirteenth, doesn't she know I have a dentist appointment on the thirteenth? I can't go, I just can't. I mean I'd love to, it was lovely for her to invite me, but really how could she expect me to show up after going to the dentist? She's a sweetheart but it's like, 'Hello?' there are other people to think about other than yourself, you know? I said there are other people to think about, Julian. Julian, are you there?"

Julian cradled the phone between the side of his head and right shoulder. He was crouched down on his haunches in the sunroom, adjusting and re-adjusting the configuration of the automatic litter box. The machine consisted of a globe-shaped chamber which rested on motorized gears that rotated the apparatus counter-clockwise and back, separating the waste from the litter and letting it fall into a basin below. Unfortunately, the chamber had slipped off the gears, with the front opening, meant for the cat to enter, stuck in a transitory position and the litter siphoned into a side-pocket, unusable in its current state. Julian had tried the reset button, plugging and unplugging the motorized basin, and manually lifting and repositioning the globe, to no avail.

Franny paced back and forth between Julian and the sunroom door, processing the scene before her. A functioning litter box was by far her preferred option, one she had utilized many times in the past with a high rate of satisfaction, but the reality that it may not be available was gradually creeping in, transforming the pointed glare on her face from annoyance to concern. She had gone outside the box a few times before, mostly when Julian returned home after disappearing for a few days, and it wouldn't really be all that much trouble for her to head over to the foyer by the front door and do her business. To Julian, it appeared as though her current dilemma -- flee to the front door or wait for the litter box to work -- was less about the pros and cons of each alternative, and more about whether she ought to have faith in him, to back him and his ability to fix the litter box she so coveted.

Julian did not want to disappoint Franny; she was a well-behaved cat who, outside of natural and reasonable cravings for food and attention, did not demand much maintenance. Yet he knew each loop she took around the sunroom -- intensifying in pace and agitation -- was like a timer counting down the moments until his time was up. It was all up to him, and he could feel the anxiety of the moment swell in his head, clouding his judgment even as he listened to and tried to empathize with Barbara and her consternations.

He tried to convince himself that he would be able to maintain the dialogue with Barbara even as he fixed Franny's litter box, but Barbara began to detect his distraction over the phone, and Franny started to scratch the sunroom carpet in the rhythmic, cyclical swoops that signalled her moment of release was fast approaching. His anxiety rapidly morphed into panic and despair. He was failing both of his companions at the same time and for a brief moment the weight of his shortcomings felt like it would buckle his ankles and send him sprawling to the ground.

Franny, you deserve to shit in your box, and I really wanted to make that happen for you, he confessed to himself. Upon resigning to her fate while preparing for the moment which was now imminent, Franny stopped in the middle of the sunroom carpet, faced Julian, braced herself in a hovered squat, and commenced her business.

"Linda is just trying to be friendly. She probably didn't know about your appointment. I wouldn't take it personally," Julian blurted back. To his surprise, his response was both appropriately within the context of Barbara's lamenting as well as reasonably sound advice. Despite the few seconds of dead air that had passed, Barbara accepted his reply in stride and continued with her appeal for his sympathy.

"But I told her about the dentist three weeks ago! She could have invited me any other day. Now I have to go change my appointment."

As her business concluded, the grimace on Franny's face receded, and she gently began to purr. Julian stood up, releasing the lactic acid which had accumulated in his quads from the prolonged squatting. Whatever had formed behind Franny was obstructed from his view for now, a debt of guilt he knew he would have to pay back later with a copious clean-up job and sustained affection by way of several uninterrupted belly scratches once Franny had forgiven him.

"What's preventing you from going to both?" he probed again. He decided he would stay put until Franny decided to leave. He felt bad for his cat and he was peeved at himself, but the agony of the moment was fading, and the urgent ramifications of the malfunctioning litter box began to dissipate.

"Well after the dentist I'll have to go home, get dressed, drive over to her house..." Barbara trailed off slightly.

"Sounds like you can do both, though, right?"

"Yeah I guess. But still, it would have been nice for her to schedule it another day so I didn't have to rush."

"That's technically true, but she didn't, so are you not going to go just because it's not exactly when you want it to be?"

"No, I guess I'll go."

"Great, sounds like fun. Seems likes she's really --"

"I have to run Julian," she interjected. "I'll talk to you later."

"Okay, bye."

Julian hung up the phone. Franny was on her way out of the sunroom, tail flipped all the way up, in either a sign of protest or relief he couldn't tell. She seemed relatively at ease with the state of affairs. He wasn't sure what to expect from Franny in such a circumstance, but in any case he was glad she didn't want to dwell on it. As she exited, the aftermath of her calamity came into full view. *Well shit*, he thought to himself, then chuckled at the unintended pun. The pile was smelly enough, but pretty manageable compared to what could have been. Based on its presentation he expected a straightforward clean-up and, if he was lucky, no material stains to the carpet. He gave the the litter box a sudden but sturdy jab with his foot, and the globe-shaped chamber snapped into place. The motor kicked on, the chamber rotated back to its resting position, and Franny's litter box returned to working condition. *Well shit*, he thought again, this time with no pun.

As he rummaged through the cabinet underneath the kitchen sink looking for his cleaning products, Julian reflected on his phone call with Barbara and its abrupt conclusion. It was typical for them to spar over her bickerings and complainings, and neither side took it personally, or so he thought. He questioned whether he was too blunt in pointing out that whatever Barb's ill-will towards Linda, it could not possibly be related to a dinner invitation. The argument seemed innocuous enough on its merits, but perhaps his tone of voice was too aggressive in making the case. He was also finding the exact sequence of statements difficult to recall, having occurred in the throes of his lost battle with the litter box.

He didn't beat himself up over it. Barbara was pleasant enough to converse with, but if this was the straw which broke the back of their correspondence, he supposed things could always be worse. Barbara was a sixty-two-year-old woman from Lincoln, Nebraska whom Julian had only met in person once, some ten years ago when he was in college. Her daughter was dating his roommate at the time. The four of them had gone for an enjoyable if awkward brunch, with build-your-own omelets and freshly-squeezed juices coupled with disjointed conversations that inescapably terminated with someone claiming, "Yes, that *is* interesting." The daughter and roommate broke up a few weeks later, at which time Barbara reached out to Julian via email, wanting to know if her daughter was as emotionally unfazed by the split as she claimed to be (she was not, but it wasn't something Julian was going to divulge). Emails about the daughter turned into emails about him, then phone calls with him, and despite Julian losing touch with everyone else from that fateful brunch, he and Barbara stayed in touch ever since. During that time, he could probably count on two hands the number of times he called her. For whatever reasons, she repeatedly decided to call, and he for whatever reasons, he chose, and kept choosing, to pick up.

They mostly talked about her and the collection of details which approximated her life. How she works as an accounts manager at a local fitness center, and drives a Rav4 that broke down two years ago while she was in the middle of the highway. How she vacations in Destin, Florida with her husband though they mostly keep to separate schedules (her: fried oysters and the beach, him: "He doesn't tell me and I don't ask"). How she does not attend a church, but identifies as Episcopal and does not understand the fuss over transgendered people and bathrooms. How she visits her daughter twice a year in Omaha, but her daughter does not visit her. How she has a friend named Linda.

Julian was sure Barbara would call again in a few days. Or mostly sure. They might discuss what happened with Linda's dinner and whether it was enjoyable after her dentist appointment, or they might not. He didn't particularly *enjoy* talking to her, but he wouldn't say that he didn't enjoy it either. He likely would be somewhat unhappy if she were to stop calling altogether, mostly because there was a chance it would create a vacuum of discourse and interaction that would ring like tinnitus in his ears, and he didn't particularly feel like risking the possibility. Though not engaging enough for him to recall any highlights or sense of fulfillment from their relationship, his correspondence with Barbara was preferable to no correspondence at all.

After cleaning up the sunroom, Julian retired to the den in his apartment. Unlike the sunroom, which had floor-to-ceiling windows that faced the open air, the den had one small window which faced an office building. Even though it was Saturday, he noticed that the man who works in the office directly across from him was at his desk, sipping a glass of water and browsing his LinkedIn profile. He was balding at the top of his head, the open ring of white scalp piercing through the window glare. The den had two pieces of furniture, a Murphy bed and a television. Julian liked watching TV in the den, but while doing so he could never figure out if he should sit or lie down on the bed. Sometimes he started a show while lying down only to fall asleep, other times he sat with his back perfectly upright all through the night only to be stiff the next day. He thought about buying a chair a few months ago, but never did it.

This time, he settled on a hybrid sitting-up, lying-down position, letting his legs and chest lie flat, shoulders and head propped up by pillows. He grabbed his tablet and checked his news feed with an opening headline of *Civil Engineer Retires at Thirty-One with Nest-egg of $1.1 Million*. The story described the life of Betty Thom of Toronto, who started working right out of college at 21 years of age. Her starting salary was $70,000 (all figures converted to USD) per year, of which she saved $50,000 by renting one room in a house and eating either Ramen, Spaghetti-o's, or canned tuna for lunch and dinner each day. There was no mention of what she ate for breakfast. Each year her salary grew but she did not change her living and eating habits, investing in a stock market which accrued a healthy 9.7% per year annually. Coupled with a small pension and some government funded assistance, Betty plans to live on $33,500 per year without gainful employment for the rest of her life.

Julian began to think about his life, and how it compared to Betty's. At thirty, he was a year younger. While she was a civil engineer, he was a business analyst for Chimera Solutions, a medium sized management consulting group with offices in six major metropolitan areas. He had roughly $150,000 in assets tucked away in his brokerage accounts, seemingly on course for someone of his age and expertise. He couldn't imagine what he'd do with himself with no job or career, and it also seemed kind of arbitrary that one would choose to live on only $33,500 a year. Yet while reading the article he couldn't help but to feel that he was falling behind, as if he were falling short of others who were doing more and better than him. It made the prospect of returning to work on Monday much less promising. He looked out the window at the man in the office; despite facing away from Julian, he seemed to be nodding his head in agreement.

Franny, seemingly unfazed by her recent turmoil with her little, entered the den and decided to join him on the bed. Curled up near his feet, purring away, she exuded a peace and tranquility which calmed Julian in his current mood.

Sunday

Bo's Diner serves omelets, waffles, pancakes, breakfast plates, fresh juices, bagels with accoutrements, and coffee from an in-house espresso bar. The establishment opened in 1974, seats 14 tables and 60 customers at max capacity, and asks customers to order at the front register before seating themselves and waiting to be served. The restaurant's namesake, Bo, was a semi-retired commercial real estate developer who enjoyed taking pictures with loyal patrons, photographs of which decorated the tables underneath the fiberglass tops. Julian was picking at a beef brisket and egg hash, accompanied by his friend and Chimera colleague, Zane.

"401(k)s and traditional IRAs are a total crock of shit," Zane opined, chomping on cut-up sausage patties in between sentences. "Roth's are the way to go. You see, with Roth IRAs you pay taxes on the contributions upfront but you get to withdraw from the account tax-free. Those other options have it backwards. Then when it's time to retire you get hit with a huge tax that eats up half your money. No thanks, man, no thanks."

Zane was a few years younger than Julian, but always asserted himself as the older and wiser half of the friendship. Zane had lots of guidance and directives to offer the world, and Julian had no problem absorbing them, if only to make sure the world didn't ignore them altogether. With a crew cut, trimmed beard, white, splotchy skin, and a steadily-expanding waistline to pair with his tall, barrel-chested frame, Zane was made to fold seamlessly into corporate America, and seemed to know it despite anyone telling him so. Two years ago, Zane was an intern at Chimera, inserting terms like 'synergy' and 'operational excellence' into everyday conversation as much as he could. It was likely that within six months, he would be promoted to assistant project manager, and technically, Julian's superior. And thus, it was vital for him to fully understand all the financial investment options which could ingest the large inflows of cash that would be imminently arriving in his paychecks.

"That's the thing about retirement accounts, any account really. Bunch of Wall Street bigwigs pushing them out to clueless busy-body workers, don't know better than to pour whatever money they got into investments they don't understand. Not gonna be me, man, not gonna be me. Hey Julian, whatcha looking at?"

Julian was staring at a red sparrow that had flown into Bo's and came to rest on a chair at an empty table across the room. The din of the customers' chatter, the clanging of plates and cutlery against one another, the jostling of waiters and waitresses gliding from in and out of the kitchen, none of these external distractions seemed to faze the sparrow as it perched on the seat of the chair, propped up with a sense of pomp and formality, as if it were no different than any other patron who entered the restaurant. Julian was drawn in by the sparrow's earnestness which was only slightly tempered by a tinge of perplexity as to why the tabletop was vaulted above its head and not better positioned to serve a diner of its stature. He was not, as Zane was beginning to surmise, paying attention to Zane's theses on the relative benefits of the Roth IRA.

"Julian, whatcha looking at?"

"Nothing. Thought I saw a guy I know."

"Where?" Zane, turned over his left shoulder and perused the general space where Julian had fixated.

"Doesn't matter. He just left."

"Do I know him?"

"Probably not."

"Who do you know that I don't?"

"Lots of people. Mostly college friends, other folks from my last job."

"How come you haven't introduced me?"

"Just different circles, man. They mostly like to hang out and smoke weed at house parties. Not the lady-killing socialite you are." Julian replied, lifting his eyebrows and flashing a smile, allaying any concerns Zane might have had about threats, real or perceived, to his social standing.

"Hehe. Guess so. Not that I'm a playboy or anything like that," he insisted, despite his appreciation for the indirect praise. "Just living in the moment, ya know? That's what I tell all these girls trying to date me. Don't mind having fun with them but then they start asking to go on real dates and get exclusive and all that and I'm just like, 'Hey, that's not who I am.' What about you, got any irons in the fire?"

"Not really. Was dating a girl a few months back, but nothing really came out of it. Everything was going fine at first. Cute girl, smart, fun. Went out a lot and had even taken some trips to the coast. Not sure what happened next. Just one of those things where you go a few days without texting, then a few weeks, and after that I guess neither of us really cared about doing anything about it."

"Huh, that's never happened to me before." Zane remarked, flummoxed by the contrast of Julian's wilted romance to his own endeavors, and wondering whether he was missing something essential about the dating experience.

"Not a huge deal. Not like I was going to marry her or anything."

"Yeah, true." Zane affirmed, hoping that that somehow settled the issue for him.

They let a few moments of silence pass, reflecting a natural and required break in the dialogue to allow both of them to mentally process the thoughts they were too averse to say out loud. For Zane, knowing that someone else out there had had a promising relationship that slipped away for unknown reasons created within him an inner turmoil, a kind he sometimes felt when there was even a small chance he might not reach his life's full potential, even if he was never sure what that potential was supposed to be. For Julian, he wanted to check back in on the sparrow and its quest to be respected in the land of brunch-eaters. The sparrow was still on the same chair, patiently awaiting its turn to be recognized. Julian was of two minds, one which admired the sparrow for its fearlessness, and one which bemoaned it for the existential disappointment which it was imminently about to face. A waitress came through, ushering a family of four and with a mind to seat the family at the table that the sparrow had until now staked as its own. As the waitress drew near, the red sparrow, sensing the inevitability of its eviction, rose up and flew out of the restaurant. Julian was glad the sparrow took flight in advance of being shooed away.

"Tomorrow. I hear you have a meeting with the CEO. Know what that's about?" Zane inquired, rekindling the dialogue. "No offense, but I don't really know why she wants to meet you. Not that you're not worth meeting or anything, but she's the CEO and you're, you know, well like me too...down the totem pole."

"Yeah, me neither. I was just told about it on Friday. 'Be at Kendra's office Monday at 10.' No context, nothing. Guess we'll find out."

"You're not nervous?"

"Why would I be?"

"Because it's the CEO!"

"Yes, that's true."

"Well, I'd at least prepare a bit or something."

"What do you think I'm having lunch with you for?" Julian fired back, flashing another grin.

Julian, after poking at the last half of his hash, decided he was finished. He and Zane split the bill, walked out of the restaurant, and began to part ways. Zane was going to a female friend's afternoon gathering at her apartment's rooftop patio, and offered for Julian to join. Julian declined.

"Well let me know if you change your mind. See you tomorrow, and let me know what Kendra wanted to talk to you to about."

"No problem. By the way, Roth IRAs only save you money if you have more income when you retire than when you are saving and making contributions. If you are retiring with less income, 401(k)'s are the better way to go."

"Well...yeah." Zane paused, then regrouped. "But I don't plan to retire with less money than I do now, do you?"

"Of course not."

"Right. See ya."

Bo's was 8 blocks from Julian's apartment. He had walked to brunch, and opted to return the same way. It was a sunny Sunday, with clear skies and a crisp, cool breeze blowing toward him, gently lifting the locks of his hair just above his eyes.

As he began his jaunt home, he pondered why he felt the need to lie to Zane about his friends, or more accurately, lack thereof. The truth was Zane was the only person with whom he had regular face-to-face contact. He had lost touch with whatever friends he had had from college. He made work acquaintances at previous jobs, but save a few beers at happy hour and the occasional holiday party he did not see any of them outside of the context of the job. Zane was the first colleague to have forced the issue of becoming friends, an act Julian had not necessarily longed for but was appreciative of nonetheless. He wasn't particularly embarrassed by his dearth of other companions, but in the moment of Zane's interrogation he had felt the path of least resistance was to dodge the issue altogether. He questioned whether not accompanying Zane to his friend's party was a mistake. It no doubt would have been a good opportunity to meet more people. Perhaps next time he would.

He had not lied about his previous relationship, however. Angie (short for Angela or Angelina, he couldn't remember) was by all accounts lovely. He had met her at The Savory Pass, a small cafe on the floor of his apartment building, about six months ago. He was sipping an Americano, and updating a spreadsheet for the project he was working on at the time, when Angie tripped over his backpack protruding in the walkway adjacent to his table. Her lemon poppy cake flew forward and crumbled on the ground. He offered to buy her a new one on the condition that she sit at his table while she ate it. She was a graphic designer for a children's toy store, a divorcee still in her 20s, and had flowing auburn hair that would dazzle in the sunlight. They got along seamlessly at first. He didn't find himself to be all that charming, but Angie was smitten, from her immediate and glowing responses to texts and invitations to dinner, to the first (and only) time she confessed she might love him. Two months in, they drove out to the coast for a weekend getaway with an afternoon picnic on the beach and romantic lodging in a beachside cabin. As they sat on the cabin porch watching the sun set over the water, she began to tear up and whimper gently. He asked her what was wrong. She told him nothing at all, that she happier than she had been in a long time, and wanted to embrace the moment. He took her at her word. The last time he saw her was when he dropped her off at her friend's house the next day.

Though he reminisced pleasantly on their time together, he did not miss Angie now. However, he wondered if having only one person in his life he could claim to be a friend -- or claim to be close to at all -- was enough. There was Barbara, and of course Franny, through perhaps cats didn't count in this equation. There were also Julian's parents, who lived in Vermont. He had last seen them two years ago, and last spoke two weeks back during their monthly, cordial, and mostly routine phone calls. He had a brother in New York City, but they never talked, except when they visited one another every few years, and relished each other's company like long lost best friends, up until the moment it was time to go back to their separate, estranged lives. Put together, Julian questioned if he -- between friend, family, persistent mothers of past friend's girlfriends, and a cat -- he had sufficiently approximated the full spectrum and richness of human interaction.

He turned the final corner on his way home, and spotted an elderly gentleman, doubled over a toolbox on the sidewalk, muttering indistinctly. The gentleman was standing on a small plot of land about five blocks down from Julian's apartment building. A worn, single-story shack with an adjoining garage was located on the back half of the plot, allowing an expansive and unkempt front lawn to creep onto the sidewalk lining the street. Julian had seen his neighbor before, sitting quietly and alone on a beach chair plopped right in the middle of his lawn, gazing into the distance with a can of something in one hand and a dwindling cigarette in another. Julian decided he might introduce himself today.

As he walked towards the house, he saw the garage door was open, and began to understand why the man was rummaging through his toolbox. The garage was filled -- from back to front, floor to ceiling, save the room from two openings for getting in and out -- with old appliances in various states of dismemberment. Refrigerators, car engines, computer monitors, coffee makers, lawn mowers, boomboxes and walkmans which must have been at least twenty years old, all spread out on shelves adorning the walls or work tables in the center. The neighbor was still bent over his toolbox when Julian approached.

"Hello. Nice day today."

"Fuck, fuck, fuck it all." The neighbor continued to mutter, ignorant of Julian's overture.

"I'm Julian. I live down the road in the building above The Savory Pass."

"Just one fucking thing I need..."

"Well I thought I'd just say hello." Julian turned to continue his walk home, slightly bewildered at the exchange. Just as we was about to get going, the man stood up from his toolbox, sweat dripping down the side of his head and vice grip in his hand.

"Oh hey. Sorry, I'm Herb."

Julian could see that Herb was in his forties, with brown but greying bushy hair and leathery wrinkled skin. He was wearing a Hawaiian shirt, buttons opened down to the mid-section, and khakis stained with dirt and other multi-colored substances over which Julian cared not to ruminate.

"Nice to meet you Herb." Julian offered again.

"What do you want?" Herb asked curtly.

"Nothing. Just thought I'd say hello. I've seen you sitting on your lawn a few times before."

"What's it to you?"

"Nothing. Nothing at all."

Herb's expression transitioned from malice to pensiveness, realizing that the inquiring pedestrian might be sincere in his introduction.

"The Savory Pass, eh? Their coffee is shit."

"Their Americano isn't bad."

"Are Americanos coffee?"

"Yes."

"Then they are shit."

"What are you doing with that vice grip?"

"I bought an old typewriter at a flea market. I am going to take it apart."

"Wouldn't you rather repair it?"

"No."

"Why not?"

"Same reason I take apart everything else." Herb pointed at his garage. "Sometimes you have to break things to figure out why they were built in the first place."

Julian returned to his apartment building, entering the front lobby and making his way toward the mail room. He checked his mail every Sunday, and only on Sunday, just to see how empty or full his mailbox would be over a week's time. It was a high-risk, low-reward venture. On some occasions he would open his mailbox only to find a few bits of coupons or junk mail, forcing him to question his relevance to anyone he's ever known or anything he's ever been a part of. On most occasions there would be at least one or two personally-addressed envelopes, just enough to allow him to remain emotionally indifferent to the implications of receiving written notifications to confirm one's existence, and defer the issue to the following week.

On this particular instance, he opened the mailbox, and a pack of bulletins, folded newspapers, and letters sprawled out and onto the floor, desperate to vacate the cramped cannister. He bent down to determine the sources of all these items addressed and sent to him in the last seven days. Reminders to visit the dentist, auto insurance statements, and alumni fundraising requests were among the first culprits when he spotted two blue high heels, and the feet within them, in his periphery.

"You should check your mail more often," said the voice above the shoes.

"I usually never get this much. Not sure what makes me so interesting now."

"Who says you're interesting?"

Julian stopped compiling the mail on the floor and looked up to see who was this stranger giving him unsolicited sass. She had olive skin, short dark hair cropped below her ear, hazel eyes, and a jade stud pierced into her left nostril. The blue high heels were paired with white jeans and a black sleeveless top which exposed her slender but toned arms. She had an impish smirk on her face betraying an amusement at both his physical and argumentative position.

"No one, I guess," he tried to diffuse. "Sorry if I'm in your way."

"You're not. Your mail is."

"Well, shouldn't be much longer." He hurriedly collected the mail from the floor and the remainder from his mailbox, and passed her on the way towards the elevator. "Nice shoes, by the way."

"I know."

Monday

Art on a wall, like a painting in particular, can be a strange thing. It spends most of its life in one place, and largely ignored by anyone or anything around it. With some notable exceptions which hang in climate-controlled, motion-sensored galleries across metropolitan museums, a typical painting endures long stretches of disregard from its human viewers, punctuated only by short bouts of sharp indifference. In rare cases, a painting might activate the mind of someone searching for the wonders of emotion not normally supplied by their lot of ordinary experiences. In the very best case, that someone may be induced into a calming serenity, privileged for a fleeting moment with an elixir of inner contemplation that, like clockwork, dissipates instantly upon the distraction of thoughts like why one ought to care about art in the first place. The rest of the time, paintings are more or less a burst of intriguing colors meant to chop up the monotony of the off-white panels which bridge one room to the next.

Even so, there was a particular painting in Julian's apartment which did not, and very well could not, conform to the boring expectations of its kind. The painting was an illustration of a boy and his dog, walking forward out of the frame, *through* the frame, against a backdrop of a city park adorned with a recreational shed and a small pond. The sky is greyish-blue, the boy is happy in his jaunt, and the dog is following appreciably. This painting, however, is not one of a boy and a dog in a park, at least it *may not* be, depending on which vantage point the observer takes. While it looks like a boy and a dog in the park from one point of view, one slight movement in any direction would reveal another image, that of a murky visage of a melancholy, elderly man. The clouds above -- both light and dark -- sketch out his bushy grey eyebrows and deep grey pupils, while the boy's body -- bright on the left, shadow on the right -- reveals a curved, squiggly nose pointing down to the ground. Flat, motionless lips rise up from the contours of the grass, while flecks of dirt in the ground approximate the man's stubble-ridden cheeks. Streaks of sunlight through the clouds above transform into flashing locks of hair. The dog, once longingly looking to his master, now gazes wistfully at the vast and brooding expression above.

The painting hung in Julian's bedroom, on the wall to the side of his bed. In between the bed and the painting was a small side table with an alarm clock. Every morning, Julian woke up on cue from the sounds of the clock, turning onto his side to turn off the alarm, and opening his eyes for the first time to the sight of this dual-identity art piece. Whether he saw the boy and dog or the grim-faced man is a matter of chance. Sometimes he hoped to see one or the other, but most often he was content to let the painting decide.

On this Monday morning, Julian turned to his side to turn off the alarm, set earlier than most Mondays. *6:09am*. He had already hit snooze once, and the alarm was roaring back to wake him again. He thought to himself: why are the intervals in between snoozes nine minutes? Seemed like an odd number to pick, especially since it was so close to ten, a much more conventional interval to break apart time. Perhaps Herb would have something to say about it, he figured. He turned off the alarm, and opened his eyes to the wall with the painting. On this day, he hoped for the boy and dog.

He saw the old man.

Julian rose out of bed and began his morning routine, which was in many ways Franny's morning routine as well. Brushing his teeth and scratching her ears. Taking a shower and rubbing her belly by the shower mat. Pouring coffee into his mug plus dry food into her bowl. Franny was persistent in demanding her morning needs, beginning her overtures with gentle leanings of her body on and around his legs and gradually escalating in intensity into verbal berating and clawed assaults of the couch. At which point Julian acquiesced to Franny depended on how much patience, free time, and alertness he had while beginning his day. Despite the obvious extortion, Julian rationalized his capitulation by noting that Franny did hold up her end of the implicit bargain between the two of them. After being satiated, she would quiet down and retire to the den for her daytime nap. Though he surmised the sharp turn from unceasing appeals to outright aloofness was inconsiderate on her part, he was also quite envious of her flexibility to not do anything at all. Unlike Franny, Julian's routine did not terminate in a nap, but in grabbing his backpack and heading out the door to work. It was seven forty-five, an earlier departure time than normal. He wanted to reach the Chimera office early in case he could learn more about the meeting he was supposed to have with his CEO. Though he shrugged it off when discussing it with Zane the day before, he was curious if not slightly worried about what it could all mean.

As he made his way to the front door, Julian noticed a piece of paper lying on the doormat. A flier for a local car wash, he realized it must have been from his mail pile which spilled out in the lobby the previous day. He turned the flier over to find a message in black marker:

> *You're just as bad picking up your mail as you are checking it. You're lucky I retrieved this for you. How else would you get your car washed? You can thank me later.*

'Blue Heels' (Lydia, 2-C)

P.S. I like your name, Julian.

This time when presented with her sass, he smiled. Whoever this woman was, she seemed like someone he wanted to get to know more, but checking his watch again he reckoned that would have to wait for another time.

Chimera Solutions, LLC occupied the top three floors of the Odyssey tower, a thirty-story commercial high rise in the heart of downtown's business district. Other, lower floors of the Odyssey were leased by high-end legal offices, well-funded tech start-ups, and other establishments of similar prestige, but the top three were kept on reserve exclusively for companies with enough cash and notoriety to absorb the cost and expectations of such a vaunted position. Aside from a spacious work area with an expansive view, these floors were a staging hub only for organizations in great transition, sometimes an organization in ascent, as Chimera was, with annual revenues quadrupling over the last three years and a #12 listing in the latest Forbes' ranking of Fortune 500 companies of the future; other times an organization in downward spiral, a blue-chip corporation of former glory shedding workforce and crashing into leased office space after being jettisoned from their own proprietary building. The managers of the Odyssey liked to alternate the top-floor tenant between the up-and-out and down-and-dropping varieties every few years to inspire both ambition and humility in the neighboring companies occupying the twenty seven floors below.

When Chimera moved into the Odyssey, they made an unusual request, that the elevators to the twenty-eighth and thirtieth floor be disabled, leaving the middle, twenty-ninth floor as the sole entrance point to the Chimera office. They asked that all entrants -- guests and employees alike -- walk in on the middle floor, and upon passing through reception and security be met with two stairways, one ascending and one descending. There were no offices or work spaces on the twenty-ninth floor, cordoned off by design. Whatever one's business, it would be either on the twenty-eighth floor or thirtieth. The message was clear: *you will be going either up or down. There is no staying put.*

Julian arrived at the office near 8:30am, badging through security and making his descent both in floors and corporate hierarchy. The twenty-eighth floor seated most of Chimera's front-line workers: analysts, sales reps, project managers, assistant project managers, principal consultants, and administrative staff. The floor was about half-full when he arrived, populated by a mix of go-getters eager to outpace their colleagues on the corporate ladder, and those in need of "development" (as HR might say) manically burning through last week's workload before this week's could be assigned. He spotted Zane across the hall past the stairway exit. Zane was normally in the former class of colleague, but the flush in his cheeks and the hurried demeanor he displayed while typing at his desk suggested on this day he was in the latter.

Julian's desk was in the northwest corner of the twenty-eighth floor, in a bullpen of twenty desks facing inward from the windows in concentric right angles. Julian was fortunate enough to hold a desk on the outer edge, meaning every so often he could turn in his seat and look out the windows onto the rest of the city. He could see his apartment building if he bent down and to his right, peeking through two buildings surrounding it. He liked to spot it a few times a day and imagine that he could see Franny straight through from his seat, either napping by the window or on the bed or on the carpet floor. He didn't do it too much, however, so as not to flaunt his window-viewing privileges in front of others with less-appealing seating arrangements, nor signal to any passing executives or other influencers any hint of lethargy or want of work ethic.

Settling into his desk, he began to mull over in earnest his 10:00 am meeting with Kendra McManus, CEO of Chimera. The appointment was in her office, and from what he had gathered in last week's email notification, there would be no other attendees. He had never seen Kendra McManus in person before, let alone meet her, learning about her only through a few magazine articles he skimmed before his job interview and second-hand anecdotes from those co-workers claiming to have made her acquaintance. She joined Chimera five years ago as a junior accounts manager. Prior to her arrival, she had successful stints as an executive in media and telecom. She infamously started at Chimera in accounts to "put the firm before herself," insisting she learn the company's fundamentals from the bottom up. Eighteen months ago, she was anointed CEO, pledging to "rekindle the power of human compassion in creating a better tomorrow." He recalled the day it happened and the hushed water-cooler talk, incredulous but optimistic about her vision. But whether Chimera was doing better or worse with her at the helm is an assessment he thought best left to someone with thirtieth floor pedigree.

He opened his email and started reading through the weekend notifications when Zane approached his desk.

"*Morning.*" Zane proclaimed with emphasis, trying to make a point. "Saw you come in, didn't want to say hi?"

"You looked busy. Work catching up to you?

"Not really. Just some stuff I was planning on doing yesterday, but man that party I went to after brunch was legit. Flip cup and tequila shots on the roof. I am paying for it now though."

"Ha. Sounds fun."

"Ready for your meeting with the CEO?"

"Not really."

"What?! Why not?"

"Co-workers keep bothering me." Julian razzed.

"Bah! Funny guy. You don't know what it's about?"

"Gonna find out soon enough."

"Yeah guess so. I heard that we missed our revenue targets last quarter, and the board is pissed. Something about change in culture, reactive mentality, so on and so on. Don't know what is has to do with you though."

"Me neither."

"It's just weird though, right? No offense to you but *no one* from twenty-eight goes up to thirty even to drop off a report, let alone take a meeting with the CEO," Zane explained. "Thing is just so, *bizarre.*"

"It's why I'm trying not to read too much into it. By the way, how many people were at that party yesterday?"

"Mmmmm...15 or 20 maybe. Most of them friends of the girl I know, which kind of sucked because I didn't know anyone at first, but by the end I had met just about everybody. Why?"

"Just curious. I was thinking I could join you next time, if that's still okay."

"Totally. I'll let you know. Couple girls there that looked like your type."

"What's my type?" Julian asked.

"Um...one that doesn't disappear all of a sudden?"

"Ass."

"Ha! Let me know how that meeting goes."

"Yeah okay."

Julian returned to his monitor and tried to find emails to answer and any other Monday morning tasks which could distract him until his expedition to the thirtieth floor. Unsurprisingly, there were no to-dos of sufficient substance to tie him over. As a business analyst, his responsibility was to conduct data analysis on financial statements, cost structures, competitors' performance, etc. and insert nuggets of insight into pitch decks, reports, or whatever interfaces Chimera used to convey the value of their services to their clients. Practically, this usually meant long stretches of idleness -- attending update meetings, checking email, appearing busy at his desk -- sporadically interrupted by the arrival of a cache of raw data files from a project manager and an obligation to churn out numbers within 48-72 hours. His latest fire drill, a two-day blitz consolidating missing costs from a food distributor's tax filings, occurred early last week, opening up the latter half for catching up on online news articles and extended lunches in the first floor food court. He received the meeting notification with the CEO last Friday during one such lunch, sent from a no-reply email address linked to Kendra's office. He was hoping more context would be offered either then or now but it didn't look like there would be.

The thirtieth floor, against his preconception, looked quite similar to the twenty-eighth. Upon reaching the top of the stairway, Julian observed the same basic hallways and communal areas, only with the bullpens of inward-facing desks having been replaced with private offices stacked against the windows. Lined against one another around most of the floor, the offices were about 8 feet across with floor-to-ceiling glass panes forming the fronts. The only bullpen to be seen was directly in the middle of the floor, where a host of executive assistants manned an assortment of television monitors, fax machines, telephones, and food and coffee trays. From what he could gather, the individuals inside the private offices were executives of some kind receiving guests in their visitor chairs or speaking intently into a hands-free phone. He caught the eye of a man in one of the offices, dressed in a silver-grey suit matching the color of his slicked-back hair. The man looked surprised when he met Julian's gaze, and for a moment, Julian couldn't decide if the glass panes were installed to keep him out or that man in.

He scanned each glass pane for the name of Kendra McManus until he spotted -- in the northwest corner, two floors above his desk oddly enough -- a significantly larger office with frosted panes instead of clear glass. On his way over, he was blindsided by a middle-aged lady of unexpected height and menacing approach, who must have come from the assistants' area.

"May I ask what you are doing?" she asked threateningly.

"Sorry. I received a notification on Friday for a meeting this..."

"Wait -- are you Julian?"

"Yes I am."

"Right this way."

The lady motioned for Julian to follow her as she escorted him the remainder of the hallway to the office of the CEO. After checking her watch to confirm the time, she gently knocked on the door, opened it a few inches, and spoke softly into the opening, averting her gaze from anything which might be happening inside.

"Ms. McManus, your 10:00 am is here."

"Send him in Janine, thanks."

Janine turned to Julian and gestured for him to enter.

"You have fifteen minutes," she instructed. "Don't run over."

Julian entered the office to find, much to his wonderment, a balding man with thick, round, black eyeglasses staring at him, sitting from behind a conference table. This was not Kendra McManus, he understood well enough. He felt compelled to continue through with his entrance and close the door behind him.

"Julian, this is Mort Browning, VP of Creative Intelligence. I'm Kendra, it's nice to meet you."

Kendra McManus stood tall by the window behind her desk, concealed by the door as it opened inward. As she turned to face him, Julian observed a slender woman wearing black flats, a fitted black skirt wrapping her legs from her hips to her knees, and a lavender oxford shirt with the top two buttons undone, revealing a loose silver necklace speckled with amethysts. Her hair was long, blond, straight, and impeccably parted in the middle, with two bobby pins on either side protecting her smooth forehead from the threat of straying strands. Julian knew from her corporate profile that she was fifty-two, but she could have passed for 15 years younger, and the calm, even warm expression on her face suggested she rarely, if ever, let stress get the better of her.

"Please sit down." Kendra offered the seat across from Mort, and Julian hesitatingly complied. Mort never took his gaze off of him.

"Julian, I have a wonderful opportunity that we'd like to share with you," Kendra began. "But first, let me ask you, how do you like working at Chimera?"

"No problems at all. I like my job and hope my performance has been satisfactory."

"Oh, of course, of course. Don't worry about that. Do you know Julian, what are they keys to employee productivity?"

"No, I'm afraid I don't."

"Most people overlook them, but they are *vital* to the sustainable success of any organization. You see, first employees must be given autonomy. That is, a sense of independence from their managers and those who might be considered to have authority over them. After all, we are all human and wish to have some sort of control over our day-to-day lives, don't you agree?"

"Sure."

"And do you feel like you have autonomy in your position, Julian?"

"Sometimes yes, sometimes no. I have a lot of freedom to make my schedule and how I work, but when assignments are given to me there is no real choice except to do exactly what has been asked, and deliver it on time no matter what."

"Very well, very well," Kendra replied. "And the second key is the opportunity to be challenged, and to master the skills which allow you to overcome those challenges. You see, the modern-day workplace is simply an extension of the classroom, and a career a curriculum of lifetime learning. Employees without a challenge are the equivalent of students without course material. In both cases, there will be no learning, and without learning there is no growth. Julian, do you feel like your current roles and responsibility challenge you and allow you to grow?"

"Not really."

"Oh dear," Kendra lamented. "How so?"

"Most of my work consists of repeating the same analysis over and over again, just for different clients. Unless I do it the same way as before, the project manager will send it back and ask me to fix it, even if the new way is better. I don't feel like I am doing analysis to learn new ideas, but to repeat old ideas in a different form."

"Well, I think what you are referring to is known as quality assurance. By making sure our services are delivered exactly as described, we ensure a positive client experience."

"But how can the quality be assured if the analysis is wrong?"

Mort furrowed his brow slightly but kept his eyes on Julian. Kendra continued, as if she hadn't heard his question.

"The third key to productivity is purpose. Purpose of the company an employee works for. If a company has a clear and inspiring purpose, employees view their work not as a job but as a calling, and feel invested in the success of the company as they would their own success."

"Makes sense."

"But you wouldn't say Chimera has a clear and inspiring purpose, would you?"

"No, I wouldn't."

"What would you say is the purpose of a company like Chimera?"

"Help other businesses make money?"

Kendra smiled. "Right, I suppose that might be true." Her eyes widened a bit, and her hands became more exaggerated with her words. "And not just any money, right, but money generated by directly undercutting and exploiting their customers. It's all a big scam, you see."

Kendra's gleeful confession unnerved Julian. He shifted the weight in his seat, and glanced back at Mort, who added a subtle smirk to his unwavering stare. Unsure of what to say next, Julian looked back to Kendra, who had gathered a smirk of her own.

"Well that's what some folks in the press, and certainly our competitors would say, wouldn't they? Yes, from the outside we can be perceived as a soulless instrument of corporate greed, and to be fair, until now, we as a company have not done or said much to offer proof against that claim. You see, back when the board asked me to become CEO of Chimera, I did so only on the condition that I would be given the latitude to transform this company into an institution whose purpose would inspire not only our clients and employees, but the clients and employees of our competitors as well. Simply put, I want Chimera to be the gold standard of a purpose-driven organization."

Julian remained silent. He had not considered by a long shot that this would be the topic of conversation when he stepped in her office. He also was not sure if the topic at hand was the actual reason for the meeting or just a prelude for what was to come.

"I suppose having purpose for a company would be useful," Julian offered flatly.

"Not just having purpose," Kendra corrected, "but knowing and feeling that purpose. Companies today don't *feel* their purpose, in their hearts, in their minds. It's like they are automatons, with no character, no moral compass, no conscientious thought of their own. This is why I brought you in here today. I want you to help Chimera find its humanity. Mort."

Mort straightened his back and offered his hands forward across the conference table. "Your next assignment will be different than your previous work here. We want you to write a novel under the name of Chimera Solutions, and become a finalist for the Man Booker prize."

"What?"

"The Man Booker Prize for Fiction is a literary prize awarded each year for the best original novel, written in the English language and published in the UK."

"I got that. Why do you want me to do this?"

"We at Chimera feel the best way to enhance our brand is by demonstrating to our shareholders that our organization can feel, think, and act as exceptionally as any individual. What better way to make that demonstration than by writing a novel? A successful story captures the essence of humanity in a way that all readers can relate to. We at Chimera believe we have the potential to make this impact on our clients every single day. We also believe that settling for anything less than excellence would send the wrong message about who we are and what our purpose is. That is why you can only write a story which contends for the Booker, an accomplishment at the pinnacle of the literary world, and one to draw acclaim which rebirths our image in the eyes of the public."

"You see," Kendra joined in, "this is the opportunity of a lifetime. Just four years ago, the Booker prize opened its eligibility to authors from all countries, so long as novels were written in the English language. Last year, an American won the prize for the very first time. We are going to make even grander history, and become the first *corporation* to win the title."

"I don't know what to say," Julian thought out loud. "Why me? I'm not an author."

"Why *not* you, Julian?" Kendra fired back. "This company is brimming with potential, from people just like you. It's time that we unshackle you from the ordinary requirements of your current position. It's time we challenged you to achieve something truly great. It's time we reconsidered the possibilities of what you can do with the right purpose."

"When do you want me to start?"

"At Chimera we give employees the autonomy to find and cultivate the right solutions for themselves and for the company," Mort intervened. "With such a task such as writing a story, we recognize any author would need the time and space to be successful. And we want you to be successful, absolutely. You are free to work on the book whenever you like, wherever you like. We believe that with this autonomy and freedom, you can thrive and succeed for yourself and for us."

"And what if I don't?"

"Julian, no, no, no, that mindset simply won't do," Kendra contested. "You have the full support of myself and everyone at Chimera behind you. With a clear mind and purpose, I have absolutely no doubt that you will make us all proud. I'd like you to leave here today full of confidence and with only positive thoughts for the wonderful journey you are about to take." Kendra returned to the chair behind her desk and began to read from her desktop monitor.

Mort took over for Kendra. "Do not ask your manager or anyone else for assistance. It's also important that you do not disclose what you are doing to anyone outside of Chimera personnel." Mort stood up, walked around the conference table, and out the door.

Julian also got up and headed toward the door.

"Best of luck Julian. Take care," he heard. He turned around, but Kendra's eyes had not withdrawn from her computer. Julian followed Mort out of the office.

"You went over," Janine chided. "Any longer in there and I would have come in and pulled you out."

"Sorry."

"I told you not to go over. Kendra's time is extremely valuable. Try not to go over next time."

"I will."

Franny rushed to her bowl in the kitchen the moment she heard the door unlock and open. Before Julian fully entered his home, she was crying incessantly, demanding to be fed her dinner allotment of food. It was 11:30am.

Julian had decided to return home shortly after leaving Kendra's office. The meeting itself was public knowledge well before he showed up to work that morning, yet upon his return to the twenty-eighth floor, seeming everyone from deskmates to colleague of tenuous connection found convenient excuses to drop by his desk and inquire as to what Kendra had to say. With each evasive reply, the responses turned from disappointment to hostility, as a sense of entitlement towards the content of his privileged conversation grew around the floor. He was thankful that he was able to escape before Zane could approach him. Julian did not want to either disappoint or anger him.

As Julian dropped his backpack in the closet and headed to the den, Franny grew intransigent for the food she felt she was rightfully owed. Her expression intimated that Julian's early arrival was only a technicality and should not preclude her customary serving of both dry and wet cat food. Her cry raised in pitch, volume, and intensity, until Julian capitulated and gave her some tuna flakes, treats he normally saved for vet visits and other stressful occasions. He returned to the den, laid on the bed, and closed his eyes.

Franny finished her flakes and joined Julian on the bed. She circled around her preferred spot left of his legs and laid down, placing her head against his knee. She began to purr in content, as she normally did after meals and before naps. With his eyes still closed, Julian felt another vibration outside of Franny's purr, from his back pocket, and reached for his phone to answer the call.

"Hey Julian, it's Barb."

Julian lifted his head and sat up on the bed, leaving his knee unmoved for Franny. The office visible from his window was empty, though the monitor on top of the desk was illuminated. The balding man from Saturday must have been on an early lunch break, he supposed.

"Hi Barbara, how you doing?"

"Oh fine. I can't seem to get a hold of my daughter. She was supposed to call yesterday but I didn't hear from her. I've called three times today and nothing. I don't think it's right. Why should I be the one who has to call her?

It's not like I have all day and night to just sit around making phone calls. If someone says they are going to call they should call, plain and simple. I know other people can be rude sometimes but to get that type of behavior from your own daughter? Same as when she doesn't visit here at all; *I* have to drive over to Omaha to see her. Why won't she come to Lincoln? Who knows. She never tells me and I don't ask. I just want to make sure she's alright; I'm her mother after all. Just once a year would be fine. Come by, stay a day or two, go have a nice dinner, catch up on what she's doing, how's her job, simple things. But no, can't even get that much. She really wasn't all that considerate, even when she was younger. I remember she would drink orange juice straight from the carton, all the way to bottom and just leave one or two ounces of juice left. Then she would put the carton back in the fridge, let someone else find an almost empty carton and throw it away. I must have told her a thousand times, *if you are going to drink orange juice, pour it in a glass, and if it's empty, throw it away.* But I guess you just can't count on anyone anymore, can you?"

"Not sure what her drinking orange juice has to do with her not calling you."

"What's going on with you?"

"I have to write a book, apparently."

"Oh writing, that sounds fun. I took a writing class once. It was in community college. A professor named Wayne Contro. What kind of a name is that anyway, Wayne Contro? He must have been in his thirties but he looked like he was my age. I remember he made us write ten ideas a week. Ideas on a character, a scene, whatever could be used to start doing creative writing. His class was okay. I liked thinking about ideas but he was always too harsh in grading the papers. I mean it was community college, it's not like we were going to go on to become journalists or something. I went to office hours one time and asked him why I got a C on one of my assignments. I remember he looked at my paper, and without even looking me in the eye said, 'because this was a C effort.' Can you believe that? The nerve of that guy. Take something kind of interesting like creative writing and just insult the students taking the class. I didn't like the class much after that, though I wish I could do more writing now to be honest. My job doesn't really make me do much reading or writing, just a lot of customers asking questions about their gym memberships and how to get more gym benefits or something like that. I have to tell them, 'Hey, all the memberships are the same, if I give you something then that wouldn't be fair to anyone else, would it?' Some people, I tell you."

Julian did not respond. He saw the man in the office across the window return and sit at his desk, the bald spot on the back of his head reappearing. On his monitor, it seemed like he was reading news articles of some kind, not browsing LinkedIn as he had done previously.

"Barbara, do you like your job?"

"Well yeah, sure, I suppose so. Why?"

"Just curious. I don't know if I like my job, or like it enough to work hard to keep it. Sometimes when I'm at work I just stare in the gap between the two monitors on my desk. Not at anything particular, just staring forward. It looks like I'm in deep thought about something on my screens, but I'm just zoning out, thinking about what my cat is doing or if there's something else I ought to be doing instead of being there."

"I wish I could zone out. But I have 660 membership accounts that have to be checked each month and there is just not enough time to waste doing --"

"I know."

"I know, I am just saying, gotta get the job done, ya know?"

"Yes."

"Why are you writing a book?"

"My CEO assigned it to me. Something about making a good impression on the shareholders."

"Well if the CEO says 'jump' you say 'how high', right? I had a boss like that once. I was working as a temp for a law office. There was this one lawyer who demanded his briefs be printed in this very particular way. Oh, I don't remember exactly now, but something with top margins, and bottom margins, and line spacing and all that. And if anything was out of place, he'd make me print the whole damn thing again!"

"Sounds like a great job."

"Ha-ha. Very funny."

"You should try texting your daughter. Most people respond to texts before calls nowadays."

"I hate texting."

"Why?"

"I remember when if you wanted to talk to someone, you would pick up the phone, dial their number, wait for them to pick up, and talk to them. Call me old-fashioned but there's something to that."

"What's there to that?"

"Look I'm not going to text my daughter, okay? She's my daughter. She should pick up the phone when her mother calls. Actually, she should just call me like she said she was going to."

The man in the office across the window was greeted by a visiting co-worker at his door. He minimized the news article on his screen and popped open a spreadsheet of some kind before welcoming the co-worker into his office. The two began to chat. The co-worker smiled and nodded intermittently. The man leaned back in his chair and put his hands behind his head, covering his bald spot.

"Why aren't you at work?" Julian asked.

"Took the day off. Had some back pain and just couldn't sit in my office chair. Those chairs are so old and uncomfortable. I don't know how anyone sits in them all day. Rock hard cushion to sit on, no give on the back, and they roll around so much you can barely move around in your seat without shifting around your desk."

"Oh."

"Are you at work?"

"No."

"Why not?"

"Took the rest of the day off. Was getting distracted by people asking around about the meeting with the CEO. Had to get away."

"Do you like your job?"

"Can't really tell anymore, that's what I was just saying."

"Well most jobs are just about someone trying to screw you over for money."

"Seems like it sometimes."

"You just have to look out for yourself, because no one else will."

The man and his co-worker ended their chat, and the co-worker got up to leave. The man, bald spot reappearing, turned around toward the window and pulled his blinds down, blocking Julian's view.

"Barb, what'd you call about?"

"Well, I just wanted to see what you were doing."

"At 11:30am on a Monday?"

"Do you think that you could call my daughter?"

"I don't speak to your daughter Barb. I barely did when I knew her."

"I know, I just get so worried."

"And annoyed."

"Well, yes I suppose," and Barbara let out a soft chuckle on the phone.

"I don't know what she is doing but I am sure your daughter is fine."

"You are probably right."

"I have to get going. Got a lot of work to do."

"Okay. Well good chatting with you."

"Goodbye Barb."

"Goodbye."

Julian got off the Murphy bed and headed back to the kitchen. Franny looked up in dazed bewilderment at the loss of her pillow, then nuzzled her head into the mattress. He checked the fridge for anything he could eat for lunch. All he found was a half-carton of eggs, a jar of grape jelly, leftover turkey sausage, and six cans of lime soda water. He moved over to the pantry. Cans of tuna, Ritz peanut-butter crackers, an unopened bottle of barbecue sauce, and a bag of ready-to-heat long-grain rice. He closed the door to the pantry. He had more than enough food of varying textures and nutritional value yet not in the amounts or composition to make one satisfying meal.

Opening up his phone to order in delivery, he realized he had had three missed calls before speaking with Barbara. One was from Barbara earlier in the morning, while the other two were from Zane. Must have been on his way back from the office, he thought to himself. He wondered what Zane would think when he found out about what Kendra asked him to do.

He went back to the fridge and grabbed a can of lime soda water. He took a few sips. He paced around his kitchen and wondered what the man in the office outside his window was doing behind the blinds.

Tuesday

Julian woke up around eight-thirty on Tuesday. He was going to be late for work, then he realized he didn't have to go to work if he didn't want to. He looked at his chimerical painting. Still the old man, staring back at him. Franny was on the other side of his bed, stirring awake alongside him. Her half-open eyes and stretched-out legs suggested she was not keen to commence her typical morning routine either.

He put on jeans and a t-shirt and headed down to The Savory Pass. The cafe was located to the right of his apartment complex. It did not have an entrance from the lobby; he and every other tenant had to walk out of the building, down the sidewalk a few feet, and enter through the front door facing the street. It was something of a local landmark, the location itself anyway. A cafe -- one form or another -- had been open since the apartment building was first constructed as a hotel some seventy years ago. It had gone through new management every fifteen years or so, changed names a few times, but always kept its doors open for coffee, pastries, and ambiance. From the front doorway the place opened up to a cashier stand and display counter on the right, tables and chairs in the back, and a long bar with high chairs lining the windows on the left. It was not a sunny day but there was enough brightness coming through the windows to illuminate the place without any additional lighting required. There were half a dozen tables occupied.

Julian walked up to the counter to make an order. The barista was behind the counter, preoccupied with writing in some kind of notebook or ledger. Julian waited a few moments, then called the barista over.

"I'd like a small Americano, please," Julian requested.

"Espresso machine's broken."

"Can you fix it?"

The barista looked up with dead eyes. "No."

"Fine. What about some tea?"

"Which kind?"

"What do you got?"

"Black, earl grey, something with hibiscus."

"Any of those have caffeine?"

"I don't know."

"I'll take a medium drip then. Do you know where the beans came from?"

"Do you want the coffee or not?"

"Sure. I'll take a croissant as well."

"They're not warm."

"Is your oven broken too?"

"No."

"I guess you'll figure it out then. I'll be over there." Julian pointed towards a table for two against the back wall and walked over.

He sat down and opened the blank spiral notebook he brought with him. He set a goal of writing out at least one paragraph, maybe one page of something, *anything*, which might give him an opening into how the rest of the book might develop. He was not a writer. He had no idea why he was told to do this. He was not sure if it was even worth trying. He decided to give it a go for today and see what happened.

He took out a blue pen and put it to paper. *How the hell do you start?* He thought to himself, almost in a literal sense, *what is the very first word that a writer writes down?* He wondered if he had to know what he was going to write before he started, or, if it could evolve organically, growing from one word into a few words, a few sentences, a few pages, and eventually a finished and elegant manuscript. The second approach seemed more compelling, almost romantic even, but awfully risky. There seemed to a lot riding on that first word, and whether it was the right word to propel an entire story.

His thoughts were interrupted by the conversation of a young guy and girl two tables to his right. He did not see them when he walked in, or when he sat down, and did not look over to them.

"I quit my internship," the guy began.

"You did? Why?" the girl asked concernedly.

"I wasn't going to spend the next four months helping some corporate lawyers make the oil and gas lobby even more powerful than they already are. The world has so many problems, you know? I figure I can and should spend my career doing something more meaningful."

"Well, yeah. Those corporations, it's like they have no soul."

"Yeah, exactly. And it's like they don't even understand. Men in their 40s, receding hairlines and high blood pressure, driving BMWs but pissed off all the time. Guys and girls my age just working day and night, slaving over paperwork or client meetings. I want my career to *mean* something, to have some purpose."

"There are so many things wrong in the world today. World hunger, poverty, wars, education, climate. It's almost unethical to be concerned with anything else."

"Exactly! And they want interns to work 8-5, Monday to Friday, week in week out. On the beck and call of some pencil-pushing manager. Assignments in and assignments out. Where's the time to explore my passion? Where are the opportunities to grow, to explore, to thrive?"

"You have so much potential, Jamie. The corporate ladder is a joke. You were so right to get out of there. What will you do now?"

"Haven't thought about it yet. Just need a while to focus on myself, you know? Worry about me, not conform to everyone else's expectations. I'm tired of getting wrapped up in what society wants. My parents keep pressing me to get my own place, settle down with a job, so on and so on. It's like they don't even care about what I want or what I need."

"You shouldn't cave in. That's not who you are."

"Maybe I'll go to graduate school. MBA, Ph.D, law, something like that. People don't take you seriously unless you have an advanced degree. It would have to be a good school though. I am not going to waste my time at some know-nothing university. Maybe I'll do some volunteering. I've been thinking about this new-society co-op on the other side of town. Sustainable living. You work for free but can take whatever proceeds you need: food, clothing, whatever. Just you and everyone else coexisting as one."

"That's wonderful. You've always had such ideals and vision, Jamie."

"I just want to make a difference. Don't want to get through half my life and look back realizing I didn't do anything important. What's going on with you?"

"Oh, same old. I'm taking biology this semester. Stupid prereq for my major. I don't get why I have to take these boring science classes. It's not like I am ever going to use it again."

"Why take it then?"

"Part of the requirements for the nutritionist certificate. Can't graduate without it. Could have taken them three semesters ago but I didn't know biology and statistics were needed. It's so hard, and it's taking forever. I just want to help people be healthier."

"Hm, yeah. You'd be good at that. Never took biology but it's just a bunch of diagrams of this organ and that. Why does that matter?"

"I don't know. But I need to study. I failed it last semester and if I don't pass this time they might not let me take it again."

"Sucks. Higher-education system. Just as oppressive as corporations. Forcing you to do things that don't matter just because they want you to."

"Drip coffee and croissant," said the barista as he dropped a cup and plate on Julian's table. Julian had not seen him coming, and was startled by the clank of the porcelain on the plastic tabletop. "Anything else?"

"Yes, how about some..."

"You'll have to get it back at the counter." The barista turned around and went back to his post at the front of the cafe. Julian took a bite of the croissant. Completely cold, but not bad tasting. He returned back to his notebook after getting lost in his eavesdropping. Still no words. He resolved to write one sentence, any sentence that came to his mind.

Why do people write stories, anyway?

It was a good question, but not one whose answer would help him much in his current task. It was curious, though. Every individual has their own life experience as a story. Some maybe more interesting than others, happier or sadder, but they have all happened and have all mattered to at least one person, sometimes many more. Then there is just history, which is like a common story that everyone knows about. Famous people doing famous things that are still talked about today. It must be worth it to write down that story because otherwise everyone would wake up each day and have no understanding of what was going on around them and why. But to make up a story, about no one and of events which have and will not exist, Julian did not quite understand the reasoning.

Why do people write stories, anyway? To read back their own words and remind themselves that their ideas matter and their existence means something more than the happenstance of a life arbitrarily fixed in time and space.

He looked over to his right at the pair whose conversations he'd been listening to. The man -- Jamie, he presumed -- was in his early twenties, wearing boat shoes with khaki shorts, a teal t-shirt, and a backward baseball cap which covered wavy brown hair that escaped as curls under the rim. He was looking at his phone, swiping on the screen every few seconds. His counterpart -- name unknown -- was of similar age, with a beanie over her platinum blond hair strewn with bright pink highlights. She was wearing a hoodie over a white tank and grey leggings. She was sipping on a large iced coffee, alternating her view between Jamie and the windows behind him, After a few moments, she pulled up her phone as well.

"Check out this girl who messaged me on Bumble," Jamie said.

"What's Bumble?" his friend asked.

"It's a dating app but the rules are the girl has to initiate the communication." He turned his phone around, and his friend leaned forward to see the screen.

"She's very pretty, sounds like she's into you," she said, as her expression dropped.

"Ha! Maybe. I'm not that interested though, seems just a little too desperate, ya know? Asking if I want to have drinks in the first message."

"Isn't that the point of the app?"

"Well yeah, but not like that. I don't know, just kind of a turnoff when girls get straight to the point."

"Yeah, totally."

"I'll still hit her up though."

Julian turned back to his table. The cafe had filled up since he arrived. It was about ten in the morning, and he wondered what all the patrons were doing at this hour. He surveilled the tables and stopped at an elderly couple by the windows. They weren't speaking, both looking out the windows at passersby. He could see from his angle that they were holding hands underneath the table. They looked happy, and it made him feel sad.

The bell attached to the front door rang as it opened for a new customer. He heard a recognizable voice at the ordering counter.

"I hear your Americanos are good here." It was Herb. "I'll take one."

"Espresso machine is broken," the barista repeated himself.

"So fix it."

"Can't. Technician's coming in the afternoon."

"Well that's pretty fucking useless, isn't it?"

The barista was unnerved. "Would you like some drip coffee instead?"

"No. Your coffee is shit here."

"You just tried to order an Americano. It's just another type of coffee."

Herb smirked. "So I've heard. Just give me one of those pastries and a glass of lemonade."

"Got it. Pastries are cold, though. Hope that's okay."

"It's not."

Herb paid and turned toward the main sitting area. He caught eyes with Julian, who motioned him over to his table. After a few squinted glares, he followed suit and sat down opposite to Julian.

"Good morning. Good to see you again." Julian opened.

"You too. Thought I'd come check out your favorite place."

"It's not my favorite."

"Oh. Then why the fuck are we here?"

"Don't have to be. I just came here to do something for work."

"Where do you work?"

"Chimera Solutions."

"What do you make?"

"Well, nothing I guess. It's consulting. We go to other businesses and help them. Well, that's the promise of it, anyway."

"Nah -- I mean how much money do you make?"

"Oh. About ninety."

"Thousand?!"

"Yeah."

"Damn. Sounds like a good gig. You must be some expert or something."

"Not really."

"Why are you working here and not there?"

"Trying to focus. I have to write a book, like a novel or something."

"What for?"

"Something about making the company look and feel more human."

"That is the dumbest shit I've ever heard."

"Why do you say that?"
"Write a book because you have a story worth telling. Shouldn't matter about some corporation pretending to be magnanimous when they are just making money out of nothing. Or just make a bunch of money -- sounds like you are -- and not give a shit about what people think of you."

"You don't care about what people think of you?"

"I care. But I am not going to try to act like someone I'm not just to make them feel any differently."

"Here's your lemonade and pastry," the barista interjected.

"We're taking all this to go. Get us some take-away cups and boxes. You don't mind if we go somewhere else, do you kid?"

"Whatever. I'm about done here anyway."

The barista left and returned with plastic cups and small cardboard containers.

"Why do you think people write stories?" Julian asked, as he closed his notebook and returned it to his bag.

"I don't know. Probably because their life is so boring or depressing that they need something else to think about."

"Look at that old couple over there. They don't look bored or depressed."

"Maybe not now. But at some point they'll look up and wonder what the hell they've been doing sitting there that whole time."

They got up to go. As they crossed the sitting area towards the exit, Julian overheard Jamie again.

"I have an uncle who works at Barclays. I suppose I could always become an investment banker. I'm not going to wear a suit and tie like those other hacks, though."

"Of course not," replied the friend. "You have to be true to yourself."

As they neared the door, Herb called out to the barista, who was back behind the counter.

"Hey, what's your name?"

"Lawrence."

"Hey Lawrence, you're kind of a dick. You should be nicer to people, or find something else to do. I wouldn't hold it against you either way. Just stop being a dick."

They left the Savory Pass and walked out on the sidewalk.

"Where are we going?" Julian asked.

"My house. Got a cooler of beer with our name on it."

"It's ten in the morning."

"You don't want to go?"

"No, let's do it."

They walked over to Herb's house, pulled out two beach chairs, and set them on the lawn facing the street. Herb grabbed a cooler from his garage and dropped it in between them. It was full of beer, as advertised. They both sat in the beach chairs. Herb opened the cooler, popped open a beer for himself, and another for Julian. There weren't many people walking up and down the street, but about four blocks behind the main road was a skyscraper in the middle of construction, with crews going up and down the makeshift elevator to the top of the developing structure.

"What do you do, Herb?"

"What do I do? I do lots of things, man."

"I mean, what's your profession?"

"Does it matter?"

"Well now that you're being so dodgy about it, kind of."

"Smart ass. I suppose I don't have a profession. Retired from the army about ten years ago. Full pension. It's not a consultant's salary, but I don't really need much, in case you can't tell."

"What did you do in the army?"

"What everyone else does. Follow orders and do your time."

"Did you see any combat?"

"One tour, first Gulf war. I was general infantry back then, just a grunt really. Was in Saudi Arabia for most of it, spent about three weeks in Kuwait at the end of Desert Storm. Never killed anyone, if that's your next question. Only fired my weapon once, but it was nothing."

"You weren't in Afghanistan or the second Iraq?"

"Was noncombat by then. Hopped around a few jobs: construction, mechanic, even paralegal at one point."

"That's good."

"Why you say that?"

"Well, I mean that you didn't have to go back into combat. Must have been a relief. I don't think I could do it, even once."

"Wouldn't have bothered me."

"Why not? You liked being in a warzone?"

"Didn't say that."

"No, then what, just super patriotic or something?"

"You going to let me tell you or just keep making a bunch of stupid guesses?"

"Sorry, please go ahead."

"I meet a lot of folks like you, either confused, angry, ashamed, scared about war and military conflicts, hell any kind of conflict really. Thinking that I have some answer for them, having been in it a little bit. But there's no answer really, or if there is one I don't know it. But here's the way I see it. Since neanderthals were roaming about trying to make fire, everybody was trying to kill everybody. For food, shelter, survival, whatever. That was just life, preparing for the next encounter in which you might die.

Here in America there's really only been two real attacks on U.S. soil since the Civil War: Pearl Harbor and 9/11. That's it. The rest of the time people like you have been able to live their lives without the need for or threat of conflict. Everything's pretty nice and orderly and set up for you to just live. Get a job, get married, do what you want. It seems normal, but it's actually pretty rare, and completely unlike the vast majority of human history, to live your whole life never having to worry about a life-or-death situation every single day.

So if I had to go back into combat, ever have to do that again, no I wouldn't mind. Not that I'd like it, but I'd accept it. Because the truth is that that would be much closer to normal than what you and I are doing right now."

"Hm. I never really thought about it like that." Julian furrowed his brow.

"Most don't. Too caught up in what they have, what they want, what they think they ought to have. Don't really stop and consider how fucking great even their shittiest day is, in the grand scheme of things. Julian, grab another beer for me."

Julian popped open the cooler and fetched another beer and handed it to Herb. He took a large swig of his own beer and looked out at the building under construction. He saw three men on the topmost floor, sitting in a small circle, sipping from cans just like he was and joking around with each other.

"What's this writing thing you gotta do anyway?" Herb inquired.

"Something about the company wanting to show their human side. Asked me to put together a manuscript to submit to the Man Booker, like a literature prize. I tried writing this morning. Just tried to write down anything I could. Couldn't even get a single idea put to paper."

"I find that hard to believe. You seem like a smart enough guy."

"Not one idea."

"Hell, I can give you *one* idea," Herb proclaimed.

"Shoot."

"Synesthesia."

"Huh?"

"*Synesthesia.*"

"What's that?"

"It's when one sensory perception in your brain is involuntarily connected to another."

"What does that mean?"

"It can happen in all sorts of combinations, but the most prevalent is colors and letters or numbers."

Herb got up and walked into his garage. He returned with a pencil and blank sheet of graphical paper. He wrote on the paper and showed it to Julian.

"Can you see that?"

"It's a 5."

"Yes, it's a 5. And what color is it?"

"Grey."

"Yep. You probably don't have synesthesia."

"Why not?"

"Cause to me, that 5 is green."

"But it's not. It's grey. You wrote it in using a grey pencil so it's grey."

"That's what synesthesia is. All 5's will be green to me, that's just what they look like in my brain."

"What else is there about it?" Julian asked.

"Well for others, there's all sorts of types. Lot of people see colors in numbers or letters. Some associate colors with sounds, like a door closing or musical notes. Some of the earliest cases of synesthesia involved people who visualized numbers in particular patterns, like in a winding road or around a clock face."

"What about you, what do you see?"

"Mine's just about numbers. I see green 5's, blue 2's, and red 7's."

"See, that just sounds like bullshit to me. You wrote that 5 with a grey pencil. It can't just be red simply because it's a 5."

"You calling me a liar?"

"Yup." Julian grinned.

"Who's to say what is truly red anyhow?"

"What do you mean?"

"Name something that's red."

"A rose."

"Right. You see a rose. You have a visualization of a what a rose looks like in your brain. When you learn the English language people tell you 'a rose is red.' So whatever color you see in your brain you defined as red.

Now, let's say that I, for whatever reason, don't see the same color as you do when I see a rose. Let's say I see the color that you see in the grass, which is green. When people tell me `a rose is red' I associate the color I see to be the red in the rose, which is really green. And let's say that happened to me for everything else that was labeled 'red'. Blood, ketchup, etc. I always saw a green color similar to the rose so the 'red' definition made perfect sense.

What that means is, you and I can both look at the same rose, call it 'red', see completely different things, and be in perfect agreement with each other, even if our brains didn't see the same things at all."

"So my perception and your perception could be different, even if we are observing the exact same thing."

"Exactly. Explains a lot when you think about it. Like how a man and wife can argue over something stupid like somebody's tone of voice. Hear the same thing, but *understood* something different."

"Is that what you and your wife fought about?"

"Easy, kid. You're a decent guy and I like you. Best way to keep it that way is to not ask me stupid questions like that."

Julian did not respond. He felt a bit tipsy from the one beer he had finished, which was odd given the small amount of alcohol. He supposed it was because he rarely drank so early in the day. He grabbed another beer from the cooler, opened it, and pointed the snout of the bottle to Herb, and invitation to cheers. Herb took a moment then extended his beer to clink the bottles together.

The two sat with their beers, replenishing when needed, reducing their conversation to small bits of dialogue, usually commenting on passersby or some other stimulus to break up the monotony of the mostly-empty street and the building in construction in front of them.

.....

"You see that guy just walking by?" Julian prodded.

"That guy?" Herb pointed.

"Yeah."

"What about him?"

"You can tell he hasn't had sex in a while."

"How?"

"Walking too fast and upright. And the frowning. Like resting-bitch-face for guys. Guys who are getting laid just casually walk by, like they don't care, cause they don't, cause they are getting laid."

"Guess that explains why you walk around so pissed off all the time!"

"Bullshit. You don't know me."

"The hell I don't. Only someone who isn't getting laid has got time to think about something like that. Write that in your stupid book."

"Maybe I will."

.....

"What was there before that building under construction?" Julian wondered.

"Not sure. What does it matter?"

"Because. It's good to know what's being removed when we build new things on top of them."

"Not it's not."

"Sure it is. Once you lose it you don't get it back."

"Yeah, but that's everything isn't it? Let's say before that building was an orphanage house. Or a crack house, so what? What was there before that, and before that? It doesn't matter. Shit moves on, always."

.....

"How long have you lived here?"

"Ever since after my first tour. Back when the Savory Pass was called something else. Coffee was much better then too."

"Oh yeah? Why is it so bad now?"

"Guess no one cares if the coffee is good or bad anymore. It's all the same to order it, pay for it, drink it, say you did it, and talk about it with your friends. As long as it checks the box who cares what the experience was."

"Then why are the spinach croissants so cold?"

"Huh? I don't know. What are you talking about?"

"Not really sure. I'm pretty drunk. Do you drink like this everyday?"

"Only days when I need to take the edge off from such horrible company."

"You're such a dick, Herb."

"You're welcome. Cheers."

.....

"Hey Julian, check out the girl walking towards us. Cute."

"Oh shit. I know her. She lives in my building."

"Nice, dude. You guys bangin'?"

"Herb, shut up. She's coming this way."

"Ohh. Sensitive. Guess you like her."

"Not really. Just don't want to have explain why I'm getting drunk with an old man in the middle of the day."

"You might be getting drunk but I've been wasted for a solid hour or two. And fuck you, I'm not old."

"Herb, please just stop."

"Well hey! If it isn't the building's messiest mail recipient." Lydia was clearly enjoying the setting of Julian and Herb on Herb's front lawn. She had exchanged her blue high heels for short brown boots, alongside skinny dark jeans and a loose white top. Julian was struck by how put together she looked despite her casual attire. The hand on her hip and the bedeviled smirk she had on her face suggested he and Herb presented much more comically, and probably more drunk, than he would have wished.

"Hey there. Lydia, right? In 2C?" Julian replied.

"Nice memory. Guess you got the envelope I put under your door. You know it's rude not to come by and say thank you, don't you?"

"Yeah Julian. *So* rude. Shame on *you*," Hank chimed in. Julian shot him a curt look, but the giddy smile on Herb's face let Julian know perfectly well that he didn't care.

"What do we got going on over here?" Lydia wondered aloud.

"Lydia, this is Herb. He lives here. We were just hanging out."

"Hi Lydia, pleasure to meet you." Herb got up to shake Lydia's hand, and stumbled on his step when reaching out to her.

"It definitely is," Lydia replied, with a soft chuckle.

"And I already spoke to Julian. He said as much as he likes you, he agrees we'd be better with each other, and he's prepared to get out of the way so that you and I can give it a shot."

"Herb!" Julian cried out.

"Oh my!" Lydia played along. "What a love triangle we have. To what do I owe the honor of both of your affections?"

"About a case of beer and no lunch."

"Oh my god." Julian was mortified.

"Sounds like a fun time," said Lydia.

"It was it was. But, I think I need to call it a wrap. You know, got some things I got to do."

"Aren't you going to walk me home?"

"Not sure I can walk myself home."

"Well then."

"I'll walk you home, Lydia. Was on my way there anyway." Julian blurted out. He rose to his feet, steadied his legs under him, and walked towards Lydia on the sidewalk.

"Herb, I'll see you later. Was great hanging out with you today."

Herb was halfway back towards the front door of his house, but turned his head for one last toothy grin. "You too, Mr. Hemingway."

"Ha! Sleep tight asshole."

"Lydia, make sure to let him down easy. He has feelings, you know."

"Of course I will, Herb. Have a nice evening."

Lydia and Julian started the walk toward their building. Julian's heart was beating fast, from some combination of Lydia's presence and an afternoon's worth of drinking. He knew he was quite a bit drunk, and he knew she knew he was at least a little drunk, but he tried to compose himself as much as could.

"I am sorry I didn't come by," Julian began.

"You should be. That gym membership coupon is quite a deal."

"I think it was a car wash."

"I think you might be right. Oops."

"I do what I can."

"I can see that. Tell me more about Herb. He's quite a character."

"Oh, don't mind him. We actually just met two days ago. He's a bit odd, but I suppose we're all a bit odd in some way. I like him."

"I like him too. Sounds like you were having quite the party."

"Yeah, I guess it looked that way, huh. I don't know. I was in Savory Pass this morning doing some work. He came by, we got to talking, and then we just spent the afternoon drinking beer and hanging out on his lawn." Julian checked his watch. "My god, how is it five already?"

"Well for most people, they go to work and spend the day there, and then at five, they go home."

"Is that what you do?"

"Not at all. Never could, never would."

"What do you do then?"

"It's an odd thing to ask someone when you are getting acquainted, isn't it?"

"How come?"

"I mean, you meet someone. There must be a million things about them that you don't know, and would like to find out. Why start with their job?"

"Jobs are important, I guess. Everybody has to do something to provide for themselves, so it's a natural point of commonality."

"Could be. But there's so many others, more interesting ones. I much prefer to start there."

"Let's do that. Where would you like to start?"

"I don't know. Just pick something else."

"Why did you write that you liked my name?"

"Because I do."

"Why?"

"It sounds very...Roman, I guess? Like it has a rich history, a character to it, like an ancestry of experience that personifies itself in you. I think that makes it quite interesting and, attractive, compared to other names."

"I wish that were true. My mom was a fan of Jules Verne, the author. But she thought Jules would be confused as a girl's name, so she went with Julian."

"Oh I love Jules Verne books."

"How come?"

"Because of the imagination of it all. Like Journey to the Center of the Earth. I know that underneath the ground is lava and all that, but wouldn't it be lovely if there was another world there, to see and explore? I know it's not true but I love to imagine it were."

"But it's not true, so what's the point?"

"Oh my dear Julian. And I was just starting to like you."

Julian blushed, and looked away so Lydia wouldn't see. He was walking faster than her, and slowed his pace so she could be slightly ahead.

"You'd probably do much better at the job I have to do," he said.

"Oh, jobs again. Fine, I'll go with it. What's that?"

"Write a book, like a novel."

"My goodness! Is that why Herb called you Mr. Hemingway?"

"Yeah."

"That sounds like so much fun. I've always wanted to publish something. But I could never think of what I'd want to write about."

"I don't believe that. I'm sure you have lots of ideas."

"Sure, it's easy to have lots of ideas, but writing can't be about lots of ideas, just one idea. And how do you choose? Picking one would be insulting to all the others."

"Well, that's a problem I'd like to have."

"What are you writing about?"

"Great question."

"Wait, what do you do?"

"Aha! So much for not asking about jobs."

"You started it!"

They arrived at the final block before their building. The day was still bright, despite the sun having set already behind a wall of downtown buildings.

"What do you think of when you hear my name, Jules?" Lydia asked, with a wink.

"I think of someone, something very elegant, classic, calm, persevering. Lydia sounds like a name that would have sounded beautiful 1000 years ago and will sound beautiful 1000 years from now."

"My, what a romantic you are."

"It's mostly the alcohol talking. If Herb was three sheets to the wind, I'm at least four and a half."

"I can tell. Well I certainly appreciate you walking me home. I'll take it as your apology for not visiting.

"I was planning to. It's only been a day."

"You make it sound like waiting a day doesn't matter."

"Does it?"

"I suppose not. Until the day before you die, when one day is literally the rest of your life."

"Wow, um, well, I'm sorry. I should have come."

"Jules, I'm just teasing. I'm glad we ran into each other down the road. Your life seems fascinating."

"It's really not. I'd say until the last few days my life was about as dull as you could imagine."

"Imagining a dull life, that seems like an oxymoron, doesn't it? If it's alright with you, I won't do that. And neither should you, really. Because good or bad, everything thing that's happened in your life has led you to this moment, here with me."

"And you are not dull at all, Lydia."

"No. I certainly am not."

They arrived at the front of their building. The Savory Pass was closed, but the window blinds were up and Julian could see the table where he sat earlier in the morning.

"Let me walk you to your apartment," he offered, before mistiming his step up through the opening doorway, and taking a quick stumble.

"How about I walk you to yours, though I still expect you to come by eventually to offer a formal thank you."

"I will. Promise."

"I mean, if a lady can't be thanked for offering a car wash deal of a lifetime, what *has* society come to?"

"Where is the decency?"

"Probably left it at Herb's."

"Whatever decency which may have been there has been gone a long time."

"Oh, stop it."

They arrived at Julian's apartment.

"I'll let you in, but be warned there's a very hungry cat on the other side of this door, and she will be all over us demanding food the moment I turn the lock."

"How rude. Don't refer to your girlfriend like that."

"I don't have a girlfriend."

"I know, Jules."

"How can you can tell something like that?"

"Oh, I don't know. Maybe the fact that you've barely taken your eyes off me since you saw me coming down the street."

Julian unlocked the door to the delight and immediate annoyance of Franny, who began to meow and run towards the kitchen. He went over to feed her, while Lydia trailed behind and lingered in the open area by the door. Julian tried to hurry with the feeding, but he was starting to build a headache from all the beer and each successive cry from Franny made it harder for him to focus. By the time he finished getting her food in her bowl and setting it down on the ground, Lydia had found him in the kitchen.

"Lovely place. Pretty clean, for a single man. I'm going to head out, Jules."

"No, please stay, for a drink or something."

"I think you've had enough for today. But rain check, for sure."

"Great. You can help me with the book I have to write."

"That's your story, Jules, not mine. It should come from, and be from, no one but you."

"Sometimes a story gets better when it weaves into another."

"Sometime it doesn't."

"When will I see you again?"

"I don't know. Maybe I'll go get drunk with Herb sometime and you can come find me there."

"I'm sure he'd love that."

"Bye, for now."

She smiled, turned towards the door, and exited. Once she left, Julian realized that the room was spinning from the beer. He felt sheepish that he got so drunk in the afternoon and walked home with Lydia in that state. It was not what he planned or wished for.

Franny was finishing her food, and periodically looked up to Julian, curious to see if she would be given more. Julian became edgy, feeling unresolved. He poured a glass of water for himself, guzzled it down, left his apartment and headed down to 2C.

He knocked on the door, in three distinct and separated knocks. The door opened suddenly.

"Jules, what is it?" Lydia was wearing the same clothes she had one before but had her hair pulled back in a clip.

"What are you doing this weekend? I know it's a bit spontaneous but would you like to drive out to the coast with me? There's a nice park there on the beach, with trails to walk and grassy fields to enjoy the sun. We could have a little picnic, what do you say?"

"I'd say you make a compelling offer, but you're probably getting a little ahead of yourself."

"I'm sorry, I didn't mean to be so forward."

"Don't be. I'm flattered. Let me think about it, okay?"

"Okay."

"Good night, Jules."

"Good night."

Wednesday

"Two Americanos, to go please."

Julian arrived at the Savory Pass at eight on Wednesday morning. There was no sign of a morning coffee rush, with a handful of customers either on their way in or way out. Lawrence the barista was not working, replaced instead by another man, a bit older, heavier, and happier, who had a pleasant and gregarious demeanor, even if he didn't appear to complete orders very quickly.

Julian had had an early start to the day, brought on by his inability to sleep neither heavily nor for long after drinking all afternoon with Herb. Despite waking up early, he was happily surprised that he was not hungover. He had spent the evening rehydrating and eating high-carb take-out. He would have fallen asleep earlier than he had, except he couldn't help but to replay his conversation with Lydia over and over in his head, analyzing every comment he made and her reactions to each one. He fixated on his decision to knock on her door and ask her out for the weekend, and what it meant that she'll think about it. It all happened so quickly, so rashly, without any planning or organization, and he felt chagrined that he didn't consider other options. He eventually fell asleep late in the evening, comforted by his bedroom painting which displayed unequivocally as an exultant boy and his loyal dog. He started the day with a shower and a shave and a walk down to the Savory Pass.

"Coming right up. Leave room for cream?" Lawrence 2.0 was a dramatic improvement from his predecessor.

"No thanks."

Julian grabbed the coffees and made his way over to Herb's. It was a cloudy but warm morning. The street was mostly residential but the din of professionals walking in heels or boots toward their cars, toward bus stops, or directly to work was beginning to pick up.

He arrived at Herb's to find the chairs they were sitting in and cooler they were drinking from yesterday splayed out on the front lawn, untouched since he had left. He walked up to the door and rang the doorbell. After a minute of waiting with no answer, he rang it again with the same result. Then, he knocked on the door aggressively. After a long pause the door slowly swung open.

"What the hell, man? What the fuck time is it?" Herb looked out of sorts, same clothes as yesterday and greying stubble around his chin. Despite the cloudy day the light from outside was blinding, forcing him to squint and cover his eyes with his hand.

"Good morning. You look like shit. Here's an Americano from Savory Pass."

"From that dick barista?"

"No, new guy's much better."

"Well, it'll probably be shit but I could use it. Thanks. You want some breakfast?"

"What do you got?"

"Just come inside and shut up for a second."

Herb opened the door and Julian followed him in. Julian found a simple and surprisingly organized layout, with a living room to the left, a kitchen galley to the right, and a hallway in the middle which presumably led to a bed and bath in the back. The living room contained a matching couch and armchair, with a simple brown rectangular coffee table in between and an orderly pile of National Geographic magazines on the side closest to the far wall. The walls were sparse except for a framed and dated photo of a sunset over desert sands. The kitchen galley included white countertops, plain wooden cabinets, and stainless steel appliances, whose facades were all bare and uncluttered save a small bowl of uncut fruit by the refrigerator.

Herb left toward the back room and let Julian linger by the kitchen. Julian dropped the coffees on the counter and opened the fridge. Inside he found a carton of eggs, packages of different lunch meats, cheeses, and bacon strips, fresh greens wrapped in plastic bags, and a loaf of home-baked bread still resting in a baking dish. A sufficient but not excessive amount of food to complete a meal, unlike his own fridge, he thought himself.

Herb returned from the back wearing a fresh t-shirt, a pair of slacks, and a splash of cold water on his face that was dripping down his neck. He grabbed one of the coffees and took a long gulp.

"Not bad, right?" Julian asked.

"Still shit. Good shit, though," Herb replied. "Want that breakfast?"

"You bet."

Herb took over in the kitchen while Julian grabbed a seat at the table across the galley counter. Herb grabbed the carton of eggs and bacon strips and heated up a saute pan on the stove. Within a few minutes he had scrambled eggs, bacon, and toast plated and on the table.

"Gotta admit Herb, I'm a bit surprised."

"You're surprised? You're the one showing up at my door at the butt crack of dawn."

"It's quarter to nine."

"Tell that to my hangover."

"Hangover? We didn't drink that much."

"*You* didn't drink that much, nursing your beers all goddamned afternoon."

"I was savoring the flavor."

"Just shut up and eat."

"That was my point, this is delicious. Where'd you learn how to cook?"

"Army, man. Everyone has mess duty eventually."

"Always thought you'd be the MRE type."

"Well I was when I was on tour. Now that I'm not, figure I should eat real food as much as I can."

"Like a case of beer in the afternoon?"

"Hell yes. Beer is one of the oldest prepared beverages there is. Was used in Egyptian times for nutrition and refreshment. Preferred to water because it's sterile too. Speaking of sterile, how'd it work out with Lana last night?"

"Lydia. And fuck you very much."

"What'd I do?"

"Acting like an ass when she showed up."

"Girls like that stuff. You'll thank me later."

"We'll see. I asked her out last night, she said she'd think about it."

"Ask her out to do what?"

"Go on a picnic near the coast."

"What the hell is a matter with you? Should have asked her to have your child while you were at it."

"Piss off. Wasn't that bad."

"Next time you should ask her if she wants to change out your catheter when you became old and incontinent."

"You're a dick."

"Ease up, Julian," said Herb. "I'm sure she'll come around. I may have been a little sloppy yesterday but I could tell she was interested in you. Seemed like a nice girl too. And eat up, too. We've got a long day ahead of us."

"Long day? Doing what?"

"Some grown men work. A change of pace for you I presume, Mr. Hemingway."

"Shit. I didn't do any of that yesterday."

"And I'm guessing that's why you're here now, so you don't do any of it today?"

Julian didn't reply, and looked down at his plate while he finished his food. Herb did the same, and quickly downed the last few bites of his.

"Come on. Like I said, you're going to work for me today. Real salt of the earth shit. It's going to be great."

"Thought you were hungover?"

"Sure am, so? You going to help me or not?"

"You still haven't told me what we are doing."

"Well alright, then let me show you. You're not worried about breaking a fingernail or anything like that?'

"Let's get on with it. You must have really hated that coffee."

Herb gulped the last of his Americano down. "Total shit, I don't know why you like that place."

Herb took their plates, rinsed them off in the sink and let them dry on a rack in the kitchen. He walked out the front door, and Julian followed him out to the lawn where Herb picked up the beer bottles, cooler, and chairs from the afternoon before. Julian grabbed the garbage bin from the end of the driveway and brought it back so Herb could drop in the empty bottles and other trash. Herb rested the chairs and cooler against the front door then walked around to the garage which had its door down. "Help me lift this up," he told Julian. They hoisted the door up and over, to reveal the packed room of assorted appliances in various stages of deconstruction. Julian recalled what lay in the garage from his initial introductions with Herb, but up close and on second view he was taken aback by the sheer volume of hardware densely assembled in such a tightly confined space.

Herb pointed to the back right corner, where a large, white rectangular structure with curved corners stood, separated from shelves of smaller materials on either side.

"See that? That's a 1950s GE refrigerator and freezer unit. Bought it for $200 from a guy whose mom passed and was cleaning out her house. She had had it since it first came out, and it still works just like it did back then. You know what we're going to do to it?"

"No, what?"

"We're going rip the whole damn thing apart, piece by piece."

Herb reached into a cabinet on the left side of the garage, and pulled out a folded black tarp. He handed it to Julian, who went out into the lawn to unfold it and lay it down on the grass. Herb grabbed his toolbox and placed it at the edge of the tarp.

"You got anything under that blouse?" Herb inquired. Julian was wearing a button-down short-sleeved shirt, something he would normally wear on a workday. He shook his head.

"Let me get you something." Herb walked in the house and returned shortly with another t-shirt in his hand, and tossed it to Julian, who swapped it for his button-down. Their next job was to remove the refrigerator from the back of the garage, out to the tarp in the front lawn. Herb fetched a flat dolly and rolled it to the fridge. Julian and Herb grabbed it from either side and lifted it slightly onto the dolly, and rolled it out of the garage and to the edge where the driveway meets the lawn. Herb tipped the top of it over gently towards the lawn, where Julian caught it from falling too far forward. Herb picked up the bottom off the dolly, and together they gently rested the refrigerator down on the tarp.

"So tell me, Mr. Hemingway. Do you know how refrigeration works?" Herb asked. Julian shook his head. So did Herb, but in frustration. "Millennials," he muttered. He grabbed a flat-head screwdriver from the toolbox, and quickly unscrewed the back panel, revealing a grill of coils, a small black compressor and wiring at the bottom.

"First thing you got to know, kid: conservation of energy. Can't create or destroy energy, no matter what. The energy in the universe is exactly the same today as it was in the beginning, only difference is where it is and in what form.

The problem of refrigeration has been around for a few hundred years and is a pretty simple question really: how do you get rid of heat? You can't destroy it, so how do you take heat from one location and put it somewhere else, so the original location gets colder? Not only that, but how do you do it over and over again so that location stays cold once you've made it cold? You could say that refrigeration is a tough problem because you not only have to artificially create an unnatural environment, but maintain it infinitely. This means you have to build something that fights against the universe's natural tendency -- to spread heat evenly -- and doesn't capitulate. To not only create a distortion, but to prolong it, even as the distortion wants to right itself.

It all starts with a coolant, or refrigerant. These are substances that go back and forth from gas to liquid, as heat is added and removed from it. They are the vessel in which heat is removed from the inside of a refrigerator and deposited on the outside. Coolant cycles through the compressor here, the coils here, the throttle which you can't see, and coils on the inside of the back panel. It's pretty neat to think about how versatile and accommodating a coolant has to be. Able to change its state, pressure, and temperature, on command and over and over again, in order to make the process work. And how hard it must have been for those original inventors to conceive of this idea. To understand how the elements work, how to build such a contraption, and to get it to succeed. I mean, refrigeration is taken as a given for everyone today, but back then, it wasn't even a concept, people didn't even know they wanted it or needed it because the thought didn't even enter their brains. The genius and bravery it took to think so far ahead of their time, to march on a road with such a high risk of failure, and in the process make humanity all the better, is really breathtaking when you think about it.

Back when refrigerators were first being invented, people used ammonia as a coolant. And ammonia worked great. Same for sulfur dioxide, which also worked quite well. But both of these are poisonous to humans, and couldn't be used without a high degree of safety measures. So there you have something peculiar: the same thing that is preserving food and helping to reduce starvation and save lives can also kill you. Again, seems kind of unnatural, a kind of imbalance, that these two effects go together.

Then in the thirties, they introduce Freon as a coolant, which is not poisonous to humans, so now household refrigerators become very popular. Except, Freon damages the ozone layer, which protects the earth and its atmosphere from harmful radiation from the sun. So what's helping us keep our food around longer is also killing the earth's conditions to make that food. Now they've replaced Freon with tetrafluoroethane, which isn't as bad for the ozone, but who really knows if that will last or if they'll find something else wrong with it?

That's why I love breaking stuff apart. Gadgets, devices, you name it. Because you see a long history of people trying to grip and squeeze and mold nature and its elements into something so unnatural, to make us happier, or healthier, or to make things easier or better. And look around, our whole lives are dominated by these creations, and they take so much invention and effort to make them work as intended, and even working as intended often means damaging or destroying something else.

At the end of it all, I can't decide whether we're making progress or we're just hamsters running on a wheel and haven't figured it out yet."

Herb trailed off, then started rummaging through his toolbox. Julian was at a loss for words, unsure of how to respond, until he bent down to get in the toolbox as well.

"How can I help?" Julian asked.

"Grab those wire cutters. We got some stripping to do."

"You know I'm not really into that Herb. Not with guys, anyway."

"Trust me, you're not my type." Herb quipped back.

"You know, even if we are hamsters on a wheel, it's a pretty entertaining wheel to be on."

"Is it as entertaining once you realize it's a wheel, though?"

Over the rest of the morning, the two of them stripped and scrapped the refrigerator. They cut the power cord attached to the back of the fridge. They cut through the coils with a hacksaw and arranged them in lines on the tarp. "Good value at the scrap yard," said Herb. They removed the compressor. They took apart the cooling fans in the back and front of the fridge, and excised the small motor powering those fans. Then they removed the shelves and cut them into small pieces, and set them aside by the pipes. Finally, they removed whatever plastic remained from the interior and set it in a separate bin for recycling. By the time they finished, it was near mid-day and the sun was high and bright above them. Julian, dripped in sweat in Herb's t-shirt, wiped his brow and stared up towards the sky.

"It's pretty hot. You work out here every day?" he asked.

"Most days, when I can. Want a beer?"

"Ha! Sure man, I can make day-drinking part of my routine. Why not?"

"Yeah, why not."

Herb went into his garage near the door to the house, where a working fridge was plugged in and of service. He grabbed two beers, popped them open, and brought them back to the front law. He gave one to Julian, and they both took their chairs from the day before and sat back down in the lawn.

"Don't think I can spend all day drinking again, Herb."

"Neither can I, but a little hair of the dog won't kill anyone though. Who's that guy waving at you over there?"

"Shit, that's Zane, my friend from work."

"Man, aren't you Mr. Popular. Had no idea I was in the midst of such a celebrity. Do I need to behave for your boyfriend too?"

"Nah, he's pretty cool. No idea what he's doing here though."

Zane made eye contact with Julian from down the street, and walked over to join the two of them on Herb's lawn. Zane was dressed in work clothes -- khakis and a button-down with penny-loafers but no tie -- and had been walking outside for a while based on the beads of sweating forming on his temples and the red flush of his cheeks and neck.

"Hey Zane, how's it going man?"

"It's cool man. What are you up to?"

"Just spent the morning working on some stuff with my friend Herb. Herb, this is my friend Zane. We work together at Chimera."

"Hey Zane. Pleasure to meet you. Geez, you're a big dude. And super red. You want a beer or something?"

The flush in Zane's cheek brightened even more. "Shit, Herb, can't you be decent to anyone?" Julian scoffed.

"What? I'm offering him a beer aren't I?"

"No, thanks," replied Zane. "I just came from work. But maybe next time."

"How do you know there will be a next time?"

"Don't mind him," Julian interrupted. "What brings you here from work?"

"Actually, Kendra sent me over. Or, I suppose it came from her assistant, but from her all the same. I went by your house this morning but couldn't find you. Checked that coffee shop underneath your place, and the barista said you had walked this way after you left his morning. Honestly, didn't expect to find you, since no one knew where the hell you were."

"Me too. Sorry I didn't return your calls, just been a bit busy. But we're wrapping up here now, aren't we Herb?"

"You're the boss, kid."

"Figures. Well hey Zane why don't the two of us get some lunch?"

"Are you sure?" Zane asked. "You two look like you're in the middle of something."

Herb finished his beer. "You two go ahead. I got some cleaning up to do here."

"You sure?" Julian checked.

"Positive. You're only slowing me down anyway." Herb got off his chair and headed back to the scrap piles and empty frame of the fridge.

"Of course I am. Alright Zane, let's get out of here. Any idea where you want to go?"

"Not sure what's around here. You know your friend can come too if he wants."

"Oh yeah, don't worry about him. Let's go to Nero's down the street. A slice with spinach and mushrooms sounds pretty good, what do you say?"

"Yeah definitely, let's do it."

"Good stuff. So long, Herb! Catch you later."

"Thanks for the help this morning. You two lovebirds enjoy your romantic lunch."

"I'll be thinking of you the whole time, sweetheart." And with that Julian took off down the street, leaving Herb behind assembling the scrapped copper into piles. Zane watched the whole scene with a puzzled look on his face, then turned around and caught up to Julian.

"Nice friend you got there," Zane offered.

"Some friend, indeed. He's pretty sour at first but once you get to know him he's pretty interesting."

"I'll take your word for it. Is this where you've been since Monday?"

"For today and most of yesterday, yeah. Monday I simply stayed at home. I guess you heard about my work assignment?"

"Jesus christ man. Everyone has."

"Yeah, I suppose that was bound to happen."

"What are you going to do?"

"I don't know, man. But let's eat first, I just realized I'm starving."

They walked a few blocks from Herb's to Nero's, a franchised pizzeria. A relatively small, express-style outfit, this location had a few tables set inside a covered portico, but mostly serviced take-out and delivery orders, particularly for weekday lunches. Glass-covered trays contained insulated pre-made pies from which customers could order by the slice. Julian ordered a spinach and mushroom, Zane ordered a four-cheese and a Coke, and they both grabbed a small table with two chairs to sit down and eat.

"Man, did not realize how hungry I was." Julian exclaimed.

"What have you been doing all morning? You look like you worked up quite a sweat."

"Helped Herb take apart a refrigerator."

"Seriously?"

"Yeah seriously."

"You seem pretty relaxed, given the circumstances."

"What circumstances?"

"You know, your work assignment."

"Oh yeah, that."

"See that's what I'm talking about. Aren't you freaking out?"

"Not really, why should I?"

"Cause the CEO of the company just asked you to write a freaking book, that's why!"

"Yeah, well it's kind of ridiculous, isn't it? I mean, professional authors can't always write a book, why would anyone expect me to?"

"So you're just not going to do it?"

"Didn't say that."

"Well then what?"

"I don't know, dude! Geez, get off my ass, would you? What's with you today?"

"What's with *me*?! Dude you don't answer my calls for two days when you're in the middle of the craziest fucking situation at work, then I come drag my ass over here to find you and you're playing handyman with some weird old dude. Now you act like nothing's out of the ordinary."

"Strangely, it's not. I feel...fine. And besides, what does it have to do with you?"

"It doesn't, I just, it's like this big thing happened, and I didn't hear from you, and just wanted to make sure you're okay, which sounds like you are, so that's good I guess."

"Yeah, sure is. And I'm sorry I didn't answer you. I mean, what kind of shit is this anyhow? I have no idea what I'm going to do or what's going to happen to me. But I guess what I'm trying to say is, I don't really care. I mean not that I don't care completely, but I'm just not going to freak out over something I really can't control."

"Yeah, I guess that makes sense."

"How is everyone at work reacting to it?"

"Strangely, it's been...normal. Like everything is the same. I don't know how many people know about your assignment from Kendra, but no one has said as much, at least not to me. To be honest, it's kind of frustrating, cause I know people know about it, or know that *something* is going on, and how crazy it is really, but everyone is just kind of keeping on, just putting their head down and not trying to make a fuss over it."

"Well what are they going to do about it? They are probably freaking out too, just not out loud. I mean think about it from their perspective. Hard enough to do the job you're hired to do, then have to put in that extra time and effort to do things on top of your job that your boss expects you to do if you want to get ahead. Doing more is expected, doing what you're supposed to do means you're falling behind. Then on top of that, they want you to *love* your job, like it's your passion to work there. Like that's the only thing in the world you ever dreamed of doing. Like you don't even think of it as work because you just love it so much. Like nothing else in your life ought to matter.

So people are working harder than they're paid to work, have to fake it like they're doing it voluntarily because they just care so much, and then, they hear that someone like me was just been called into the CEO's office and work on something special, *for my job*. They're probably scared shitless that someone is going to ask them to run a marathon or something like that, to show the company really means it when they say they are champions. Perform open-heart surgery in Uganda because Chimera wants to show it cares about the needy. It's like, what more can they expect from someone who wants to do just enough to make sure they and their family have a decent enough life?

But the truth is, they are probably not worried about having to do something like that. I mean, sure, maybe they can do it, or maybe they can't, but either way everything would work out one way or the other. What they are really upset about is that they know that, if it really came down to it, they'd be too scared to say no. That they're caught on this one path, which, like a lot of us, including me, we went down by choice, only to realize at some point later on that we really don't have the strength nor conviction to head back and find another path when we realize the current one isn't working out anymore. What? What are you looking at?"

Zane didn't respond, just continued to stare unwaveringly at Julian. Eventually, he responded.

"Nothing, I just realized, well...how long have we know each other?"

"Let me think. Probably, a little after you joined Chimera as an intern. So, two years ago?"

"Yeah, that's right."

"What of it?"

"I've never really heard you talk like that before."

"Like what?"

"Well, to be blunt, like you gave a fuck about something."

"Ha! Who says I give a fuck about anything?"

"You know what I mean."

Julian and Zane finished the last of their pizza. The lunch crowd was growing, and a couple stood impatiently a few feet behind them, casting disapprovingly looks every few seconds to signal their displeasure at Julian and Zane's loitering.

"What are you going to do now?" Julian asked.

"Go back to work I guess."

"Forget that, man. Let's go do something else. This has been fun."

"No way, I can't."

"Sure you can. Just tell them tomorrow that you had to spend all afternoon finding me. Who will really care?"

"But what would we do?"

"Well let me ask, what do you want to do? And I mean, really, like if you could do any one thing this afternoon, what would it be?"

Zane paused for a few moments to reflect. "Can I tell you what I'd really do?"

"Yeah, fire away."

"Paintball."

"Huh?"

"Let's go paintballing."

"You serious?"

"Yeah I am. I used to love it as a kid, and used to play regularly up until college. Then I just stopped. We should go."

"Fuck it. Let's do it."

"For real?"

"Yeah let's do it. Sounds like a good time."

Julian and Zane arrived at Willow Ridge paintball park just outside the city limits at one o'clock in the afternoon. The park was set up on a few acres of green pasture, separated into 12 distinct fields, or 'terrains,' in which to play. Each field had a different landscape corresponding to a different playing format. Some were set up to simulate urban warfare, with small houses, old cars, and open walls strewn about randomly. Others were set up with clear battle lines for two teams, with inflatable plastic objects set up as defense posts behind which one side could mount their attack against the other. One field was just completely open save two or three narrow, vertical posts, leaving almost nowhere for anywhere to hide.

They walked by all the fields to the far end which looked to be the headquarters, with a small shed which housed the paintball equipment, and a registration table with some employees handling sign-ins and payments. There were about 15-20 guests in the vicinity, either beginning or ending their paintball excursion. They reached the main table, where a Willow Ridge employee was assorting some masks which had just been returned.

"We'd like to play a few rounds, please." said Zane.

"Do you need gear?" the employee asked.

"Yes."

"What about paintballs?"

"That too."

"Just the two of you?"

"Yes."

"Minimum group on a field is 4. You guys are going to have find another group to pair up with."

"Who should we go with?"

"You'll have to ask around."

Looking around, they found a group consisting of two fathers and six young boys about the ages of ten to twelve. They went up to the men and asked if they could join. The group was a collection of friends which included the sons of the two men. They were there on an afternoon outing to celebrate the boys making the playoffs in their youth baseball league, and though it was a Wednesday, they were allowed to take off from school as long as they caught up on their assignments by the end of the week. The fathers agreed to let Julian and Zane join, on the condition that for two-team battles the adults equally split against the children. Julian and Zane went back to the registration table, paid for their gear and paintballs, and suited up for the day's play.

The first round was to take place on one of the urban warfare terrains, with a capture the flag challenge. Julian and Zane split up on opposite teams, who had to defend their flags in opposite corners of the field. The round lasted 15 minutes. If neither side captured the other's flag, it would be called a draw. Each contestant had one paintball gun, which could hold up to 50 paintballs in its chamber at one time. The guns were semi-automatic, meaning that pressing and holding the trigger would fire off up to 5 paintballs one after the other. Each player could carry two canisters of ammunition holding up to 100 paintballs each on their belt. Aside from a clear plastic facemask which covered one's face from the forehead down to the chin and across to the ears, there was no other protection required, although some of the boys who had played before came in with knee pads and elbow pads to cushion themselves.

A Willow Ridge referee explained the rules of fair play to the group. Don't aim for the head, or intentionally shoot at someone within ten feet. The universal signal for being out or surrendering is to raise your hands and gun, high in the air. Anything outside the yellow ropes which marked the boundary is out of bounds. The referee split up the group into two teams, and Julian and Zane took their positions opposite one another. The teams lined up by their respective flags, and the referee blew an air horn to commence the game.

Julian rushed out in front of his team to take cover behind an open wall to his front and left, which shielded him from any fire coming from the center and right of the opposing terrain, while exposing himself to the left most flank. Zane, from the opposite side, resolved to track about 30 feet to his right, towards Julian, to an elevated ridge, protected by a row of waist-high stumps forming a crescent in front of him. This put Zane almost directly in front of the wall protecting Julians. Zane crouched down to conceal his whole body behind the stumps, which had just enough space between them to squeeze his paint gun through. Though he was in direct sight of the wall protecting Julian, Julian himself was protected from view. He would only be exposed if he were to step out towards the left flank, which he would need to do to get a clear shot at Zane or anyone on the other team.

The boys in the group quickly scattered about the terrain, with seemingly little application of tactical maneuvers that might improve their chances of capturing the enemy's flag. One boy on Julian's team enjoyed running as fast as he could between defensible positions, chortling in glee each time he fled from one to the other without being hit. Another boy on Zane's team secured the high ground on the opposite side of Zane, and spray-shot his paintballs with no concern for who or what he was hitting. The others did some combination or running or shooting, content enough to emulate the machinations of real-life commandos. The fathers hung back, cheering on their group of boys occasionally or offering suggestions for someone to claim a particular area or shoot at a particular enemy combatant.

Between Julian and Zane, there was no dearth of trash-talking during their opening skirmish. Julian darted out behind his wall to fire a volley onto Zane's stumps. "Stop hiding!" he shouted. "These ten year-olds are braver than you!" Zane, both riled by the insult and surprised by Julian's jeering, stood up tall to return a volley, forcing Julian back behind his protective wall. "Who's hiding now?!" he fired back in response.

Zane used Julian's retreat to race down the hill to a closer strike point. The defense offered -- just three four-feet long planks arranged next to each other vertically -- was less secure, barely covering Zane's torso and forcing him to bend at the knees to shelter his head and shoulders. However, he now had an advantage: when shooting from above the planks, Zane was able to shoot behind on the wall on Julian's left side, preventing Julian from using that side to mount his own offensive. With each spurt of fired paintballs, Zane shouted out a "How do you like that?" or "Come out come out!" as Julian was cornered further and and further behind his wall. Realizing that moving to his left was no longer an option, Julian eventually whipped out from the right side of the wall, away from Zane, but into the center of the field and out in the open. Two of the boys and the father from Zane's team team rained paintballs at him. He fired back while running forward, pegging the father in the leg and nearly tagging one of the boys before he dove down into a small path underneath a ridge, protecting himself from the fire directly in front of him. The boys on Julian's team, inspired by his act of selfless defiance, began to charge ahead, with his team's father marshalling the troops forward with exalting cries of "let's go!" and "move forward, men!" While crouched, Julian turned to his left to take aim at Zane, who had not seen Julian's charge and was now in Julian's direct line of fire. Julian unleashed his own volley and sprayed the side of Zane's protective planks. Zane, alerted to his Julian's new position, began charging towards Julian, hopping, zig-zagging, and leaping up intermittently to become as evasive as possible. Julian continued to fire, but was unable to make a direct hit. Zane lurked closer and closer, thirty feet, twenty-five feet, before he unleashed a volley at Julian's torso, who was lying prostrate on the grass ahead. The paintballs landed directly on Julian's back and side, creating mini-explosions of color up and down his midsection. As Zane finished his volley, Julian say him flinch once, then twice, before stumbling forward. Zane turned around to find the father on Julian's team standing high on the ridge behind, with his gun locked on his arm and posing like a statue after picking off his target. Realizing he was out, Zane raised his hands high in the air. He turned back around to find Julian, who was writhing in the grass.

"Ah! Those hurt, you fucker!" Julian cried out.

"Yeah no shit! I just got popped in the back too!"

"Serves you right!"

"God, this hurts a lot more than I remembered."

The two of them slowly got up and retreated off the field to let the others conclude the game. The charge Julian instigated had paid early dividends for his team; three boys had stormed the right side of the opponent's terrain, and had eliminated one of the opposing boys by firing at both sides of his defense post. The father from Julian's team took up Julian's old spot behind the protective wall, and used his position to keep the remaining boys from the opposing team from escaping his way. Eventually, one of the boys from Julian's team made a run up the middle, past where Julian was gunned down, and reached the unprotected flag while his opponents were preoccupied with fire from their left flank. The referee blew the air horn, signalling a victory for Julian's team.

"Fuck yeah! How do you like them apples, Zane?" Julian gloated.

"You mean the apples where I shot your ass out?"

"Yeah as a suicide mission, apparently."

"Yeah that father really put a few in me."

"That's what she said."

"Zing!"

"You had some pretty good evasive maneuvers at the end there. Like a ninja coming at me, could barely get a shot near you."

"Told you I used to play quite a lot. The key is to make yourself small and quick, and there's almost no chance you'll catch any spray."

"That's what she said."

"Hm. Not quite there but I'll give it to you."

"Ha! Thanks."

The referee ran over to the two of them, who continued to jaw on the sidelines. "Gentlemen," he said, "please watch your language. The children might not have heard your profanity but I did. Next time, I'm going to have to ask you to leave."

"So sorry, sir, won't happen again," Zane responded remorsefully. The referee turned around to advance to the next field.

"...dick." Zane finished.

"Oh, snap."

"Well I mean what gives? We were just having fun. Plus, these kids probably have heard worse."

"I know I did when I was their age."

"Me too."

"Fuck it, it'll be fine."

They spent the next hour or so sequencing through rounds of elimination knock-out, sudden death, and target shooting with the group of boys and the two fathers. Sometimes Zane was on the side of the victor, sometimes Julian, but in all cases they engaged fully in the challenge, and did their best to censor their language. The boys, after mostly keeping their distance, began to attack and defend with Julian and Zane as if they were one group, and the two of them returned the favor in equal kind. In one game, the fathers decided to take a break to grab water and snacks for the group, and breaking protocol, the boys decided to battle against Zane and Julian directly. They lined up on opposite sides of a field and at the sound of the airhorn, raced out towards each other with furious volleys from both sides. Within seconds, the group of boys had Julian and Zane surrounded, giggling maniacally at their victory over the two adults. As Julian and Zane surrendered, the boys whooped and hooted and one in particular dropped to the ground to perform a celebratory "worm" dance, something his friends must have anticipated, as they began to clap and cheer on their companion as he moved back and forth with long, loopy gyrations. Julian and Zane could only laugh and clap along as the boys started running in a circle around them, surrounding their new caught hostages.

The day of paintball finished when the hour was up and the boys had to leave with their chaperoning fathers. The group said goodbye to Julian and Zane as they walked towards the registration table to drop off their gear on their way to the parking lot. Julian and Zane stuck around, finding an open field with circular targets marked on square wooden boards. They each grabbed a bottle of water from a cooler near the registration stand and took alternating turns firing their paintball gun at the targets.

"Hey Julian, thanks for doing this with me."

"No man, thank you, to be honest I don't think I've ever been paintballing, and this was incredibly fun."

"Really? You moved around and shot like you'd done it before. I would have never noticed."

"Sure beats going to work, doesn't it?"

"I'll say, though I don't think my boss will be very happy with me spending company time like this."

"Of course not, but you got your whole life to worry about what your boss thinks. When's the next time you're going to get to do something like this?"

"Good point. Though next time, perhaps some advanced preparation would be nice, particularly as it pertains to attire." Zane looked down at this outfit, khakis and a button-down shirt, which were covered in grass and paintball stains.

"Oh shit! I hadn't even thought about that. Those stains will probably come out though. Tell you what, let's go back to my place. You can shower and I'll give you some clothes to wear home."

"No, you don't have to do that."

"No I mean it. I was the one who put you up for this today anyway."

"Alright let's go."

Julian and Zane returned to Julian's apartment, covered in grass, exploded paintballs, and sweat from the day's play. Franny greeted them at the door, only to run away upon seeing Zane.

"I didn't know you had a cat," said Zane.

"You didn't?"

"This is the first time I've even been to your place."

"Oh, well I don't think I've been to your place either, really."

"Yeah, guess not. Cool digs though, you like living here?"

"Yeah it's not bad. Easy commute to work, plus the coffee shop downstairs is a good fallback to have close by."

"Know anyone in the building?"

"Up until recently? No. But just met a girl a few days ago."

"Woot! When was this?"

"Sunday. Actually, after we had brunch."

"So you guys already had sex then?"
"Ha! I wish. I asked her out the other day, but she said she'd think about it."

"Ouch dude, sorry."

"I know, probably wasn't the smoothest."

"Eh, who knows. Maybe she'll say yes. Just don't introduce her to your crazy old man friend down the road."

"Too late."

"You're killing me, bro, just killing me."

"You still want that shower?"

"Yeah for sure, I'm a mess."

"Here, let me get you some stuff."

Julian went into his bedroom and found a towel and a washcloth. He dug into this back closet and picked out an old pair of gym shorts and t-shirts which were a couple sizes big on him.

"Here you go," he said, "hopefully the clothes fit."

Zane held them up in front of him. "Should be fine. You sure I can borrow them?"

"Yeah definitely. You can keep them if you want, I never wear them."

"No, I'll get them back to you next time you're back at work."

"Who said I am coming back to work?"

"Funny."

"I'm serious."

"What, really? You are just going to up and quit like that?"

"I've been considering it."

"No way, you've been stirring up too much shit to just bail now."

Zane departed to the shower. Julian changed out of his clothes and into a pair of sweatpants and a ribbed thermal t-shirt. He rinsed off his face and hands, and returned to the kitchen to grab a can of lime soda-water. He cracked it open and stood by his window near the sunroom, staring out towards the view beyond, which started with the road below and the cars and pedestrians walking back and forth, followed by a city park with an external boundary of trees forming the perimeter of open green fields and a large, circular pond in the middle, with small fountains around the rims. It was near the end of the business day. Individuals, couples, and families alike were assembling near the pond, where the fountains went off in an orchestrated sequence every 30 minutes. The sun was on its way to set behind a bevy of clouds, creating a bright but grey sky over the park.

Here, Julian paused and reflected on his day, and the powerful, driving feeling of satisfaction permeating from within. He was hot, sweaty, sore, and scraped up from the paintballing with Zane and the handyman work with Herb. He had not been to work in two days. Franny began to make figure-eights around his legs, purring and crying in tandem to create a soft high-pitched growl, signalling that she was both hungry and happy, a feeling Julian shared as well.

Zane finished his shower and walked out of the bathroom. The gym shorts fit rather well, but the t-shirt, while broad enough to cover his shoulders was not long enough to drop fully to his waist. His cheeks still flushed from the hot water from the shower, he continued to towel off his head and face as he gathered his old clothes and compiled them in a white plastic bag.

"You want anything to drink? Don't have much but there's a lime soda in the fridge," Julian offered.

"Thanks, I'll grab it. Let me see that view."

"Come check it out."

Zane walked over to the window and stood next to Julian. Franny once again departed from the scene, torn between bonding with Julian and evading Zane.

"This is a great view. You must stare out here a lot."

"To tell you the truth, this might be the longest I've looked out here."

"What, really? Man if I lived here that's all I would do."

"I guess I just never cared to look out at the park. But now that I am, I agree it's pretty impressive."

"Didn't realize how many people hang out there during the evenings."

"If you could be anyone down there, who would you be?"

"Anyone? Her." Zane pointed down towards the pond, at a small girl running in a grassy area, by an opened picnic blanket and a couple who was presumably her parents. The girl was blowing bubbles in the air, projecting them forward even as she ran straight through them, allowing them to pop on her face and blouse. Periodically she would look back to her parents with joyful laughter, who would smile back at her while they held hands and sipped champagne from plastic flutes.

"Why her?"

"Because she's just so happy. And she's too young to have the weight of the world on her shoulders. There are times when I want that, to not have to worry about stuff all the time."

"What are you worried about?"

"Everything, really. Money, my job, if or when I am going to get promoted, what I'm supposed to do with my life, what I *want* to do with my life, girls, relationships, friends. I just can't shake this feeling that I'm missing something, that I'm doing something wrong."

"I suppose it's natural. How old are you now?"

"Twenty-seven."

"Yeah, so you graduated college five years ago and that was the last time you got to achieve something that was already set up for you, laid out for you where you just had a follow the path and get to the finish line. After that, there is no one path, there's seemingly infinite paths, and who's there to tell you which one is the right one for you? It's an impossible task really, and it's only natural to look around at other people and wonder if they know something you don't."

"Yeah. That's exactly what I mean."

"Well, my advice to you is don't worry about it. You're smart, and people seem to like you. And those two together means you're going to do just fine."

"Thanks. Who would you be down there?"

"Easy. Him." Julian pointed at a bench some one hundred yards from the pond. The bench had one elderly gentleman, wearing a three-piece suit and a fedora hat, sitting with a straight back and knees touched together, staring blankly into the jumble of bodies before him. His expression emitted neither jubilance nor sadness, bewilderment nor animosity. It was simply one of peace.

"Um, seriously?" Zane asked. "He looks kind of crazy."

"Probably is, but, I want to be like him," Julian began. "I don't know what he's thinking about, but if I had to guess he is reminiscing about something that happened in his life, and whatever it was, he is satisfied with it. He's proud of whatever he's done, and feels at peace knowing his life in its full arc was lived fully and with purpose. He has lived well. That's what I want. Or maybe what I really want is to avoid the opposite. Getting to the end and looking back and being disappointed at what I did with my life and why."

"Damn, that makes everything seem kind of depressing when you think about it."

"I didn't mean it to be. I just want my life to be something good to look back on when it's all said and done."

"Yeah, can't argue with that. Listen, Julian, I am going to head home. Thanks a lot for hanging out today, I had an awesome time."

"Yeah, me too. Maybe not playing hooky from work, but we should do it again sometime."

"Yeah definitely."

Zane finished his lime soda, gathered his old clothes, and walked towards the door. Julian followed him to see him out.

"Good luck with that girl," Zane offered.

"Thanks, I'll let you know what she says."

"And if it doesn't work out, text me her number."

"You wish, asshole."

"See ya Julian. Are you going to come into work tomorrow?"

"Yeah sure, why not? Although I don't have to, I suppose I should check-in and see what's what."

"Okay cool."

"Hey Zane."

"What?"

"I wanted to tell you something. The other day, at brunch, you asked me what other friends I had, and I told you I knew some friends from college who liked to smoke weed at house parties. Truth is, that's a lie. I don't have any college friends around here. In fact, I barely talk to anyone from college, and I don't really have any other friends either. In fact, you're probably the person I'm closest to."

"Oh, I see."

"Yeah, sorry, didn't want to make it weird or anything, just felt bad lying to you. I don't know why I did, just felt kind of embarrassed I guess."

"Don't be. Having lots of friends isn't all it's cracked up to be. But if you want, you can come with me to whatever parties I go to."

"Yeah thanks, maybe I'll take you up on that."

"Please do. See you tomorrow."

Zane headed out the door and walked down the stairs to the front lobby. Julian closed the door behind him and returned to the kitchen in order to feed Franny. He then went into the shower to rinse off and put a fresh set of clothes on. He was hungry, but opted to kick back and watch some TV on the Murphy bed, relishing that feeling of being spent from a day's worth of physical exertion, where one's energy is drained and muscles ache, but the mind feels fresh and clear and focused. He turned on the TV, scrolled through his Netflix, and resumed an episode of One Way Trip, a novelty travel series. The protagonist, Shelby Connors, is held at the whims of an app which offers bargain-basement prices for private jets that are on their way from one city to another to pick up a client. These "throw-away" flights are lost costs for the carrier anyway, so the app pairs those flights with passengers who are flexible and willing enough to hop on the flight at the last minute. Shelby's mission on the show is to hop on a flight anytime one is leaving from her current city, regardless of its destination. Each show, she arrives in a new city, and improvises her touring of the local culture and cuisine, and by the end, she learns where the app will require her to travel next, which according to the show, is left to chance and is not known in advance to anyone, including Shelby.

This particular episode, Shelby is in Tarifa, Spain. She samples the local flavors (she loves the Halal influence in the city juxtaposed with traditional Spanish offerings) and walks along the long, windy beaches where kite-surfers jump out of the waves in the background. She spends a few minutes off camera talking with her production crew about whether the bylaws of the show allow her to take a ferry to either Gibraltar or Tangiers. The production crew determines that no, she cannot, which disappoints her and limits her options considerably. She takes in the local history by visiting the Castillo de Guzman el Bueno and the Church of San Mateo, which she finds interesting but not exceptional especially when compared to the historical structures in the rest of Spain, and finally, she concludes by returning back to the beach, facing towards the water, watching the sunset, and waiting. This happens every few episodes or so, particularly in cities that are less populated or less traveled, when she runs out of things to do and places to see while waiting for another jet to offer a one-way trip out of there. The first time Julian watched one of these pauses in an episode, it unnerved him, seeing her wait somewhere in a city she didn't really know for a duration she could not know, but eventually he got used to their recurring cameos, knowing that a flight would always show up, somehow, from somewhere, eventually.

Julian enjoyed One Way Trip, in part because of the irony of the show. After all, any person at any time has the freedom to travel anywhere they want to. Aside from having money in the bank, and occasionally the right documentation, any major city on the planet was within a day's length in travel. By this argument, the possibilities are endless, and the excitement of such possibilities ought to arouse even the most sober of observers and contemplators. Even so, Julian himself, and most other people he gathered, did not feel this excitement much, if at all. Despite the limitless opportunities to travel, explore, *live*, back and forth across the globe, he could not help but to think that on any given day, he was confined, even constrained to spend that day in the same ruts which had formed across his home, work, and social lives from the day before that, and the day before that. Yet, for Shelby -- who, conditional on arriving in one city, must, through threat of breach of contract, remain in that city until an unknown time, at which point she will be transported to an unknown destination -- the absence of choice in how long she would stay and where she would go next felt, at least to the viewer, exhilarating. That through the removal of excessive choices, the show could garner a sense of true joy and wonder on behalf of the viewers who had many more places to go than Shelby ever would.

The show concludes, as it always eventually does, with Shelby hopping on a one-way flight out of Tarifa, to Sofia, Bulgaria. What awaits her in Sofia can only be known in the next episode, which Julian would save for another time, despite Netflix's kind but firm suggestion to stream it immediately after the current episode's conclusion. Julian turned off his TV. By this time Franny had made her way into a curled-up position between his legs, and he slid his legs down so as not to bother her while he laid down on the bed. He put his hands behind his head and closed his eyes, and let the accumulated exhaustion of the day wash down his body, from the crown of his head to the bottom of his toes.

While laying there, in the waning moments before he fell asleep, he recalled a memory he had since he was a small child, when he, his brother, and parents visited the island of Maui in Hawaii. They took a boat tour off the coast to watch dolphins and whales, and swim and snorkel by a reef, watching the fish swimming nearby. Julian was proud of himself for learning how to control his breath through the snorkel while keeping his head just below the surface. The first few times, he could not control his head nor his breath, so he'd either spill water down the air pipe, or breath so haphazardly that he'd have to come up for a few normal breaths above water before he could start again. Eventually, he learned how to keep his head flat in the water and control his breathing, and could spend minutes on end gazing at the aquatic life underneath. He was too young to know the types and names of all the fish, but he remembered seeing blue ones, orange ones, black and yellow ones, and some so translucent that he could see through their bodies to the reef below.

On this particular reef, the tour guide informed the group that about twenty meters toward the edge, the reef dropped off to a deep ocean floor beyond, with a richer, denser underwater terrain of rocks and plants. This drop-off, about twenty feet in total, was where turtles were known to visit, to pick off tiny fish leaving the main reef. In order to see these turtles, one needed to swim out past the reef a few feet, turn around, and stay put, waiting for a sea turtle to make an appearance.

Julian was eager to see a turtle, and darted out past the main group of snorkelers to the edge of the reef. Keeping his head under water, he swam a few feet past the reef as instructed, to find the drop-off was not only deep, but dark. The color of the water changed to a dark, rich blue, and the visibility

94

decreased even as the ocean floor opened up. Julian turned around to face the reef and wait, hoping a sea turtle would appear looking for a bite to eat or just to give him a personal visit. After a few seconds, while waiting patiently, he was overcome with fear, no, more than fear -- terror -- of floating out in the ocean past the reef, past any sense of origin offered by the rocks and active fish underneath. The terror overcame him, and he felt that at any moment the tide would take him out to sea and he would be pulled away forever, from the reef, from the boat, from his family. He panicked, knifing his arms vigorously into the water in order to return to reef, and for a few moments it felt that no amount of force in the world would return his body back to safety. He swam as hard as he could back onto the reef, and back further to where he could stand with his head above water. He stood up, looking above for the first time since leaving the reef, only to find the rest of the tour group calmly swimming and snorkeling in the vicinity around him. His parents and brother were all together, scanning a separate part of the reef, and paid no heed to Julian's explorations. The water itself was flat, with no tide to speak of pulling or pushing anyone around.

He thought of this memory while lying in bed, thinking about that moment out away from the reef, waiting for a sea turtle, and how much longer he would have stayed there in order to see one, if he could do it again. How long would it have taken? Would he have been sucked out to sea eventually, as he so feared? If he waited out there indefinitely, would anyone, would his family, have come and retrieve him? He wanted to return to see that turtle, only to turn his back to the vast, shapeless ocean once again and hold his nerve for as long as it took to conquer the challenge he had set before him.

Thursday

Julian heard a knock on his door. He was half-dressed, and less than half-awake, having overslept his alarm and running late. He came to the door and looked through the peep-hole, and found Lydia waiting and smiling on the other side. She was wearing a purple shirt with one shoulder missing, draped over her left arm and cropped at the navel, with tan capris and bright pink flats. Her hair was clipped behind her head, with one loose strand falling across the bridge of her nose. She knew he'd see her from behind the door, and she knew she looked stunning. "Just a minute," he cried out, as he ran back to his room to grab a t-shirt. He swung it over his head and let it fall over his shoulders as he darted back to the door, unlocked and opened it.

"Hi, Lydia"

"Good morning, Julian."

"What are you doing here?"

"I wanted to see you. Is that alright with you?" she asked with a gentle, knowing smirk.

"Of course. Please come in. Sorry but I need a couple of minutes to finish getting ready."

He led her into the kitchen and living area and returned to his room. A few minutes later, he returned in khakis, a royal blue polo, and high-top brown sneakers.

"Sorry about that. Welcome to the place, can I offer you anything?"

"How about a tour? It's a wonderful spot and a gorgeous view of the park. I don't remember it from the other night."

"Probably intoxicated by my charm."

"Pretty sure just one of us was intoxicated."

"Fair. Well you are looking at the most of it here. The sunroom would be a lot nicer if I didn't have to keep Franny's litter box in there. Bedrooms and baths are that way."

"And where is Miss Franny?"

"Probably in the bedroom. Let's see."

They walked into Julian's bedroom, and found Franny lying on top of the clothes dresser, tucked into Julian's clothes which he had left there from the previous evening. She was half-asleep, in her typical post-breakfast daze, though she flashed her eyes open once she saw Lydia enter. Lydia, unfazed, walked up to Franny and began petting her, scratching behind her ears and on top of her head. Franny, after a few seconds of aloofness, capitulated to the affection and began to arch her neck back and forth to embrace the unexpected massage.

"So cute. How old?"

"Six. She usually doesn't take well to strangers."

"My neighbors had cats where I grew up. I'm used to them."

"Do you have one yourself?"

"No. Thought about it a few times, but could never quite the pull trigger on getting one. Surprised you don't have a dog, given that painting on the wall."

"A dog you say? Interesting. Try standing a few feet closer."

"Sure." Lydia walked closer to the painting. "Oh I see. It's a dog and a boy, same as before," she added somewhat sarcastically.

"You don't see anything else?"

"What am I supposed to see?"

"Well, some people see an old, sad man."

"That wouldn't be a very fun painting now, would it? Besides, why would you want to see the sad old man if you could choose the boy and his dog?"

"Don't think it's about choice. You either see one or the other, based on your perspective and disposition."

"No, I think at some level you can make a choice about what you want to see."

"And you would choose to see the happy side of the painting?"

"I would, but that's just me. Is this what you wear to work?" She pointed at Julian in his outfit. "I didn't know writers had to dress like they are in a Dockers commercial."

"I'm actually not a writer. Just assigned to do some writing for my job. I'm a consultant, at Chimera."

"Chimera? Sounds scintillating. And so exotic too. Hard to believe it's some boring consulting company. Though I guess not really, if you have to write a book for them."

"Definitely can't call that boring, at least not at the moment, though I haven't been in since I found out about this project of mine. Was planning to go in today."

"Well, I hope I'm not holding you up."

"No, I'm glad you're here. Maybe to let me know about my invitation for the weekend?"

"Hmmm, maybe," she replied, with that smirk again. "How about we have breakfast? Do you have time for that?"

"Sure, I can make time. Where would you like to go?"
"Let's just go downstairs. I don't want to take you too far out of your way."

"Okay, let's do it."

The two of them walked down the building stairs, out of the lobby, and into the Savory Pass. The portly, pleasant barista from the day prior was manning the counter when they arrived, and recognized Julian.

"Two Americanos?" he asked.

"You remembered from yesterday. But just one for me, plus whatever she is having."

"And what would you like, ma'am?"

"Which herbal teas do you have?"

"Chamomile, raspberry hibiscus, and cherry currant."

"The hibiscus, please. And I'll take the pesto tomato panini as well, if this guy insists on paying."

"You got it. Any food for you, sir?"

"A croissant, along with the fruit cup, please."

"Coming right up."

"Can I ask you, what is your name? I don't see your badge."

"Nelson, sir. Thanks for asking."

"Don't mention it. You've been awfully polite to me these last two days. I appreciate the service."

"It's my pleasure. You two have a nice morning."

Julian and Lydia grabbed their beverages and walked toward an open table near the windows. Once they sat down, he realized that it was the same table where he saw the elderly couple having breakfast two days before.

"So, are you also on your way to work?" he asked her.

"I am not" Lydia replied flatly, with no intention to offer more detail.

"Ah yes, not a fan of talking about your occupation."

"I'm just so much more interesting than what I do to make money would imply, don't you think?"

Julian blushed. "Of course."

"Aren't you sweet, Julian."

"You know I was in here two days ago. Over there, by the wall. But at this table, where we are sitting now, I saw an old couple, looking out the window in silence, holding hands underneath the table. I thought it was nice, but it also made me feel, I don't know, disappointed."

"How so?"

"Well, in some way part of me longs for or wishes that when I am that age I will have a similar companion by my side, with whom I am so content and at peace that we can sit in silence and still enjoy the moment. At the same time, I don't think I ever want my life to just settle into a monotonous routine where I am spending all morning staring out a window. Think it would depress me to no end if all I had to look forward to was gazing into oblivion, saying nothing to the same person day after day after day."

"How do you know that's what they do everyday? Maybe the rest of the week they are off scuba-diving, or snorting cocaine, or playing bingo with their friends."

"Ha, maybe. I suppose I just worry about getting to the end of my life and regretting what I've done, or not done for that matter. Seems like if you settle down with someone, you don't get to explore and experience and achieve everything you could. But if you focus on all that, you miss the fulfillment of a spouse, a family, a legacy. Hard to choose one way or the other when you have to give up so much."

"My goodness, you make life sound so terrible!"

"I'm sorry, I don't mean to."

"You should be, because the way I see it, what you see as a 'damned if you do, damned if you don't' conundrum, I see as a golden opportunity, to have many many chances to do whatever you want to do. I mean, think about how rare that truly is. It's a gift, really, the license to take your life in whatever direction you please and have it turn out very well, no matter choice you make. You see it as suffocating, but to me it's the most liberating circumstance anyone could possibly imagine."

Julian paused. "I hadn't thought of it that way."

"And why straitjacket yourself with fears of regret? Let's say you live every day of your life minimizing regret. You play it safe, do everything you should, for all your days until your very last. All for what, so you can spend that last day of your life sitting on a high-horse of righteousness, congratulating yourself that you've lived the 'best' life? It's just one day, you know. Does that make up for all the days before then, when you were scared out of your mind that any wrong choice you made might screw up your perfect life story? But put it the other way around. Let's say you live every day of your life doing what you wanted, what you thought was best, what you felt was right. You might get to the end and realize you regret some things. But, it's just one day of regret, no more. And you'll have lived most of your life -- every day except one -- doing everything you wanted.

I like the fact that an old couple was here, sitting in silence, holding hands. They probably woke up and decided 'hey, this is what I'd like to do today.' And maybe right now, they are doing something else that they felt like doing. And tomorrow it will be something else. And so it will go for them. I bet they are quite happy."

Julian smiled. "You know what, I think so too."

"Hey now, even though I am making some pretty stellar arguments, you don't have to just capitulate and agree with me."

"I know. But it's actually quite nice. And on this day, I think I choose to make myself happy by listening to you tell me about what you think happiness is about."

"Oh dear, aren't you a clever one."

"I think Herb would call it, 'being a smart-ass.'"

"Ha! I bet he would. Where is he today?"

"At his home, I presume. I haven't seen him since yesterday, and after this I'll have to go to work."

"Ah yes, *work*."

"I know I know, we shouldn't talk about it."

"Well, normally I would agree, but your job seems quite fascinating, given that one of your assignments is to write a book. How interesting."

"It's only interesting if I actually do it. So far, I've barely written a thing."

"Oh my!" Lydia feigned a dramatic response sarcastically. "You mean to say you haven't written anything in two days? I would have assumed you'd be halfway finished by now."

"Cute."

Lydia smiled. "Well, I certainly think so."

"I'm sorry to have to wrap up like this, but I have to go into the office. I actually haven't been in since Monday, when I first found out about this whole book-writing thing. Think I should go back in just to check on things."

"Of course, I didn't mean to keep you. I know I just popped in this morning unannounced."

"I'm glad you did."

Lydia wrapped up the rest of her panini and grabbed her tea, while Julian finished his food and drink and returned the cup and plate back to Nelson at the counter, who thanked him. They walked out through the front door.

"Well, I'm this way," said Julian, pointing the way towards his work.

"And I'm that way," said Lydia, pointing in the opposite direction.

"Where are you off to?"

"Oh, who knows? Maybe I'll go buy a new shawl."

"What for?"

"I hear it gets a bit windy on the coast. I don't want to catch a chill this weekend."

Julian paused, then began to grin. "No, I guess you don't."

"What time will you pick me up?"

"How about ten on Saturday? I'll come by your apartment."

"Sounds lovely, Jules. I can't wait. Goodbye for now."

"Goodbye."

Lydia gave Julian a small hug, the type of hug you give acquaintances when a simple handshake feels too callous a manner to conclude and engagement. At first, Julian held his ground as Lydia softly embraced him, roping her arms over his shoulders. As she lingered for a few moments, he leaned in slightly and clasped his hands together on the small of her back. Her body was slender, but felt firm and strong in an upright posture against his. As she released from his grasp, she let the fingertips on her right hand trace along his left arm, from the top of his shoulder to the end of his fingernails. He wished that he did not have to leave her.

Julian turned around and began his walk to Chimera Solutions in the Odyssey tower, to the twenty-ninth then twenty-eighth floor. He walked at a leisurely pace, slowing his steps at each intersection just enough to miss the light which would signal him to continue. Eventually he arrived. He rode the elevator up, took the stairs down, and walked through the web of desk bullpens and colleagues on his way to his own workstation. He noticed that everyone was looking at him, with furtive glances from across the floor or sideways stares as he walked by. Many of these people he did not know, or if he knew them not very well, and on the few occasions when he met their gaze with his, they would soon enough turn away. But before doing so, seemingly each person would hold their stare, as if they had a deep, intimate connection with him, and made a point to confer their solidarity (or was it empathy?) before abandoning their view. He searched for Zane, who was neither at his workstation nor among the throng of unfamiliar faces around him.

He reached his desk, sat down, and connected his laptop to its docking station. He opened his email, to surprisingly find only a handful of messages since Monday, most of which were company-wide notifications not directly addressed to him. However, at the top of the heap was a note from Janine, Kendra's assistant, with a red exclamation point denoting high importance, and a subject line reading "come find me when you get in. EOM."

No sooner than when had he read the note he saw Janine walk up to his desk, come around to his side and lean on the edge, partially blocking his monitor.

"Did you get my note?" Janine asked. "I told you to come find me when you got in."

"I just saw it, because I just got in."

Janine looked at her watch and grimaced. "It's nine-twenty."

"Is there a problem?"

"Kendra wants to see you. Come with me."

Janine got up and walked briskly towards the center of the floor. Julian rose from his chair and followed her, but no matter how quickly he walked, he could not catch up with her, always remaining a few paces behind, having to resort to occasional leaps in order to not fall too far behind. He followed her up the two flights of stairs to the thirtieth floor and around the hall towards Kendra's office. As he passed a row of window offices, he stopped when he saw Zane, or the back of Zane, sitting in a chair across the desk of a middle-aged executive, who was gesticulating wildly with his hands and flashing a wide smile as he described something only audible from the other side of the glass. For his part, Zane appeared to be nodding furiously, his hands clutched tightly to his thighs as he sat upright in his chair.

Because he stopped to take notice, Julian fell significantly behind Janine, who arrived outside Kendra's office, turned to find Julian, then grimaced again. She double-backed to fetch him, her heels clacking forcefully against the floor as she stepped in quick cadence. The sound awoke Julian from his distracted pause, and he continued on, as Janine frowned and about-faced again. She paused outside Kendra's office and waited for Julian to finally catch up.

"You'll see her at nine-thirty. You were supposed to see her at nine but you were late to the office."

"I was unaware there was an official work starting time. Is there a policy handbook somewhere which states that?"

Janine did not answer, but crossed her arms and turned from Julian to open her phone and scroll through it.

"Can I ask you, do you know what Zane is doing up here? Whose office is that?" Julian asked, pointing in that direction.

"It's confidential," she replied, without looking up from her phone.

"You mean you don't know either, do you?"

Janine stopped scrolling and looked up. "Perhaps you should wait over there," as she pointed at a water-cooler about fifteen feet past the door to Kendra's office.

"No thanks, I'm good here."

They both stayed put, but remained in silence without making eye contact. A few minutes passed by, and at nine-thirty, Janine knocked on Kendra's door, and pushed it slightly ajar. Before she could she say anything, Kendra called out from inside "Let Julian in please, Janine. Thanks." Janine, startled by the break in their normal back-and-forth, stammered a few words before pushing out a soft "okay."

Julian walked into Kendra's office for the second time in four days and, once again, found Mort Browning, VP of creative intelligence, sitting at the small conference table and peering at Julian with an aloof, emotionless expression. Kendra was seated to his right, her back to her own desk, leaving an open seat for Julian to his left.

"Please sit down, Julian," she offered, to which he complied. He said nothing, as did Mort and Kendra, for a long-enough interval that Julian began to nervously look around the room for any stimuli which might break the tension building between the three of them. At that point, Kendra began to speak.

"Tell me, Julian, what do you know about power?"

"Power?"

"Yes, power, or more specifically, authority."

"Not much, I suppose."

"For centuries, scholars -- historians, sociologists, anthropologists -- have studied the application of authority in communities and civilizations all over the world. They have studied why some individuals gain authority, while others succumb to it, what makes authority durable and long-lasting, and what doesn't. It's a remarkable subject, one that tests your cognitive abilities to abstract yourself outside your own perspective, and see things from a meta point of view. These scholars have determined that the successful application of authority relies on three important characteristics. Do you know what they are, Julian?"

"I suppose you are going to tell me."

"Why don't you posit a guess, then?"

"I'm not sure. I would think people respond to authority when it's credible, when it's effective and aggressive enough to deter most individuals from rising against it."

"That's a very astute observation Julian, because it is exactly what most experts had thought as well. I said had because there is a new, more modern philosophy that is revolutionizing the way people think about authority, and making the old view seem antiquated and obsolete. Here is what this philosophy proposes:

First, for authority to be considered legitimate, it must allow for *feedback*. That is, it must allow for the group under authority to have some voice or influence in the administration of authority. Even if it is just to voice complaints or suggest changes, members of the group must feel they can be heard, and that the authoritative body can be reasoned with, and amenable to the concerns being raised. Though you might think this would be a sign of weakness, studies have shown that authoritative regimes which are too dismissive of the concerns of their subjects become more prone to civil unrest, leading to instability and eventually, revolt. Thus, it turns out there is greater staying power and success if the authorities adjust to the ebbs and flows of the community's needs. Like mesh netting around a captured animal, it can restrain that animal more safely and for a longer period of time than a wood or bamboo cage, whose bars can bend or snap if treated with enough force.

Second, the authority applied must be considered *fair*. Fairness in this definition means the same system of rules and consequences applied to one individual or group is applied the same way to another individual or group. This seems fairly intuitive and not that controversial, but what's interesting is just how much we humans seem to care about it. For example, there is this wonderful experiment called the Dictator game. The Dictator game is played by two people, one of whom gets to decide how much, from a fixed amount of money, they will receive and how much the other person will receive. The other person, after seeing the deal that the first person proposes, can either accept it, in which case both parties walk away with their allocations, or reject it, in which case both parties are awarded nothing.

Now, anyone with a basic understanding of game theory knows that it is optimal for person number one to award themselves the lion's share of the fixed amount, practically the whole thing. Person number two, when faced with either a little amount of money or nothing, will choose to accept the deal, despite the vastly unequal allocation. Academics have commissioned countless studies where they ask participants to play this game. What's notable about these studies is they consistently come to the same two conclusions. The first, that person number one tends to choose an allocation that's closer to equal than game theory would predict. For example, if the pool of money is $10, they will choose a $7/$3 split instead of a $9.90/$0.10 split, even though the latter would be in their better interest. Post-study interviews with the participants find that they did not feel comfortable nor think it was right to award themselves too much money. The second finding is that on the occasion when person number two is faced with a grossly unequal allocation -- exactly the type game theory would expect -- they will tend to reject it, so that both parties receive nothing. When asked to defend their decision, participants will claim that it was justifiable for them to forfeit their small allocation in return for withholding the large allocation from the first person, as a punishment of sorts for the first person being so unfair. This is just one example of people valuing fairness, even at the expense of their own self-interest. Therefore, the philosophy on authority states that rules and policies should be applied fairly, so that each individual knows they are given neither preferential nor non-preferential treatment, which keeps them acting in their own interest and not out of spite or malice toward another group, or worse, the authority itself.

Third, the authority applied must be *consistent*. Consistency means the rules and consequences applied today will be the same as those applied yesterday and the same as those applied tomorrow. Of course, rules can change, and often should, but should be done with proper forewarning and with reasonable justification. Outside of these occurrences, the rules should not change unexpectedly, such that people cannot trust or rely on them. When this happens, people no longer can plan for the future because they don't know when or how rules might change. They grow suspicious of the administrators of those rules, who cannot defend those changes, and in general the goings-on of the group will slow and then stop, as people worry less about what they were doing or planning to do, and more about grasping for straws of answers about when things might change again and how.

Consistency of rules and consequences turns out to be critical for people not only to plan and prepare for the future, but to believe in it altogether. There was a study done on children taking the Marshmallow test. Are you aware of the Marshmallow test? It's an insightful, and sometimes, hilarious test given to small children. They are left alone in a room with one marshmallow on a plate. They are told by the administrator that they can eat the marshmallow, but, if they wait for 30 minutes, they will receive two marshmallows which they can eat at that time. I say the test is hilarious because if you go on YouTube you will find videos of children trying, but often failing to resist the temptations of the marshmallow. They will squirm, twist and turn, fight against their impulses, then eventually succumb. Researchers have suggested that a child's ability to resist the marshmallow -- that is, to delay gratification in the present for something better in the future -- is indicative of their ability to enroll in school, save money, start a business, and all sorts of other productive behaviors in their adult life.

However, one researcher conducted a study where the children were allowed to play in a playroom before they were asked to take the Marshmallow test. They were told that should they want any additional toys, they could ask for them from the administrators and that the toys would be given. For half the children, the toys were given when requested, but for the other half, they weren't. The administrators would simply take the requests but do nothing. When both groups of children then took the Marshmallow test, the children whose requests were rebuffed were much more likely to fail the test than the children whose requests were honored.

Do you know what this means? Passing or failing the test had little to do with the children's inherent patience or foresight. Instead, it was the children's trust in the authoritarian regime, their belief in its legitimacy, which influenced their decision to plan for a better future. Without assurances from the authority that promises will be kept, there was no benefit to making sacrifices today, and so they didn't.

Now, my goodness, I've certainly been going on and on, haven't I? What I've been meaning to ask you, Julian, is whether Chimera lives up to these three ideals of authority. Do you think we are fair, consistent, and allow for feedback?"

Julian had spent so long listening that he was caught off-guard when it was time for him to speak. "Um, uh, yes, I think so. At least the first two. I don't think that at my job level I know enough about how the whole company works to provide useful feedback."

"Mhm, I see. And how would you feel based on the last three days? Do you think it is fair, in the terms I just described, that you haven't shown up for work since we last spoke? That your co-workers came here and worked a full day, while you didn't, and when your colleague, when sent to go find you, ended up taking a half day off as well? Or that it's consistent, by the same logic, that you were allowed to show up late this morning, when others are expected to show up on time? So I ask again, how do you feel about my use of authority given your recent experience?"

"Well, I'd say you're probably right, by the looks of it I'm getting preferential treatment. I do seem to recall you instructed me to work whenever I like, wherever I like."

Kendra frowned, and for the first time since he arrived she averted her eyes from his. Mort, recognizing the cue, stepped in.

"The expectation for all Chimera employees is to report to work for any and all normal business hours," Mort began. "Any liberties you may or may not take related to the duration and location of extracurricular efforts, should be applied to times of the day and week which occur outside those normal business hours."

"Hold on -- are you saying you expect me to write this book on top of my regular job?!"

"Employees at Chimera are expected to be not only workers, but pioneers. At Chimera, we don't recognize dated concepts like 'regular' when describing what they do. Employees should feel liberated and inspired to take on whatever efforts will maximize their potential, both for themselves and for Chimera.

As much as we care and thrive upon potential, we cannot ignore the ever-present reality of the expectation to deliver results. Chimera as a dynamic entity must excel not only in the future but in the present as well. With regard to your assignment, we believe it is not unreasonable for you to complete it by next Monday."

"Oh good, next Monday. And I thought I was going to be pressed for time."

"We believe the challenge of high expectations breeds innovation and resourcefulness that powers your personal growth in the long run," Mort responded flatly.

"Well, I certainly appreciate that. Say, didn't you mention that you wanted some feedback? That your authority required it? Well, here's some feedback for you." Julian turned to Kendra. "First, why on earth do you care about writing a book, let alone having me write it? You run a huge company! You should just focus on making that company more money, or making its customers happier, or something in between. Second, what's with the 'personal passion' routine? Whose passion is it to work in corporate consulting? Folks do it because they're looking for a successful career, or scared to death of losing one. Because of that, you can get them to do all sorts of things, work harder, work longer, take more crap, get paid less, and they'd probably just do it, so long as you were blunt about what they're getting out of it. What's the point of trying to convince someone that their doing all this for their own personal benefit? They don't really buy it, and if they do, well, that's just kind of pathetic. And finally, stop pretending you really care about what I or any standard-fare employee thinks about you or this company. It's just obtuse, really. Before Monday, I had never even spoken to anyone on this floor, let alone been up here. Your assistant talks to me like I'm less than human, like my very existence in her life is an atrocity for her. It's crystal clear to everyone like me that our purpose is to stay on the twenty-eighth floor, do what we're told, don't rock the boat, then rinse and repeat. And you know what, *that's totally fine*. But if you end up making a habit of talking to people like me, do yourself a favor and stop trying to convince us that you are genuinely rooting for us, cause we both know it is just not true."

Kendra stared blankly at the wall behind Julian for a few seconds. Her expression did not change, but Mort briefly took his gaze off Julian and shot a quick glance to Kendra. Seeing that she was unmoved, he turned back to Julian.

"Mort, give us a moment, please."

Mort appeared startled, and peered inquisitively at Kendra, who was still unmoved. Finally, he offered a diminutive "sure" as he got up and left the room. Julian followed Mort with his eyes as the office door opened, then closed. At that moment, Kendra got up as well and walked toward the window behind her desk, observing the view outside. It was from that position which she began to speak again.

"Julian, do you know what all of this is?"

"All of what?"

"*This.*" She pointed back toward the building. "Chimera. Everything that I'm in charge of."

"It's a company."

"And what's a company?"

"Um, a business and people and a building headquarters, maybe."

"Maybe. Exactly. It is not any of those things, nor all of them. The people could go, I could go, the building could go, the work we do could go, and Chimera would still be here, in some form. Do you know why?"

"No, I suppose you're about to enlighten me."

"Careful, Julian. It's just you and me now. We don't have to be hunky-dory here, but particularly after your outburst just now, all I ask if that you remove that steeliness in your demeanor, and just talk to me. Just for right now, we can be two equals having a discussion."

The frankness and coolness of her plea stung, and Julian felt his growing aggression recede. He gently muttered an acquiescence to her request.

"Right then. So what is Chimera, actually? It's not tied to any physical presence. And so how does it exist at all? Much like the book I am assuming you have yet to start writing, Chimera, it turns out, is a fiction."

"A fiction?"

"A fiction. A myth. A fabrication. It is a figment of the collective imagination of you and I and everyone else who chooses to believe it. Chimera exists because we all believe it to exist, and if we all woke up tomorrow and stopped believing in it, it would no longer exist."

"Sorry, I don't follow."

"Let me ask you, why do you do it? Why do you come to work here, sitting at a desk through each day, five days a week, all through the year? Money, I presume. You are made the promise that in return for your work, you will be given money. And up until now, Chimera has fulfilled that promise.

But what good is money? It's a number on a screen which you believe is the balance of your bank account. There is no stack of dollar bills sitting in a bank vault somewhere with your name on them. And even if there were, what good would that stack be? It's just paper or coins, which have limited use for much more than to be money.

So the money is good for one thing: to act as money. People will take money from you in exchange for food, rent, a movie ticket, all the things you consume in your life. They accept the money because they can convince others people to take the money for a particular good or service that they want. On and on it goes.

All that Chimera does, hiring people, writing reports and analysis, paying money for certain goods and services and getting paid for others, it is all part of a fiction, a fiction where everyone accepts Chimera as a legitimate entity that can take part in such affairs. An entity legitimate enough to have its shares of ownership bought and sold on a stock exchange, to lease land and buildings, to sue or be sued. And legitimate enough for thousands of employees like you to consider it their benefactor for a career, a livelihood, a way of living. This is a reality that is both incredibly powerful as well as absurdly fragile at the same time. The power that this company has, that I hold by proxy, to shape countless lives both inside and outside company, is unlike anything most humans have had throughout their existence. At the same time, all that power could disappear in an instant, the moment enough people realized they did not have to cooperate with or take seriously something which only exists in the shared constructs of our imaginations.

The same logic holds for me, in my position as CEO. What is a CEO, really? What do I do, here? I don't run numbers and analyze data like you. I don't write the reports, or deliver services to our clients. Hell, I rarely even meet our clients these days anyway. Yet, it is remarkable to see the power and influence that I have. The authority to give orders to every single person in this company. I could fire you on the spot, and no one would bat an eye. I have the power to speak, and to be listened to, and to be followed. To spend millions of dollars as I see fit, or not, with much if any incredulity.

And why does everybody follow along? Why do *you* follow along? Do you believe that I'm worthy of this power and standing, to give orders and make decisions, despite not contributing to the effort and the production of this company in any material way? What would stop you or anyone else from simply not listening to me, or making your decisions without regard for mine? People don't challenge me because they believe I have all the authority, but because they believe that others believe that I do. And if everyone believes that altogether, then the authority stays mine. Think about just how precarious that makes my position. Knowing that my power, my salary, my entire identity rests in a fragile, unstable network of fictions believed by everyone else, outside my direct control but absolutely vital to my livelihood.

So you see, Julian, when I ask you to write a book, I am not asking you to write a bunch of words on pages. I am not asking you tell me a nice story with some characters and a plot. I am asking you to continue in this tradition of fictions. Fictions which reinforce the value of companies as benevolent stewards of modern economies and societies. Fictions which stoke the meaning and purpose of working at a corporation that serves other corporations. Fictions which win over board members and shareholders alike on the value of the executives which are currently in charge. These fictions, at their core, mean nothing and everything when it comes to what you perceive as the natural order of things.

You know, I used to think these fictions were a bunch of crap. I started my career in Wall Street, selling municipal bonds. The value -- funding for bridges, roads, dams -- was clear as day, and the investors knew that as well as I did. My salary, oh my it seems so paltry when I look back on it now, was based on a very real and very material transfer of funds and construction projects. Once I worked my way up to management, I started to accept these fictions as necessary evils. Instruments used to keep up team spirits, or convince a client to come around on a deal. I remember being skeptical of the whole idea, but went along with it once I saw how effective they were, and how my career rose along with them.

But by the time I was a junior executive in telecom, I had not only begrudgingly accepted these fictions, I had made them part of my repertoire. Buzzwords like corporate vision, big picture ideas, organization culture, the legitimacy of corporate social responsibility, all these were just so, *useful*, to get things done. To gain influence and have your pursuits and ideals churned to life through the efforts of others, convinced to follow your leadership. I remember encountering other executives -- good people, more senior than me but clearly falling behind -- incredulous of my success, bristling at how they were being passed over. But they, like so many others before and after them, just could not understand how fictions, created by others, about nothing, meaning nothing, had completely done them in.

And now Julian, the truth is, I *thrive* off these fictions. I don't know how to describe it, but they keep me, *alive*. That feeling of having the whole world at your fingertips, catering to your whims, the ebbs and flows of your life defined by the success you have wielding the conductor's baton in front of this grand symphony of followers. It swells in me a rush of excitement and euphoria like nothing else I experience anymore. There's no financial reason for me to keep this job, I have enough money to retire in luxury many times over, but to me, a lifetime of mai tai's and sandy toes would be a prison sentence compared to this arena. Whether today or tomorrow or the next day will be the one when my fictions no longer win the day, I can't say, but I know there's nothing else I'd rather do than to thrive in this lattice of myths and imaginations until that day comes.

So what now, Julian? Cards are on the table. What are you going to do?"

Julian gathered himself in his chair. In the long stretch of listening to Kendra, he had begun to slouch. He wanted to stand and stretch his legs, but didn't feel it appropriate or appealing to position himself eye-to-eye with Kendra, who had stiffened up and refocused her steely expression on him after her monologue.

"Kendra, I don't have a fraction of the knowledge, experience, or pedigree as you, nor the responsibility and pressure of the job you have. I get what you're saying about these fictions and how they wield order and influence on people and their behavior. But there's a fine line between being the master of these head games and just being delusional. And you know what I think? I think you crossed that line a long time ago, because right now, I think you sound fucking crazy."

Kendra froze in her expression for seconds on end. For his part, Julian kept his eye contact with her and refused to look away this time. Eventually, she let out a smile, a quick chuckle, and then returned to her desk to log back in her to computer.

"Julian, you'll need to deliver the first twenty-thousand words of the book on Monday. I know Mort said the whole thing, but let's be realistic here. Perhaps this is me responding to some feedback, hm? I am inviting some of our board members and largest shareholders to the office for a preview. Everyone is very excited about it and its potential to revolutionize the image and vision for this company. I can't wait to see what you've come up with."

"Twenty-thousand words?"

"It's what I said, Julian. This is your job, and you know the expectations. That will be all."

Julian got up to leave. "Fine then," he chided. "Nice chat, Kendra. See you later."

"Good luck, Julian. Let me know if you need anything."

Julian walked out of her office, leaving Kendra idling on her computer. When he left, there was no Janine waiting for him, nor Mort, who had exited earlier. Retracing the steps from where he came, there was no Zane as well, and all of a sudden the thirtieth floor looked as foreign and distant as it had the first time he walked up.

He arrived back at his desk. Scanning his email, nothing had come in since he'd been away. The glare from the sun beaming in through the windows created grey spots on his monitor, making it difficult to see the screen. He walked to the window to lower the black-out screens half-way down, to remove the glare from his monitor but leave the light coming in to rest of the office.

When he returned to his desk, he noticed a body to his right, which had not been there before. A woman, young in her early twenties, with long dark hair and brown, ethnically ambiguous skin. She was scanning a series of handouts inside a manila packet, which Julian recognized as the set of materials Chimera distributes for new hire orientation. When he sat down in his chair, the commotion interrupted her reading, and drew her attention to him.

"Hi, are you Julian?" she asked inquisitively.

"Yes, I am. Hi, what's your name?"

"I'm Anita. New business analyst, started this week. It's nice meeting you."

"Yeah, you too. Say, do you know what happened to the guy working here before? I can't quite recall his name."

"No, I can't say I do. When I got here on Monday, the desk was clear. You didn't know him?"

"I guess not. I'd see him here when we were both in the office. We would wave to each other in the hall and make small talk at the desk. But now that I look back at it, I don't recall ever knowing or asking about his name."

"Hmm, well I guess it happens. I wasn't sure you worked here, and I've been here all week."

"I suppose that's true. I was here on Monday morning. I'm guessing you didn't get here until the afternoon."

"That's right. Orientation most of the morning and through lunch."

"How was it?"

"Um, pretty good I guess. I don't know, this is my first job, so I don't really know how orientations are supposed to go. I have to say that I didn't care for lunch though. My lunch buddy took me to the canteen down on the first floor. Ordered two sandwiches and barely said a word before dropping me off here. Is that what everyone is like?"

Julian smiled. "Sometimes. I'm sure you'll find your way around to the right people soon enough."

"Thanks. I'm glad I saw you today. I heard from some other people that this was your workstation, but I didn't know what to think until just now."

"I didn't realize I was the talk of the town around here."

"Of course you are. It's all anyone can talk about. Is it true what they say?"

"What do they say?"

"You know, that you have some secret project that you are working on for the CEO?"

"Well, if it were true, then I wouldn't be able to tell you then, right?"

"Ohhhhh. So I guess it's true then."

"Trust me, it's not nearly as cool as you probably think it is."

"Well, I'd only know for sure if I knew what it was."

"So you're a business analyst. So am I. How are you liking the job so far?"

"To be honest, I don't really know what the job is. I've asked a few people what is the specific role and what I am expected to do, but I mostly get boilerplate statements about commitment to the team and making a difference."

"I'm afraid that's because the actual role is quite boring. Lots of charts and tables in Excel, reading and analyzing industry reports, and the occasional report to write yourself. But the upside is that there's lots of downtime if you have other enjoyable ways to pass the time, and most people prefer to leave you alone and communicate mostly by email."

"Really, you don't get to talk with anyone?"

"Not really, well unless you really want to. I've just found most of the business people who use our work have no problem interacting with us as nameless, faceless entities."

"Perhaps I can put an end to that! I don't know, I just can't understand how you work here and not really know your colleagues. I mean, not you personally, just generally. Just not what I was expecting, I guess."

"What were you expecting? It's not like your favorite college class or a book club. People come here to get paid to do their job, and leave. The rest is just window-dressing."

"I know I know. I knew it wouldn't be like summer camp, but I figured people would at least be friendly to one another. Can I ask you, you're kind of older, right?"

"Ouch."

"That's not what I meant. I mean, you've been out of college a while, right?"

"It's ok, yes. I'm thirty. It's been a while."

"So, who are your friends? Did you meet them at work?"

"I have one friend from work. The rest, well this will sound kind of strange, but the rest I just met a few days ago."

"Oh."

"It's okay. I know it's weird. I am just kind of a loner, that's all. Introvert, keep to myself. Guess that's why I never knew my old desk-mate's name."

"It's not weird. It's actually exactly what I'm talking about. I've just left college. I still have a lot of friends from there, but we've all gone our separate ways. New cities, new jobs, and I am terrified that after a few years I'll lose touch, and have no new friends to replace them. Until now, everything about life was so organized, going from grade to grade and then onto a university. It was simple enough to make friends, but now, it's like I have my whole life to plan for myself and even simple things like making a new friend seem incredibly difficult."

"Wow, Anita, you are too young to be this jaded."

"Hey! I'm not jaded. I just…want to make sure I am setting things up well for myself. It's important to me."

"I think you're going to be fine. And don't take everything I say as gospel. I told you I keep to myself. Maybe I just turned this job into what I wanted it to be, and you can too."

"How long have you been working here?"
"Couple of years, maybe a little longer."

"Why did you join?"

"A headhunter messaged me at my old job. It was a bump in pay and a good name on the resume. Tell you the truth, I didn't expect to be here this long. But I do decent work I suppose and the job is easy to manage, and a few months became many months and then a couple years. And then one day you get called in to the CEO's office…"

"What did you think you were going to do next?"

"I didn't really know, to be honest. Still don't. I figure with the way the economy changes all the time, it's better not to make any grand plans which might flame out. One of the reasons this is a good job for the resume is the variety. You get to study a lot of different industries, and do analyses that are quite versatile and attractive for a number of other positions. You can work this job until you know what you want to do next, and by then you will be in a pretty good position to jump to the next gig."

"That's a good way to look at it. Play it safe and limit the risk of committing to any one thing."

"It was. But at some point you have to pick something you want to do and just go all in. A business analyst is a respectable job in your twenties. No one can tell the difference between someone who is just trying things out from

someone who's shooting up the corporate ladder. For people who are thirty --
like someone I know -- if you are not moving into a manager position or
starting your own company or something like that, it starts to look like you've
plateaued and that you'll spend the rest of your career in a dead-end support
role."

"Maybe you should think about moving to a new job."

"Yeah, maybe I should. "

"Any other career advice?"

"I'm no wise sage of careers, but I truly envy people who find a calling that
fulfills them for their whole career. I just haven't found that for myself yet.
Some people focus on their family, and have no problem sucking it up at their
nine-to-five, which is pretty admirable to think of it, if they really love their
family. My dad was like that. Pretty sure he hated his job but did what he had
to do to support us. I guess the most important thing is that whatever you
choose, you do it mindfully and know what you are getting into. Work to live,
right?"

"Yeah, right." Anita's face dropped, and she fell silent as an inner thought hit
her that distracted her from the conversation. The pause extended long
enough that Julian took it as a cue to conclude their chat and return to the
work. He turned back to his desk, until Anita spoke again.

"Hey, can I ask, who was your friend that you met at work?"

"Zane." He turned back to face her. "He started as an intern two years back,
and now he's full time. We started out as acquaintances. Work happy hours
and things like that. But now, I'd say we're friends. So there's an example of
how you make new friends, you see?"

"Yeah, that's nice. Does Zane work here still?"

"Yeah, he does. He usually sits over there, on the other side of the floor. I
don't know where he is right now though."

"Maybe I can meet him sometime."

"Yeah, he'd really like that."

"What's that?" Anita had spotted the legal pad Julian had used for his writing. It was laying on the desk, having protruded from his bag which he had dropped on the desk when he arrived that morning. The front page of the pad included his notes and other bits that he had jotted down two days prior.

"Oh that, just some notes of mine. I like to write in my free time, what little of it there is. Haven't had much inspiration lately though."

"Writing? I love writing! What are you writing about?"

"So far, nothing. Thus, the need for inspiration. Do you write?"

"No, not regularly. I took a few classes in college and really enjoyed it. Was pretty good at it too."

"Cool. If you had to, what would you write about?"

Anita stalled for a few moments. "I've had this recurring dream since I was about ten years old. I'm walking through a field, far up in the mountains. The grass is high, wildflowers all along the way. I reach a ridge, which overlooks a broad, flowing stream below. I sit down on a wide, flat stone on top of the ridge, and look out below. And I just wait, and wait, and that's the dream. Sometimes a butterfly will come and float around me. I will try to catch it, but despite my intentions, my arms move too slowly to ever do it. But that doesn't happen all the time. Sometimes the butterfly never shows, and I just wait, on top of that ridge, looking down at the stream. If I had to write, I would write a story about that."

"Would that be the beginning of the story, the middle, or the end?" Julian asked.

"I'm not sure."

Julian spent the rest of the day at the office, occasionally chatting with Anita, but mostly passing the time between emails, internet news articles, and lots of alternating trips to the water fountain and bathroom. Toward the end of the day, he stumbled upon a long-form article on the CRISPR gene editing technology. There are certain parts of the DNA sequence inside each cell which are designed to attack foreign elements that can enter or threaten it. If altered, these DNA parts can attack or modify faulty parts of the genome, and in some cases modify or eliminate abnormalities. The technology is being hyped as having the potential to cure all genetic diseases. Julian thought about what it would be like to remove all diseases from the body. He wondered if the body would be stronger from the removal of the diseases, or whether the lack of adversity would make the body weaker, like muscles which are never exercised.

He began his walk home, passing by buildings similar to the Odyssey tower. Buildings, constructed only a few years ago but already among the largest and most glamorous in the city. They rise high and their windows shine against the sky which reflects off of them. From afar, an observer can see exactly which panes have lights on behind them and which do not. Even in the late evening and through the night, one can find lights still turned on and smattered across every floor.

Colleagues and other white-collar professionals zipped in front and behind him, some in athletic gear on their way to their local gym, others who just swapped their footwear for more comfortable walking shoes for the commute home. In either case, they are always walking, always in straight lines, never stopping. In the middle of the sidewalk, a family of four paused to stare up at the high-rises. Clearly tourists from out of town, they blocked the pedestrian traffic like a boulder jutting out in front of whitewater rapids, violently pushing the gushing water to the right or left. With each redirection, they drew the wrath of the passersby, but were completely ignorant of or immune to it based on their lack of reaction. When they angled their heads down back to ground level, Julian noticed they were all frowning, those squinty annoyed looks people give when they are stuck by themselves at a party without anyone to speak to. When they were done observing the buildings, they all marched forward in unison, maintaining their frowns as they pushed through the oncoming traffic. Julian wondering where they were from, but also where on earth were they going.

At the end of the block where the string of high-rises comes to an end, two roads intersect each other slightly disjoint from another and at an angle, creating a triangle between themselves and the main road. On each side of the triangle are three identical commercial towers, each forty stories high, with colored segments adorned vertically on the dark blue facades. On the twentieth floor of each building, a skywalk extends outwards and connects to the other two, creating another triangle in the sky, accessible only by building occupants. All three buildings are owned by the same company, a Fortune 100 tech conglomerate specializing in media and advertising. In the middle of these buildings, inside the triangle created by the three roads, rests a strip club/sex shop combo establishment, with mannequins covered in corsets adorning the window galleries on one side, and blackout shades concealing the view from the other two. It was odd that this building still remained inside the three others. Rumor has it that the tech company tried to buy out the strip club/sex shop combo on multiple occasions, but they simply refused to sell. Apparently the business from all the young single software developers made the location too valuable to ever let go.

He passed by the triangle of buildings and turned the corner towards his home. In this stretch the height of the buildings decreased noticeably, to just four or five stories, and became significantly dated as well. The odd homeless person appeared every now and then, smoking a cigarette while leaning on a building side, or panhandling for change on the curb. Julian in general did not give them any money, but when asked, he would make sure to look them in the eye and tell them no to their face. He figured that just because they did not have any money didn't imply that they didn't deserve the dignity of being acknowledged as another human being, even when being given disappointing news.

He soon arrived at the same Nero's where Zane and he had ate pizza for lunch the day prior. Opportunistically opting for an early dinner, he walked up to their counter for a quick bite.

"What would you like?" the attendant asked.

Julian looked at the displays of ready-to-go slices. "Which one has been the most popular today?"

"Probably the pepperoni sausage."

"I see, and what about the least popular?"

"Least popular? Probably the pineapple jalapeno."

"Mhm."

"Why? You want a slice."

"You know what? I'll take two."

He grabbed a table and took a seat facing the road. He ate his pizza slowly, taking breaks between bites and filling up his water glass repeatedly from the complimentary tank. As he mused over whether the combination of pineapple and jalapeno was either delightful or distracting, his mind began to wander, to a time back in college with Barbara's daughter, his roommate, and another girl, a high school friend of his roommate who was in town visiting. The four of them came together one night to go out to a local bar, both to show the out-of-town friend some of the city and have a decent night out at the same time. This was before Barbara's daughter and the roommate began dating; the three of them were friends who all lived on the same dormitory floor, and grew close through the academic year as they shared meals, classes, and personal stories. The night started out like most other nights. Pre-gaming in the dorm room, some drinking games mixed with music playing and the conversation getting cruder, simpler, and louder with each round of drinks.

Later in the evening, they hopped in a vanpool to head to the bar. Julian's roommate and his hometown friend sat in the middle seats and continued reminiscing about high school prom and summer pool parties. He and Barbara's daughter jumped in the back row. Julian spent most of the ride staring out the back window, watching lampposts fly past on the highway and passengers in neighboring cars converse with one another. Barbara's daughter intermittently tried to jump in on the dialogue happening in front of her, with limited success in breaching the tight-knit discussion. Halfway through the ride, Julian felt Barbara's daughter's hand slide over his, clasping his palm in hers. He looked over and found her paying no immediate attention to him, but smiling widely as she stared forward in the car. He leaned back and stared forward too, and reciprocated her advance by clasping her hand in return, creating a sealed and intimate grip between the two of them. They spent the whole ride in that position, even as his hand began to sweat slightly from the heat of the night, the rising amount of alcohol in his bloodstream, and from his elevated heartbeat.

When they arrived, she let go of his hand as the four of them got out of the car. Julian offered to buy the first round of drinks and headed toward the bar, which was packed from end to end. He waited quite a while to secure his place in front to make the order, wait for the drinks to be served, and pay the bartender. When he returned to meet the group, he found his roommate and Barbara's daughter dancing closely and exotically on the dance floor, the out-of-town friend abandoned by a bar stool. Julian put the drinks down and struck up a conversation with the abandoned friend, who vacillated between being bored and annoyed at being inadvertently siphoned off with him. By the time they ran out of pleasantries to exchange, Julian's roommate and Barbara's daughter were kissing on the dance floor, locked tight in each other's embrace. They spent the whole ride home making out in the backseat, Julian and the out-of-town friend relegated to the front, sitting in an awkward and miffed silence. Even as his roommate and Barbara's daughter began to date, the roommate and his hometown friend lost touch and she no longer visited. The three dormitory pals, once as close as platonically feasible, began to fissure into two and one, the brunch with Barbara a lone exception to their steadily growing separation.

By the following semester, Julian's roommate and Barbara's daughter were broken up, and Julian had moved out to his own off-campus apartment. One night, in the early hours of the morning, she showed up at his door, slightly intoxicated and wanting to see him. He invited her in, to drink hot chocolate and watch old *Friends* episodes playing through the night on cable television. She curled up beside him on the couch, slipping her arm between the pillow and the small of his back, and gently caressing the stubble on his chin with her free hand. They lingered in a state of half-embrace for multiple episodes. She laid her head down on the crevice between his neck and shoulder, and when she turned to align her lips with his, he leaned back, got up, told her he was going to bed and that she was welcome to stay the night on the couch. He fetched some blankets and left her in an embarrassed and bewildered state as he closed his bedroom door behind him for the night. The next morning, she had already left when he woke, the blankets folded neatly on side of the couch. He never saw her again.

He checked the call logs on his phone, to see when was the last time he and Barbara spoke. As he scrolled through missed calls and texts over the last few days, he heard a tap on the serving counter behind him.

"Excuse me, sir?" the attendant called out. "Sir, we are going to close in fifteen minutes. If there is anything else you would like, please let me know now."

"No, I'm just finishing up, thanks. Do you need any help?"

"Help with what?"

"Closing the shop. I'm happy to help if you need."

"Oh no, sir, thank you but that will be alright."

"Come on, let me do something. How about I wipe down all the tables? I'll start with my own."

Before she could reply, he grabbed a towel from behind the serving counter and began to clean off his own table and those around him.

"So, how has your day been today?" he asked her.

"Oh same old same old. Just glad it's over. It's my last shift of the week."

"Nice. Have any fun plans for the weekend?"

"Why yes. I am going to see my son tomorrow. I haven't seen him in three years, and he is going to come visit me."

"That sounds like a wonderful time."

"I hope so. I'm very anxious about it. I don't know what I'll say to him when he gets here."

"Just speak from the heart, it will be right no matter what."

"What about you, sir?"

"There's a girl I know. I met her last weekend, when I was picking up my mail, literally picking it up off the floor. She lives in my building, and was kind enough to return some mail which I had left behind to my apartment. I ran into her a couple days later when I was getting drunk with my friend sitting on his front lawn in the middle of the afternoon. I walked her home, or more accurately, stumbled her home and then I asked her to come to the beach with me this weekend. She said she would think about. This morning she came by my place and invited me to breakfast. We sat at the same table where an elderly couple had sat two days before, and we talked about love and soulmates and the fear of regret. At the end of breakfast, she said she would go the beach with me, and we are going to go this Saturday."

"Well, okay! That sound like you're going to have a nice time. What a sweet story, I hope she's the one for you."

"How long have you been working here?"

"Let's see. It will be twelve years next month."

"Wow! You've been here this whole time?"

"Sure have. I remember when this place was the only shack on the whole block. It was just us and a whole lot of nothing. That was back when this town was a town. Sleepy, blue-collar, wholesome. Now, there's a skyscraper on every corner and a bunch of non-locals racing around the sidewalks, looking pissed off all the time. Now I can't complain about the flux of transplants. They frequent this place, and give us lots of good, paying customers. But sometimes, I look back on the way it was when I started working here, and get a little sentimental."

"I hear you."

"Where do you work, young man?"

"At Chimera, one of those skyscraper places."

"Oh! Well I apologize. I didn't mean to offend."
"Of course not, and you didn't. Internal contradictions aside, I agree with what you said. Sometimes slower, quieter, smaller is better."

"Amen to that."

"I think I wiped down all the tables. Are you sure there's nothing else I can help you with?"

"Oh no, young man. You've already been a great help. I do appreciate us chatting as well."

"Me too. What's your name, ma'am?"

"Loretta. Pleasure to meet you. What's your name?"

"I'm Julian. Pleasure to meet you Loretta."

"Do you want any pizza to take home? I have to throw it all out anyway."

"Sure, I can take a couple slices. Maybe not the pineapple jalapeno though. Two slices were enough."

"I bet. I was wondering why you wanted those. I told you it was our least popular one, didn't I?"

"Yeah you did. I liked it, just not enough for more I don't think."

"Which one would you like then?"

"Surprise me. I trust your judgment."

"Okay. Try the zucchini ricotta. It sounds weird, but I think you will like it. I'll wrap up a few slices for you."

"You're too kind."

Loretta wrapped up the slices and handed them to Julian in a box. He waved her a final goodbye and left to finish his walk home. He was moving slower than before with a stomach full of pizza, but didn't mind the pace given the evening was reaching its twilight, with a cooling breeze passing through the air. Around the corner from Nero's, just one block away from Herb's house, he passed by a homeless man standing on the sidewalk. He had on ripped jeans, a stained grey sweatshirt, and no shoes.

"Howdy friend. How are you doing this evening?"

"Sorry man. I don't have any money for you."

"What about that box? What do you got in there?"

"Zucchini ricotta pizza. I hear it's very good."

"Hmm. I'm not really sure what that is. But I wouldn't mind some food."

"Yeah, why the hell not. Take it." He hand the box over to the homeless man.

"Thanks a lot, friend. God bless you."

"Don't thank me. I got it from a very nice lady up the road. She's the only reason I had anything to give you. Personally, I got nothing."

Friday

Julian's phone started ringing as he sipped an Americano at the Savory Pass. It was late in the morning and the early rush had come and gone from the shop, leaving only amateur writers, the occasional tourist, and him. He had arrived a half hour before, having attempted to work from home. Instead, any chance of opening his laptop or writing on a legal pad was quickly preempted by Franny, who followed Julian around the apartment, slid her body around and through his legs, and jumped on tables to step on or over whatever he was working on. Each time he would move her back down to the ground, she would look up to him, squint her eyes delicately, and jump back up to commence her non-hostile takeover, purring loudly the whole time.

It had been a rough morning so far. He woke up in a state of exhaustion feeling like he had not slept through the night at all. Halfway through his shower the hot water ran out, leaving him to quickly and miserably scrub himself down while freezing cold and dripping wet. As he rushed to his room to change into warmer clothes, he found the old melancholy man staring deeply at him. He eventually decided to head down to Savory Pass and try his luck there. Hopefully Nelson would have been there to greet him, but he was not, with only Lawrence and his general apathy behind the counter instead. He felt his phone vibrate in his pocket, and saw Zane on the screen.

"Hello?"

"Hey Julian. How's it going man?"

"It's fine, what's up?"
"Just checking in on you. Didn't see you yesterday at the office. Thought you were coming in."

"I did. Surprised you didn't see me."

"Why's that?"

"I was up on the thirtieth floor for a bit, with Kendra."

"Why would I have seen you up there? No one but execs are up there, and you now, I guess."

Julian paused. "Yeah, guess not."

"You coming in today?"

"No, probably not. Didn't get much done yesterday at the office. Too distracting."

"Yeah, makes sense. What are you doing this weekend?"

"Don't know yet."

"I got a thing tonight. Small party with a friend from college. Want to come with?"

"No man, don't think so."

"Come on man, it's not like you have other friends to hang out with. You told me so."

"Fuck off, Zane."

"Whoa, easy there cowboy. Just joshing you."

"It's not funny."

"Okay got it, sorry. Anyway, I actually need a work thing from you. You know that Pershing account? I think you worked on it a few weeks back."

"Yeah, I did."

"You mind sending me over those spreadsheets?"

"What spreadsheets?"

"The ones with the financial simulations. I gotta do a few more and figured you already had most of them built."

"Just do it yourself."

"What? It'll be way easier if I could use the ones you've already done."

"What am I, your lackey? It's your job now, you should be able to do it."

"What the fuck? Why you being so pissy? Just send me the files. It will take five seconds. It's no harm to you."

"What about you free-riding off me? I work hard at my job, most of it so that some asshole upstairs can make money off it. If that's what you want to be doing, be my guest, but don't expect me to help you."

"I don't even know what you are saying. And you work hard? You've barely been to work all week and when you're here it's just to schmooze with the boss. Get over yourself."

"Whatever."

"Yeah, whatever. I'll just get your manager to give the files to me. Thanks for nothing."

"You're welcome."

"Yeah, great."

Zane hung up. Julian left his coffee half-drunk in the mug, packed up his things, and walked out of the Savory Pass.

"Hey dude, you're supposed to clean up your mug," Lawrence said from behind the counter."

"Thanks for taking care of it for me," Julian replied sarcastically. "Jerk," he muttered under his breath.

Julian walked out with his bag on his shoulder. The sky was grey, filled with the dark kind of clouds which foreshadow heavy rain. He could feel the heaviness in the air from the rising humidity weighing against him as he walked. He continued forward, pushing against the thick, moist air even as beads of sweat formed around his neckline and under his shirt. He found himself walking faster and faster, until he passed by Herb's house. He was almost all the way past when Herb opened his front door and walked out.

"Julian, where you off to, amigo?"

"Herb, hi."

"Where you off to? I was gonna crack open a few beers and take apart a boat engine I found at a flea market yesterday. Even though you're shit with your hands I could use a number two, what say you?"

"No, I got to head out."

"What's the rush? Going to see that girlfriend of yours?"

"I wish."

"Maybe that boyfriend then?"

"Geez, easy."

"Easy? What, you got some sand in your vag?"

"Hey piss off!"

"Piss off? Up yours! I'm too hungover for this bullshit."

"Yeah, what else is new? I've known you five days and you've been drunk or hungover for six of them."

"Get off my property, Julian."

"Gladly."

Herb walked back into his house and slammed the door behind him. His front lawn was in its typical state of disarray, lawn chairs in the grass, empty beer bottles in a cooler filled with water that used to be ice. The garage door was closed.

Julian kept walking, making his way through the rest of the neighborhood. There were only a few pedestrians like him out for a walk or on their way to or from work. Each time they passed, it seemed to Julian like they were frowning at him, or avoiding him, or both. The sweat from the humidity had built up under his shirt, forming moist pockets under his arms and around the straps of his bag. He had not had any water that day, and was beginning to feel parched. Passing by a building with mirrored window panes, he saw his reflection. Sweaty, a disheveled shirt, dark circles under his eyes, and a permanently furrowed brow, despite his attempts to straighten it. He paused to study himself, and for the first few moments, did not recognize the face or body that he saw. Like a word that has been repeated so many times that it loses its meaning and turns into a nonsensical mush of syllables, it was as if the portrait in front of him had lost its relation to who he was. The hair, eyes, nose, and mouth were all familiar, but put together it formed a face that which he no longer recognized.

It was at that moment when his phone rang. He looked at the ID, and with a pained grimace, answered the call.

"Hi Barb."

"Julian, hi. What's going on?"

"Not much, same old."

"Oh, well I just thought maybe something was going on since you hadn't called in a few days."

"I never call, Barb. You always call me."

"Well that's just not true. I tell you I've had it up to here with my next door neighbors. They are incredibly nice, and they really are good neighbors, but I think they must have had some landscaping done, or some new gardening, because they have put this mulch in their backyard that smells just awful. I mean I'm sorry, but it is just appalling and I don't know how they think it's okay to just dump that stuff all around for everyone to suffer. Just rude."

"It's just mulch, Barb. Everyone uses it."

"I don't use it! I always use regular potting soil, then add coffee grounds. Much better than using Miracle-gro or something else filled with chemicals. I remember my sister-in-law used to stay with us sometimes and would try to get me to use Miracle-gro. I never liked her at all, so pushy, so judgmental. Of course she's welcome here anytime but I am glad she doesn't visit anymore."

"Okay great. Hey I have to get going Barb."

"There was this one time we went over to her house. Long time ago, I think my daughter was nine or ten. And we went over for lunch and a playdate or something, for the afternoon. I remember we walked in, and her place just a mess. Toys and clothes all over the living room, clumps of dust and hair on the ground, and dirty dishes piled in the sink. I was so grossed out. I told my daughter to go play outside in the yard, cause I didn't want her to step in or touch that filth. I offered to help her pick the place up, and you know what she said to me? She said 'why? Everything looks fine to me.' Can you believe that?! We stayed long enough to not be impolite, but that was the last time I ever stepped foot in that house. And she has the nerve to tell me how to take care of my garden?"

"I really don't know Barb, but I have to go."

"And that's not the only thing that-"

Julian hung up. He walked around the corner, and down a few blocks to arrive at Bo's. It was the late morning, patrons who had leisurely ate their breakfast were now leisurely exiting, and the wait staff were busing tables and switching out the menus from breakfast to lunch. Julian walked up to the counter to order a grilled chicken sandwich and a large bottle of water. He grabbed the bottle straight away and found a table by the front door as he wiped off his brow and neck with a paper napkin and waited for his order to come up.

After a few minutes, an elderly man, with tanned olive skin, silver hair gelled and slicked back all the way to the nape of his neck, and a loose short-sleeved button-down shirt with wide lapels and open to the middle of his chest. It was Bo himself, and he was carrying Julian's sandwich on his way to his table.

"Order up, my brother," he said in a hoarse, booming voice which effused as much authority as it did contentedness. "Best chicken sandwich you'll ever have, take it to the bank."

"Thanks, it's a nice restaurant you have here."

"I'm glad you think so. Say, how would you like to take a photo with me? I could use a new one to add to these tables."

Julian grinned. "Sure, though I'm not sure how good of a picture I'll take."

"Come on, man. Good-looking brother like you will pop in the picture. Everyone will look at it, look at me and say 'hey, who's this old fart and what's he doing here?'"

"Okay, let's do it."

"Cool runnings, brother. Let me go get my camera and I'll come get you in a bit. Enjoy your lunch."

"Thanks."

Bo walked back behind the counter and into the kitchen. Julian took one bite of his sandwich and chewed slowly as he looked out the window into the front parking area. As he took his second bite, he saw a red sparrow walking and hopping along the gravel in front of the restaurant entrance. The sparrow wandered from parking space to parking space, picking at bits of food left by either messy kids or clumsy adults. After scavenging through most of the supply, the sparrow walked up to the front door, held wide open by a firmly-placed doorstop, but stopped on a dime in the divide between the restaurant and the outside.

Julian realized it was the same sparrow he had seen on Sunday, the last time he was at Bo's with Zane. The sparrow had the same movements, the same demeanor, the same intents, and when it looked at Julian, had the appearance of recognizing him the same way he recognized it. Julian wondered about this sparrow, its life before and outside of the restaurant. Being born in a colony of thousands of sparrow parents, traveling around human establishments to feed off grain fields or insect-infested buildings, bathing in dust or water by furiously flicking its wings. It was no surprise the sparrow found its way here. For several species of sparrow, human settlements are a primary habitat. And for this particular one, coming to Bo's just extended a tradition of sparrows co-mingling with humans, across time and cultures.

Julian wondered what inspired sparrows to marry their fortunes with his kind, and what drove this particular one to Bo's doorstep. For the sparrow, it seemed to Julian, the opportunity to step across that doorway, into the restaurant with tables, chairs, humans and their food, represented a monumental milestone in its life, an incredible and joyous experience to break apart the seemingly endless spate of nomadic episodes of food-seeking and discovering. Any of which would be enjoyable in their own right, but when strung together with no beginning nor end, no peaks or valleys, are felt like a beautiful yet inescapable desert of unexplained existence. Indeed, for the sparrow to believe this place to be a destination, a key landmark or culmination to a journey through a gauntlet of adversity, would bring it a sense of purpose no other collection of happenings could offer, even if extended indefinitely into the future and summed together for comparison. Yet, as valued an outcome that might be for the sparrow, it could only be through the sparrow's eyes that that value could be seen, because for anyone else, Julian included, it would appear so trivial and inconsequential to be laughed off entirely. When a giant leap for one is but a small stumble for another, how should anyone attempt to judge their own steps through an objective lens?

Julian recalled a favorite middle school activity of his, back when personal computers in the classroom were a novelty, and adolescents used the full force of their ingenuity to subvert task their parents or teachers wished them to complete. In his case, Julian, when tasked with an assignment to tabulate statistics in Microsoft Excel, chose instead to enter a special keystroke-combination which turned the program into a flight simulator. The flight simulator allowed the user to fly from a point-of-view perspective through a backdrop of purple sand dunes with a yellow horizon in the background, dipping and lifting, swerving left and right with abandon. The simulator never let the user crash, nor float away into the sky unabated, and outside of a lone plaque which displayed the programmers' credits, there was nothing differentiating any one frame from the other, with no way for the user to infer the route they had already flown nor the one they were about to. The simulator, while thrilling to engage in real time, nonetheless grew tiresome as users like Julian discovered then ultimately capitulated to the reality that all their efforts, no matter how big or small, amateur or skillful, did not make one difference in where or how their flight would end.

Julian knew then that he envied the sparrow. The sparrow, by virtue of the limitations of its own self-awareness, does not have to consider the possibility of its life being an endless abyss, with no meaning or purpose. The cruelty of nothingness, to know that every moment experienced, from birth to death, is arbitrary and random to the unknown machinations of the universe. With a legacy destined to be quickly washed away with time, it may seem inviting to indulge in every romantic pursuit, to thrive on the enjoyment of every hedonistic pleasure and cultivate a lifestyle which holds no obligation to how it might be perceived long after it concludes. Yet, when faced with this revelation, those pursuits immediately cease to satisfy, and no extension or augmentation of them can fill the emptiness of knowing there is no higher order or additional consideration to provide any context or consequence to actions taken in the present, that an apple may no longer taste sweet the instant it is known that its sweetness makes no difference in time or space other than during the moment it is consumed.

Julian also realized there was no salvation in abiding by any construct, be it power, fame, religion, or innovation, which conjures up fulfillment or destiny into one's sense of being. A securement of a positive afterlife, a monument built to celebrate great achievement, a well-attended funeral, or a vast bequeathment to one's offspring; all seek to provide a salve to a lifetime of toil, to the man or woman who follows the rules and regulations of their family, neighbors, caste, or creed on the presumption that their efforts and the awards bestowed for such are universal, worthwhile, and permanent. These constructs, if so believed, can provide a harmony to the days and years which string together to make a life, a backbone which arcs from childhood to old age and through everything in between. They separate good experience from bad, remove from consideration many conceivable yet unorthodox choices, and instill in each person a reassurance that all existential anxiety can and will be relieved with proper adherence to them. That adherence, however, is often too demanding, requiring a firm unwillingness to inspect all the axioms and assumptions on which those constructs are built, a purposeful deception to hide the rough edges of a paradigm which promises so much to those who can believe in it intensely enough. The curiosity to explore those edges turn into a burden, a curse put upon those who shelter inside a battery of walls built on shaky foundations, and continuously equivocate between exiting back to the dangers from which they originally sought protection, or recklessly leaning harder on those walls and expecting them to become more durable as a result.

The sparrow knows nothing of these constructs, or the choice to believe in them or not. It can rejoice in its own happiness, happiness as either a random but no less special splash of colors on an empty white canvas which stretches far beyond the eye can see, or, as the next and most important stepping stone on its quest towards something better. In either case, the sparrow gets by just fine, because whichever path it takes is not one it has to choose. But if that sparrow knew what Julian knew, and had the capacity and therefore the obligation to make a choice, even implicitly, it'd be doomed to the despair of knowing all paths are equivalently littered with the same heavy doses of doubt and futility that exist solely from the realization that there is more than one path to take. And so Julian wondered if he could lull himself into a state of mind where all but one path faded away, where the existence of choice would not crush down on his psyche, and like the sparrow, each moment could be appreciated as is, without prejudice or angst of what lay behind or ahead.

His phone rang again, breaking his concentration, and Julian answered in haste to silence it.

"What is it, Barb?"

"Sorry must have lost the connection back there. I was just saying that my sister--"

"Barb, please just shut up."

"What?"

"I said, shut up. I'm tired of listening to you bitch and moan about everything and everyone you hate. It's all in your head, fueling your constant bitterness, and frankly, it's really fucking annoying."

"Oh I see, yeah I'm just so annoying. I should just never say anything then I suppose, just keep silent because of course how I feel doesn't matter!"

"Cut the martyrdom crap. If you had even one ounce of something positive or interesting to talk about, people just might care a little more. And honestly, are you giving me crap for not listening to you? I've listened to you for years, and I don't even really know you. You're the mom of someone I barely knew in college a decade ago, and ever since you've just kept calling, and I've kept answering, mostly because I didn't care enough either way to say something about it. So how about this, why don't you deal with your own life and your own problems, and leave me out of it, huh? Your daughter, your neighbor, all of that shit, just handle it yourself, because I don't give a shit, and I really never did."

Julian hung up the phone and slammed it to the table. He looked up at the restaurant and felt the eyes of the wait staff indirectly staring at him, and he realized that while on the phone he must have raised his voice to an angry yell. Still reeling from the exchange, he got up to leave, and as he did, Bo returned from the back with camera in hand.

"Say brother where you going? Let's take that photo."

"No thanks, changed my mind. I'm going to take off."

"What, come on man don't be like that."

"Hey leave it! I don't want to be in your fucking picture!"

"Hey take it easy, friend. And don't talk like that in my restaurant."

"What are you going to do about it? I said I don't want to take the photo. Go find someone else to be a superficial ornament on a table. What is this some kind of shrine to yourself? Get over it, it's all a bunch of shit anyway."

"That's it, get out right now. I don't want to see you in here again."

"Fine by me. Thanks for nothing."

Julian took his bag and stormed out of the place. The sparrow hanging by the door rose up and flew away as Julian passed by.

He spent the afternoon walking in and around the city. He walked by his office, and in the districts and neighborhoods between the office and his home. At one point, he walked by a local zoo, a minor establishment with a small collection of exotic animals housed round the year. Though admission was free as part of a Friday special, he chose not to go in. The grey color of the clouds had deepened, though the humidity had dissipated and the air had cooled since the morning. Still, Julian was drenched in sweat by the time he reached a bus stop, about four miles from his home. He sat on the bench underneath a clear awning, waiting for whatever line was due to come next. To his right sat an elderly man, with a grey thinning beard, a wrinkled but clean clothing and a large black beanie covering his head, and sitting in a wheelchair parked right next to the bench. Julian looked at him often but tried not to overtly stare, which became more and more difficult the longer the two them sat alone at the stop.

"Say young man, can you tell me when the nineteen is coming through?" the man asked.

"Excuse me?"

"The nineteen line, takes you up to the bridge. You know it?"

"I'm sorry I don't. I actually don't take the bus much. At all, really."

"What you doing here then?"

"Honestly, I'm not sure. I got tired of walking around but I don't really feel like going home."

"Man, you and I couldn't be any more different. Here I am, can't barely walk, and got no home to go to."

"You're right. I'm sorry, I wasn't thinking about what I was saying."

"Shit man, don't be, it's all good."

"Can I ask why you are going up to the bridge?"

"Well, I ain't jumping off it if that's what you're implying. Not that I could if I wanted to!" he slapped his thigh with his left hand and let out a sharp laugh.

Julian offered a soft laugh in return. "No that's not what I meant."

"I'm going to see my friend Roger. He usually hangs out there on Fridays. Some good money up there. Lots of folks heading out of town for the weekend, so the traffic is slow too. I'm just going to visit though. Never was a fan of panhandling."

"You don't panhandle?"

"No sir, never did, never will."

"How do you get any money?"

"Shit man, I've been on disability for twenty years. Can't you see these legs here? I used to work in a warehouse, but had a forklift drop heavy cargo on my back. It's been me and this chair ever since."

"I'm sorry to hear that."

"Don't be, man. It was twenty years ago. And my life turned out pretty good anyhow. Got my health outside these dead legs, got friends, a full belly. Ain't no point worrying about something else that coulda woulda shoulda happened."

"What about a home?"

"I got a small place, subsidized housing. But I'm never there. Unless it's below freezing or a thunderstorm or something, I'm out and about, even at night. Always felt better that way, even when I had my legs."

"You choose to be homeless?"

"Home-less, or how I like to say it, shackle-free. Depends on how you look at it. What's a home anyway? Walls, a ceiling, a bed. I don't need it, and I don't want it. What I do need here is that damn nineteen line, you feel me?"

Julian laughed softly. "Yeah I feel you."

"What are you doing out here anyway? Ain't seen you around her before."

"I live a little bit that way. I've just been walking around all afternoon. Just trying to clear my head."

"You don't got a job?"

"I do, technically. Maybe not after this week."

"Oh hey then you're about to be joining me on this bench for real then. Put it there partner, name's Jerry."

"Julian."

"Double J's. That's what they'll be calling you and me."

"I like it."

"Me too, but you don't look down and out. I mean, you sweaty as shit, but you look young and rich enough to take care of yourself."

"I am. Just feeling a bit lost lately."

"Shit man that's okay. I ain't known where I was going most my life. Doesn't make you *lost* exactly."

"Oh, you mean like that saying, not all who wander are lost?"

"Hmmm, I like that. You just make that up?"

"No no, it's like an old proverb or something."

"Well, that's a good one. I'm going to have to remember that. But it's what I was saying, sometimes you just have to go do stuff just to go do it. And it may not make any sense, may not be the thing you did the day before, or what you'll do the next day, but if you want to do it on that day, then I say you go do it. And you do that enough times, you'll learn enough about what you like and don't like, and boom, you figure out where you're going."

"Is that what happened to you?"

"Little bit. I remember when I was younger, I was actually a police officer out in Kentucky of all places. I was okay at it at the time. Followed a girl out here, one I thought I was going to marry, and I did, and that lasted for a while, until it didn't. I worked a little construction, a little HVAC, even had an office job for a while at a paper company. Then that warehouse job threw a little wrench in shit, didn't it? But it's okay now. Don't gotta work, don't gotta stick to no one's script but my own, and I've been making it up as I go along."

"What about the future? You got any plans for that?"

"Plans? Well I suppose I could make plans. But really now what good would it do? Always a chance I wake up tomorrow and on my way to this here bus stop I get run over. Should I plan for that? Then there's always a chance I get on this next bus and bump into some genius spinal surgeon, and they offer to fix my legs so I can walk again. Should I plan for that too? I don't know what's going to happen any more than the next guy, and can't do much about it anyhow. I just find it easier to worry about the road I can see in front of me."

"I just can't see how to do that."

"Well, you're young, by the looks of it. Chances are nothing has really happened to you yet that's going to make you think different about anything. Not saying I want that to happen to you, you look like a good kid after all, but sometimes things need to fall apart for you to understand how they work. That's my two cents on it anyway."

"I think I get that. So is there nothing you want that you don't have now?"

"Well I didn't say I don't want anything! Shit, man. Naw, I tell you what. If I could have something, it'd be a car. Not a nice car, or a special car, well, except something that would allow me to be in the driver seat. But you know why? Man, I'd really like to be one of those Uber drivers. They get to drive around all day, all across the city, and meet all sorts of different people. And you get paid too! I can't think of anything better to do."

"That doesn't sound bad at all."

"No, it sure don't. Can I make a suggestion to you, my man?"

"Sure, please do."

"In about, oh, ten minutes or so, the forty-five line is going to swing by here. It's a fun route, goes from here out into the suburbs, does a few loops and then comes back. I like that route a lot, you see a lot of families, moms or dads strolling around with their children or playing in parks, and older couples out for a post-dinner walk. I don't even get off the bus most of the time, I just look out the window, and think about those couples and families and their backstories, where they came from, how they met, what else they do for fun. I suggest you do the same, might clear your mind a bit."

"I think I will. Thanks for the tip."

"Sure thing, Mr. Julian. The nineteen line is coming around the corner now. I'll need to get going."

"Thought you didn't know when the nineteen was coming?"

Jerry grinned. "Ha! I always know, man! I just said that to strike up a conversation. A good one too. I'm glad we did this. Take care, my man."

"Take care."

The nineteen bus rolled up to the bus stop. The driver, upon seeing Jerry, clearly recognized him and began to lower the wheelchair-accessible platform. Jerry gave one last wave, wheeled himself up on the platform, and let it rise up to the bus. The nineteen then drove off.

Julian sat by himself on the bench. He recalled a time with his father, back when he was moving into college. It was the night before freshmen were to move into the dorms. He and his father were staying in a local motel, each laying down on their own double bed, watching a local news station despite the fact that they were both in a new and unknown city. In the middle of the program, Julian's dad began speaking out loud, giving advice to prep Julian on his collegiate future. The topics began simple enough, cliches about studying for classes and keeping a proper diet. His father then weaved his way into a parental sex talk, explaining the do's and don'ts of protecting oneself, from disease, from pregnancies, and from the accusation of impropriety. Throughout the talk, his father looked ahead at the television, never glancing over to Julian much less looking him in the eye. When the talk was over, his father turned the television off, suggested they both fall asleep, and turned off the lights.

Julian remembered how awkward the whole encounter was. The jump in discussion from handwriting to premarital sex was so abrupt that he had trouble adjusting to what he was hearing. Before then, he and his father had hardly shared an embrace, and so listening to him work through a detailed discussion of how to apply condoms had left him shell-shocked. Julian couldn't tell if his father knew that he had been sexually active for a couple of years, ever since he had met his high-school sweetheart. Julian had kept his endeavors covert, or so he had thought. His only lapse was one particular evening, after sneaking out of his house, when he returned early in the morning, so late as to be near the time he would normally wake up for school. He got up to his room, quickly undressed and threw his clothes on the floor, and hopped into his bed for a few brief minutes of shuteye. Unfortunately, he woke some forty minutes later, already late for school, with his clothes from the night earlier removed from the room, already gathered for laundry by his father. Julian rose in a panic. His pants pocket had included one condom, unused from the evening before. He ran downstairs to the laundry room, and while attempting not to rouse suspicion, he rummaged through the clothes pile, attempting to retrieve the condom before anyone might notice. He didn't find it, and began to brace for a stern and embarrassing conversation with his parents. Yet, neither his mother nor father mentioned the episode to him, neither that day nor any day after. For Julian, the whole episode had faded into distant memory, until his father brought up the topic of sex as if Julian had had no previous exposure. Julian offered little response except basic syllables of agreement. It was the first and only time he and his father discussed the matter.

As Jerry had predicted, the forty-five line came through after ten minutes had passed. Julian hopped aboard, and sat down two rows back on the passenger side. There were about a dozen other people on the bus, mostly on their way home from work by the look of them. Julian remained in his seat as the bus reached the suburbs, an ensemble of newly-built developments outside the main city loop. Tight, medium-sized homes packed close together around winding roads which dead-ended to cul-de-sacs, periodically broken up by a playground or man-made water fountain. As Jerry detailed, there were plenty of young mothers and fathers taking their babies out in strollers, and grandparents walking in sweatpants behind them. Small children with pegs on their bicycles rode around in gangs, on a mission to find the next best patch of woods in which to stow away before dinnertime.

Julian remembered his old neighborhood, a similar development only with bigger houses but less-friendly neighbors. Still, he had one friend from the apartment complex outside his neighborhood, who would bike over so they could roam the streets to pass the time. He remembered this one occurrence when both of them rode by a narrow gap in the woods which formed the boundary of the development. He and his friend jumped off their bikes, and walked through that gap. After some ten or twenty yards the woods opened up, onto a trickling stream which cut left to right about thirty feet below them. On the opposite side of the stream was a wide but shallow inlet, a few feet of sand forming a bank just deep enough for two people to lay there. There was no way to continue down to the stream below, and eventually, Julian and his friend walked back through the gap and returned to the main neighborhood. But before he left he imagined what it would be like to go to that bank, to take someone over there one day, a girlfriend or wife perhaps, for a picnic on a relaxing afternoon, to enjoy the seclusion and intimacy of the setting. It was one of the first romantic thoughts he had ever had, long before he ever had a girlfriend or the means to arrange such an excursion.

"You planning to get off here? It's the last stop before I head back to the city." The bus driver, a woman, middle-aged and overweight, with her hair held in a bun at the top of her head, turned around to jolt Julian from his daydream. Her tone was neither concerned nor annoyed, just engaging enough to obtain information which could potentially affect her shift. "Hey sir, if you live out here, you need to get off at this stop now."

"Oh, no, sorry. I actually live in the city, you are still going back there right?"

"I am, but why did you ride out here if you're just going back?"

"Jerry told me."

"Oh, *Jerry*. I see. Ok then, let's get going then."

Julian and the driver were the only ones left on the bus. The bus driver got on the highway to bypass the stops she hit on the way out.

"So, did you have fun on your little joyride?" she asked Julian.

"I did. You know, living in the city, you don't actually see children all that much. It was nice to see families out and about, very nostalgic."

"Ever thought of moving out here?"

"No, I don't have any family here. Plus my job is in the city. Though when I was younger I used to live in a neighborhood likes the ones we just went through. I can imagine living in one someday, just not right now. Where do you live?"
"I live on the east side. Not as nice as these neighborhoods, but it's what I can manage."

"Family?"

"Only the worst kind. An ex-wife, who has custody of the kids. And my parents who live with me."

"Oh, I'm sorry, I didn't mean to intrude."

"Don't worry about it. It is what it is. My mother has kidney failure, been that way for the last year, and my father's too old to handle the dialysis and doctor's visits."

"That must be hard, having to work and support them."

"Like I said, it is what it is. You do what you go to do, and if it's what has to be done, easy or hard doesn't mean anything. Yeah sure, it would be easier if my wife were around, and if I could see our kids more, but it's not an option so the comparison is pointless. My parents need the support, and there's no one else to do it, so it's done."

"Do you like driving this bus?"

"Is that a serious question?"

"I mean, it's not something you hate, is it?"

"Hate? No. I picked up this job a few months back for the benefits, and so far it does the trick. Fixed shifts, good health insurance, and enough down time to take care of everything else in my life. Aside from the occasional crazy person or loiterer, the time passes quickly enough."

"And don't forget Jerry."

"Of course, Jerry." The bus driver smiled. "Yes, I'd say he's a perk of the job."

"How long do you think you'll do it?"
"As long as I have to. If I'm good about it, I can save about $200 a month, and if I do that for a few years, might have enough to put a down payment on a small house. More room for my parents, and for my kids when I get to see them. Still a pittance compared to the houses we just drove around, but better than I got now."

"If you don't mind my asking, what happened with your ex-wife?"

"Boy, that's a long story."

"I got time. Again, if it's alright with you."

"Okay then. What happened? Life happened I guess. It all started out well enough. We met through common friends and hit it off from the start. Nights out dancing, trips to the beach, sharing an apartment. We got married once it became legal, a small civil ceremony and a reception in my parent's backyard. The two of them were so great -- when I first came out, brought girlfriends over, they were always so understanding, still are to this day. It's why I'll never leave them or put them in a nursing or retirement home.

After we got married, the problems started to build up the way they always do, slowly, without any one thing being too noticeable. Bickering over what to eat for dinner, which friends we were going to see, what expenses were responsible for us being over our budget. After a couple years, we were basically just roommates. The intimacy was gone, the fun was gone, and we weren't happy. Like idiots, we thought having kids would make things better, so we found a donor for IVF and decided my ex should be the mother. And then when the twins came out, it was like everything fell apart. Fighting all the time, getting no sleep, and there was nothing left to keep us in it anymore. After a year or so, she found someone else, a fellow mom at a breastfeeding support group. I was hurt, but couldn't say I was heart-broken. The only thing that really stung was when the court sided with her for primary custody, on the grounds that she carried the twins and had better financial means with her new wife. The money I understood, but I would have gladly been the mom for my kids and carried them to term, and because I didn't, I now only see them two weekends a month.

So, what really happened? What happened was I made a bunch of decisions which made sense in their own small way at the time, but when you put them all together, it just turned into a mess. A complex, thorny mess that I can barely keep up with even when I think I have it under control."

"Do you regret it?"

"No, I don't. Because as tough as it is, it's beautiful in its own way. I love my kids, the ex and I get along now, and though my mother's not doing so well, we have a happy time. To say I wouldn't do it any differently is kind of stupid, of course I would, but that's not what you or me or anyone else gets to decide. But I don't think I'd trade my life for someone else's. Because there is something special about it being mine that I wouldn't ever want to give up."

"Yeah, this is something they've found in studies. It's called the endowment effect. The fact that something starts out as yours make you value it more than if it were somebody else's, even though it's the same thing."

"What do you mean?"

"Take my bag for example. If I offered to sell you my bag, you'd be willing to buy it for less money than you'd be willing to sell it back to me if you owned it, despite it being the same bag."

"Well, I don't know if I understand all that. But all I'm saying is my life, warts and all, is okay by me. Whatever decisions I've made, I did what I thought was best at the time given what I knew and what was I hoping to make of myself. Some things turned out alright and some not quite, but either way I've got nothing to regret. What about you?"

"I couldn't tell you. I actually feel like for most of my life I haven't made any decisions at all. I know that's literally not true, but I don't think I've been faced with a decision so consequential to make me consider other paths I could've taken. Maybe that's why I'm on this bus right now, to think about what those other paths are."

"Nothing wrong with exploring a little."

"It's not just about exploring, but more like, *discovering*. I've had several jobs in a few companies, I've dated multiple women, done a bit of traveling. But lately I've been feeling like I went through all those experiences while only scratching the surface of any one of them. I can't shake the feeling that they had more to offer than what I took from them, like I left a lot on the table. I'm thirty, financially well-off, and have checked most of the boxes someone my age would be expected to, but right now, I can't shake the feeling that I've missed something, and I don't know how to find it."

"Let me tell you a story, if you don't mind."

"Not at all."

"There was a man who used to ride on my line. Kind of like you, he would ride around all day, but instead, he would get off periodically, and then he'd get back on when I came back around. He did this one day a week, for a few weeks on end. He was older, probably in his fifties, well-dressed in a suit and tie. It was always the same day of the week, a Sunday I think, and he would be going about his business before my shift started and would continue even after I clocked out.

One day, towards the end of his routine, I asked him what he was up to. At first, he kind of blew me off, but when my shift ended and I was changing out, he got off with me and asked if I wanted to see what he was doing. Normally I wouldn't go for such a proposition, but it was broad daylight and he didn't seem the dangerous type. So I went along. We walked a few blocks away, until he found a 7-eleven. We walked in, and he ordered two large blue slushies -- 'Blue Crush' or 'Blue Freeze' or something like that -- for us to have. I tried a little bit of it, but it was so sweet I could barely get through a few sips before I had to stop. For him too, he drank a few big gulps, paused a second, then threw the rest in the trash.

I asked him what it was all about. He told me that he was taking a tour of every 7-eleven in the city to try the same blue slushie we just had. I asked him why on earth would he do something like that. He told me that going to 7-eleven for slushies was a pastime of his with his father when he was younger. That they would go every Sunday, taking the bus, and that he would always pick the blue one, even though there were many options and his father always encouraged him to explore the other ones. The man said he and his father did that for years, until he grew up and became more interested in sports, girls, you name it, and eventually stopped going.

He told me that he and his father had drifted apart as he got older, and by the time he was in his adulthood the two were almost estranged. He became quite successful as a banker, working hard and playing harder, got married with kids, retired early, all the while barely speaking to his father. Then, a few weeks back, he said his father suddenly passed, a massive coronary nobody had seen coming. He told me that the last words he said to his father were, "Why don't you get it yourself?" the day before, his response to a request to bring over a glass of water.

After the funeral, he decided to take the bus to get a blue slushie from 7-eleven. When he tried it, he said it didn't quite taste the same as he had remembered it when he went with his father. So he got back on the bus, and went to the next one on the line, but the outcome was the same: they never quite tasted right. So he tried again the following Sunday, and each one after that, trying different locations, asking the managers about the ingredients, each time sampling a new slushie and hoping it would match. And then eventually, he realized that his quest to find the perfect blue slushie was his way of mourning his father, that he was never going to find exactly what he was looking for, but the quest of doing so would reconnect him to those wonderful memories he had. And so he went on and on doing so, every Sunday, tried a new slushie and considered its features, thought about his father, and smiled.

He started to ride the bus less frequently after that, and within a month, I didn't see him anymore. I don't know if he was done mourning, if he had found another route, or if talking about his ritual to me somehow ruined it for him. But whatever the case, it was done. I think of it now, because he had all the means to do whatever he wanted, anywhere in the world. He could travel, eat at fancy restaurants, or go to a private beach every day of his life. And yet, the only thing that mattered to him was continuing his pursuit of something he knew he would not find, something which from the outside appeared entirely pointless and wasteful, but to him, was the only endeavor from which he could find peace.

All that to say, perhaps it's best not to worry about what you haven't done, what you've yet to experience or accomplish, what you may or may not have left behind. There's an endless list of those, and measuring your tally against them is guaranteed to result in disappointment. But you can find something which matters to you, and if it matters enough, no string of shortcomings in pursuit of it can bend your will or sense of satisfaction."

"I'm starting to think you'd be a better life coach than a bus driver."

"Wouldn't that be nice! You learn a lot observing people come and go from a rearview mirror. People take a seat, stare out the window, and their face will let you know everything that's going on in their mind. To me, it all boils down to the same few things. They're either happy, sad, or just kind of done. It's the third one that I like the least, because it's the state of nothing, nothing worth celebrating or brooding over. Just nothing."

The bus had exited off the highway and was back into the main city. They reached a stop close to his home, and Julian stood up to leave.

"Thanks for taking me back."

"All part of the route, but you're welcome."

"Hope your mom gets better."

"She'll need a new kidney eventually, but I appreciate the sentiment. If you see Jerry before I do, tell him the forty-five line says hello."

"Sure thing."

Julian walked off and headed back to his place. It was evening now, and the sky was a rich blue even though the sun had already set. He walked by Nero's, and saw a woman sitting at a table outside. As he got closer, he saw that it was Loretta, the employee he had met the day before. She was staring out in the distance, and did not notice as he walked up to her.

"Loretta, right? It's me, Julian, from last night."

His voice startled her, and she looked up to see him.

"Oh, yes, hello young man."

"Funny seeing you two days in a row. How have you been?"

"I'm ok, I suppose. Where you coming from?"

"I've been out and about. Had kind of a rough day, but I feel better now."

"Well that's good to hear. I'd offer you some pizza but my shift ended a few minutes ago and I'm already clocked out."

"It's not a problem, some other time. What are you doing here? I thought yesterday was your last shift."

"I thought so too, but one of my co-workers got sick and I offered to cover their shift."

"But what about your son? Wasn't he coming to visit you today?"

"Yes, he was supposed to, but --" she paused, her lip quivered and she turned away from him, "he didn't show up. I tried calling him, but no one answered. I waited most of the day. When my phone rang, I got so excited because I thought it was him, but it was just work, asking me if I could come in. I was so disappointed, I figured coming to work would at least help me pass the time rather than being miserable about it."

"I'm sorry to hear that, that's terrible."

"As sad as I am about it, I can't say I'm really surprised. There's a reason I haven't seen him in three years, and it's not for my lack of trying. Every few months or so I manage to get in touch with him. He normally holes up in a public storage unit, seems to be the one form of housing he can stick with. Only way I can reach him is a pager, and then he has to call me back on a prepaid phone. He rarely does, but when I do get a call back, I just try to talk about regular things, like the weather or how our relatives are doing. He gets upset if I ask too many questions about how he's doing or what he's up to. If I'm lucky, he'll agree to come by the house to see me, but he never shows, no matter how hard I try."

"Why doesn't he come?"

"I wish I knew. He's had trouble with social interaction for most of his adult life now. He's a recluse. Hasn't ever held down a job, or had a girlfriend. As far as I can tell, he doesn't have much of a life at all.

It's a shame too. He was a straight A student in high school, and got a scholarship to study mathematics in college. But he never adjusted well, to the dorms, the classes, the campus life. His grades started to drop, he complained of being alienated by his classmates, got into some trouble. He lost his scholarship and had to drop out, and ever since he's been in the wind. He picks up disability each month, drinks and smokes a lot, keeps some friends who live a similar life as he does. When he was younger, he used to come visit me regularly, but that tapered off, and now here we are."

"Did he ever get evaluated, you know, mentally?"

"A few times he went to see a specialist, but he never told me what they told him, and after a while he stopped seeing them too. Didn't trust them."

"It's too bad he didn't come today. Maybe someday he will."

"I hope so."

"What are you doing out here, waiting for a ride?"

"I was going to hop on the bus, but I just wanted to sit out here a moment and collect my thoughts before I head home."

"It's quite late, I can give you a ride home if you don't mind walking back to my place first. It's just a few blocks away."

"Oh no, thank you Julian, but that's alright. I don't mind the bus."

"Looks like it will be a while, and it's already getting dark. At least let me call you an Uber."

"Uber? What's that?"

"It's like a taxi cab, only it's regular people who drive their cars around giving people rides. You use your phone to call a driver, they come to your location, and take you where you need to go."

"That's pretty nifty, but I don't have one of those smartphones to use."

"That's alright, I can order it for you, and when the driver comes, they'll take you to your home. All you have to do is give me the address and the driver can use GPS to navigate the way."

"How much does it cost?"

"Nothing at all."

"Now that can't be true!"

"Well, not exactly. Let me take care of it. I still owe you for the pizza from yesterday."

"You're too kind. Thank you, Julian."

"It's my pleasure."

Julian took Loretta's address and hailed a ride. The sun had completely fallen, and the streetlights had turned on to illuminate the street in front of them. For the first time that day, Julian felt exhausted, and wanted to go home. The car arrived and Loretta entered the backseat. He reiterated with the driver where to go and how to get there. As the car pulled away, Loretta waved to him, and he waved back.

Julian began his short walk home. He found himself humming the chorus of a song, over and over again, but he could not recall what it was nor how he knew it. Whatever it was, it had dark, harmonic overtones, and each loop of the chorus sank him deeper into a despairing, haunting mood. He continued to hum the nameless song. Though the brooding notes felt heavy on his chest, they also felt cathartic, relaxing his built-up consternation even as they lowered his mood. He hummed louder, taking deep breaths before each sequence and letting the final note extend and endure. He began to riff on the chorus, clumsy in his improvisation and execution, but maintaining its dark, somber theme. His face tightened and grimaced to complement the anguish emanating from his dour tune and from the painful yet soothing despondency forming within him. It was the first time he could recall being happy about being sad.

He returned to his apartment, where Franny pranced to the door to greet him. One burst of his cacophonic humming sent her in the opposite direction. He lowered his voice and followed her into the bedroom where she had ran, and when seeing him again, she immediately rolled over on her back and purred for attention. He bent down to pet her behind her ears and under her chin, before getting up to open a can of wet food for her to eat. The mere sound of the pantry door opening was enough to send her running to the kitchen, crying frantically in anticipation of her next meal. He opened the can and spooned the food into her bowl, and she began eating purposefully, soft purring coupled with forceful bites and loud lip smacking.

He opened a can of club soda for himself and paced around his apartment. The humidity from the day had seeped into the rooms and left his furniture sticky to the touch. He turned on the A/C so the cold air blowing from the walls and ceiling could spell relief from the heat of the day. He closed the blinds on all the windows to shield what remained of the sun from further warming the air. He went to his bedroom to remove the sweat-drenched clothes off his body, which stuck to his arms and legs as he undressed. He removed them all down to his underwear, feeling liberated by the touch of crisp air on the skin up and down his body. He started to make his bed, sheets and pillows strewn about from the morning, so that when he fell asleep later in the evening, the interior would be cool and calming when he entered.

He gazed at the picture hanging by his bed. The melancholy man stared at him with pointed eyes, and despite Julian looking away and then back numerous times, never wavered. For the first time, Julian saw himself in the painting, as if the man were a portrait of Julian as a much older man. The unkempt hair, dark circles under the eyes, furrowed brow, all indicators of an aging process that Julian could viscerally feel as he stared at the painting. He thought about what his life would be like at that age, what he would be doing, who would be there, who wouldn't, how many good years would be left to enjoy, or not enjoy, once he got old. He did not think much about death, but in that moment he felt a morbidity about the prospect of dying, and it froze him in his place, at the edge of his bed with his comforter half-tucked under the mattress.

He walked to the bottom of the bed and took in the painting from there, hoping to glimpse the boy and his dog. Instead he saw the old man once again, and the pangs of aging and decay sank deeper into his chest. He lunged to other spots in his room, each time checking the picture, but in no instance was he able to recapture the alternative image. The old man continued to glare at him, and the more Julian looked back he could see the old man's grimace growing more rigid and menacing, getting angry at Julian's attempts to escape it. His heart rate began to elevate, and his neck flushed with blood, as the internal panic of slipping down an abyss rose up from his stomach and made him nauseated. He rushed to the bathroom, loosened the faucet on the sink and splashed cold water on his face until he calmed himself. He looked up at the mirror above the sink to see his own reflection, grimaced and brow furrowed in imitation of the man in the painting. He forced himself to smile, to create some kind of a positive affect, but in the mirror all he saw was an awkward and uncoordinated baring of his teeth, squinting of his eyes, and puffing of his cheeks. His frustration boiled over and he splashed the water pooled in the sink at the mirror, hoping it would wash away the reflection he so acutely detested. The water beaded up and trickled down to the sink, leaving the image in the mirror as it was before, lonely and lost. He stormed out of the bathroom to stare at the painting one more time, and one more time he found the grimacing old man staring back at him, fierce and unrelenting. He ripped the painting off the wall and slammed it down on the ground as hard as he could. The clashing sound of the frame colliding with the floor startled Franny from her eating, and he heard the scatter of her claws swiping against the tile floor as she jolted away from her food. He looked down at the painting on the floor, and saw the boy and the dog, jubilant and affectionate. Only now, the boy and dog had been separate and ripped apart, the canvas ripping in half on the nail previously holding up the frame on the wall.

Julian picked up the painting and returned to the kitchen to throw it away. Franny, alarmed and hiding behind a chair, looked out, cautiously returned to her bowl, and recommenced purring and eating her food.

Saturday

Julian drove along the river road, with Lydia in the passenger seat. The river was a docile, slow-moving body of water which began from glacier run-off and ended in the ocean, curving around the city in between. The road alongside the river picked up a few miles outside the city, winding and weaving along the river's edge until it ended at a small ocean town, with a main street of restaurants, art galleries, and farmer's markets, and bookended by a boat marina on one side and a small beach on the other. The beach opened up to grassy fields, park benches and hammocks, and wooded trails which wound around tall trees and bulky rocks adorning the coast. The road itself was two lanes wide, one each way, squeezed between the river and a steep rocky cliff some twenty feet above. The river flow had cut through the rock over thousands of years, leaving a smooth multi-colored edge. The cliff revealed layer upon layer of sediment, each one displaying rich tones of red or brown and crystallized quartz which reflected sharply in the sunlight.

Julian was driving a blue convertible with the top and windows down, the wind blowing their hair straight back. It was late morning and the sun was out with clear skies, feeling pleasantly warm before the temperature would rise and become uncomfortable in the early afternoon. Julian didn't own the convertible; he had rented it earlier that day, a last-minute decision to upgrade his ride for the day's outing. It was an expensive upgrade, both in time and in money, spurred by an anxious feeling as he was getting ready in the morning that a normal drive in his normal car would not suffice. Because of the change of plans, he was thirty minutes late to pick up Lydia, something she didn't mind until she determined the reason behind the delay. Once they were on the river road, Julian lowered the windows and uncovered the top, frequently looking over to Lydia in the passenger seat and smiling at the demonstration of his newly-acquired capabilities. She offered a smile back the first few times, but between the force and volume of the wind on her face, and the inability to converse beyond pointing and nodding, she soon withdrew and kept to herself on her side of the car.

Halfway along their journey, the shoulder expanded into a resting area, covered in loose gravel and surrounded by a rocky wall formed into a semi-circle. In the middle was an illustration of an amalgamated bird-like monster, with branching red horns, bearded face, a thick wide body covered in scales, outsized talons, and a long braided tail which extending underneath its body all the way up through the horns on its head. Julian pulled off the road, parked in the rest area, and he and Lydia exited the car to observe the mural.

"What's this?" Lydia asked.

"It's an ancient Native American mural, of a mythical creature that would snatch up victims with its talons and tear them apart for meals. Pretty gnarly, huh?"

"It's...*grotesque*, I'll give you that. The face, the horns, looks like it was supposed to be intimidating. It could be that the tribe who painted this was combining all their fears and anxieties into one being, and put it up on this rock here for what? As a warning? As an homage? I can't quite tell."

"Maybe it was just a kid who was vandalizing."

"No! Come on now. Whoever painted this, it must have been a huge deal at the time. For us, it's one picture. Anyone can take a picture nowadays and have it preserved forever. Back then, they wouldn't have gone through all this effort if it wasn't something truly important. It's kind of nice to think about how proud these people were when this mural was finished."

"Not much of an accomplishment though, when you think about it. Like you said, nowadays pictures like this are pretty easy to do, and come out way cooler than this."

"But you have to appreciate achievements like this in the context of the time and place in which it occurred. This is probably one of the only works like this that existed in that age, and based on what they had before it, must have felt like a huge accomplishment. People can only be judged based on the conditions in which they act."

"Hmm, I don't know if I buy that. It's not like the human brain has changed that much between when this mural was painted and now. Why should I care more about this just because it was created in the past?"

"Well if you're so unenthused by this mural, why did we stop to look at it?"

"I heard it was an interesting thing to see, and I thought you'd like it."

"Indeed I do, but not as much as I would have if you liked it as well."

"Sorry to disappoint."

"Shall we take a picture?"

"Yeah sure, I guess."

Lydia took out her phone and moved close to Julian to take a selfie. Julian put his hand meekly over her shoulder and stood tall. She counted down from three, snapped the photo, and reviewed it on her phone.

"Jules, you didn't smile."

"Sure I did."

"No, you just showed your teeth. Aren't you happy to take a picture with me? Now, do it again and smile this time." They took the photo one more time.

"Much better, don't you think you look much nicer in this?"

Julian glanced at the photo. "Not really, my eyes are squinting and my cheeks are puffed out."

"I think you look very handsome."

"I'll take your word for it. Shall we keep moving?"

"If that's what you want, sure. Can I ask that you put the top back up on the car? I love the sun and the open air, but my hair is starting to look like Albert Einstein, don't you think?" She stuck her tongue out to mimic the iconic photo.

"Yeah we can. I just thought we could utilize the convertible, being such a nice day."

"And we did, didn't we? Plus, it's hard to hear you or talk to you with the air blowing so hard."

"Fine."

Julian and Lydia returned to the car and continued their drive. They drove mostly in silence. Julian periodically changed the radio station, but there seemed to be no song which allowed them to sit and be with each other comfortably.

"Thanks for bringing the food for lunch," Julian offered. "What did you bring for us?"

"Not just a lunch, a *picnic*. Picnics are way more delightful."

"Yes, our picnic."

"I've prepared for us a three-course meal. We will be starting with fresh-cut strawberries and honeyed goat cheese with crackers. A little blend of sweetness, the smooth saltiness of the cheese, and the crunchy texture of the cracker to bring it all together. The second course features a spinach and kale salad, with sliced almonds, mandarin oranges, figs, avocado, and lime vinaigrette dressing. And for our final course, we will be eating ahi tuna poke, marinated in poke sauce and served with seaweed salad, toasted coconut rice, and daikon radish. What do you think?"

"Very fancy. Are you a chef or something?"

"Better - I'm a food network junkie, and spend way too much money and time at Whole Foods. And let's just say I embellished a bit on today's selection. Oh, and I forgot to mention our dessert! What do you think it will be?"

"Thought you said it was three courses?"
"Does dessert count as a course? Fine, four. Now guess!"

"I don't know, cookies?"

"Come on, where is your imagination Jules? That simply won't do."

"I'm out of guesses. Tell me what we're having."

"Since apparently you are awful at this game, I suppose I can tell you. We'll be having raspberry macaroons and lemon curd yogurt. A soothing palate cleanser after a delightful meal. You're welcome."

"Sounds great," Julian replied flatly.

"Doesn't just sound great, it *is* great. Tell me, which part sounds the most appetizing to you?"

"I couldn't tell you. To be honest, I don't really like food that much."

"What?! Now that is just crazy. You cannot be serious."

"I am. Not that I don't enjoy the taste of food, but don't really care for or crave it in anyway. It's just something you have to have, like clean water or having a roof over your head."

"So what is your favorite food?"

"That is an impossible question."

"Is not. I could tell you mine."

"Spill."

"Easy. Chocolate banana pancakes."

"Wow okay, that's oddly specific."

"But that's what it is."

"How come?"

"It's from my childhood. Whenever I was sick, or sad, or just feeling off, my mother would make chocolate banana pancakes for breakfast. She would break a Hershey bar into bits and pieces, mix it in the batter with smushed bananas, cook them in the pan, and serve them with maple syrup and some fresh fruit. She'd always make me eat them one at a time, so they wouldn't go to waste. I always remember how good the first bite tasted, after watching her make the pancakes from scratch. And when I took that first bite, I just remember being so happy. From the taste, and from having that moment with my Mom, who took the effort to make me feel better. And no matter how many times we had those pancakes I'd always get that feeling. As I got older, I started to help her make them, occasionally trying to do them myself, but it was never quite the same."

"And what about now? Do you still eat them?"

"To tell you the truth, not really. Haven't in a long time."

"So I guess it's not your favorite food then, if you don't really eat them that often."

"I guess I just hold on to the memory of them more than anything. Don't you have anything like that?"

"Not really. Like I said, food is food."

"Perhaps I should just throw our picnic out the window, then."

"I didn't mean it like that. I'm sure the picnic is going to be great."

"But how would you know, Jules?"

They sat mostly in silence the remainder of the drive. At the end of the river road, they reached the ocean town and hung a right onto the main street. Julian found a parking lot near the marina at the end of the road, and turned in to park the car. Because he had no experience driving the convertible, longer and heavier than his normal sedan, it took three tries to align the car in the parking spot, with each successive try increasing the agitation with which he turned the steering wheel and applied the accelerator and brakes. Once parked, he and Lydia got out and started walking the long strip to the other side of the main street. Julian tried to walk alongside Lydia, but frequently found himself getting ahead of her by a step or two, resulting in him having to slow his pace to fall back to her.

They passed a local restaurant, Patsy's, a breakfast and lunch diner established in 1948 and known for serving their original menu and their original prices. The only catch is guests cannot ask for any substitutions, add-ons, or modifications to the spartan but economical offerings. Outside the restaurant, they caught a red light which prevented them from crossing the street, having to wait until the pedestrian signal turned green. Julian was standing next to Lydia, close to her but not so close as to betray any untoward intimacy to an external observer. As they waited to walk across the street, Julian gently raised his hand and put it on the small of Lydia's back, just above her waist, just below the line of her bra-strap, its impression visible through the back of her green blouse. His hand was clammy from the heat of the walk, and it stuck to her shirt slightly, but when he placed it on her she turned to face him and gave a soft smile. He smiled back, until a family of four walked out of Patsy's and joined them near the curb. The two children were running circles around their parents, and started to bump into Julian and Lydia, giggling through all of it. The parents tried to call them back, apologizing to Julian and Lydia for the intrusion. Lydia laughed it off and told the parents how cute the children were; Julian lifted his hand and returned it to his pocket, offering no expression to the parents and avoiding eye contact with them.

They continued their walk down the main street towards the grassy beach at the other end. Just before they reached, they passed a commercial building with a modern style and looking brand-new compared to the old dated structures to its left and right. Grey sandstone walls alternating with floor to ceilings windows, with manicured rich green grass in the front. The front doorway was all glass, opening into an entranceway which continued through to glass doors in the back that led to the ocean water behind, all visible from the curbside view.

"That's such an odd building on this street, don't you think?" Lydia questioned.

"Yeah, looks completely different than all the other ones. Let's check it out."

They walked up to the front door, which was locked for the weekend. On the door itself was the name of the enterprise: Jerome H. Baumann Commercial Real Estate. Inside the building, there was only a small reception desk to break up the vast openness of the foyer, but with no papers on top of it nor chair behind it. It looked as though the whole building had been vacated, save for one lone desk which had been left behind.

"Makes no sense. Why would a commercial real estate company in this small town have such a glamorous building?" Julian wondered aloud.

"You got to spend money to make money, I guess?"

"I don't think that's how it works."

"Hmm, maybe Jerome H. Baumann just has fancy taste, and wants his clients to know that."

"Still doesn't explain how he can afford it."

"That's true. Who knows, maybe there are some secretly rich people hiding away in this town."

"Maybe eating at Patsy's, eh?"

"Maybe."

They continued to the beach, a small patch of sand by the ocean, backing into grassy fields with picnic benches, hollowed out fire pits, and a lone unisex restroom. There were a few families there already, along with a smattering of individuals reading, listening to music, or meditating by themselves. Julian and Lydia found an open space on the grass, unfolded and stretched out a blanket which she had brought, and sat down for their picnic. Lydia rested the cooler which held their food on the blanket.

"Since you have no feelings or emotions attached to your taste buds, Jules, how would you like to prepare the first course of our meal?"

"I suppose I can lavish you with my culinary prowess on this occasion."

"Oh, aren't I just the luckiest girl in the world."

"Very funny."

"I expect a professional presentation here. I want each cracker to have a smooth, even finish of the goat cheese, and a crisp, fresh-cut strawberry resting on top. If not, I am afraid I'll have to dock you on your Yelp rating."

Julian began to cut the strawberries in fine, even triangles. He spread the goat cheese evenly across a cracker, applied the strawberry on top, and offered it to Lydia.

"What kind of premium service is this if I had to feed myself?" Lydia asked playfully.

Julian smiled, and slowly lifted the cracker to Lydia's mouth. She gently enclosed the cracker in her mouth, letting her lips softly caress his finger. She chewed on the cracker slowly, exaggerating her enjoyment with deep rolls of the eyes and long, drawn-out moans of approval.

"I take it the first course is a success?"

"All I can say is whoever picked out the ingredients really knew what they were doing."

"Oh really, no special credit given to the chef?"

"Some, perhaps. But we're only on our first course, aren't we?"

Julian and Lydia continued their meal through the second and third course, and onto dessert. They alternated preparing the food, feeding each other, and offering whimsical quips on their respective efforts. They cracked a bottle of sparkling white wine, and sipped on it as Julian kicked back on the blanket and stared out to the ocean. He saw a little girl and her father on surfboards sitting atop the waves. The father was attempting to teach the girl how to surf, gently paddling on his board as he instructed his daughter to do the same. The daughter, however, was perfectly content splashing the waves at her father and attempting headstands on her board. The father laughed in exasperation at his daughter's defiance, and the daughter shrieked in excitement from her playful rebellion. Julian imagined in that moment a vision of himself in the future, with his own daughter, playing in the water. He felt a tightening in his chest, a pang of unbridled affection for a child which existed only his mind. The thought of having unconditional love for another being, one who thought the world of him, made him feel warm and terrified all at the same time. He tried to picture this daughter, what she looked like, what she was wearing, what she was doing, but the image always evaded him in his mind. All he could picture was her shadow, her silhouette, or the back of her head as she turned away.

"What's on your mind Jules? Thinking about that book of yours?"

"Hm?"

"You were spaced out there for a minute. Everything alright?"

"Yeah, everything's great. Just lost in thought."

"What *is* going on with that book of yours?"

"Wish I had more to report, but to be honest I haven't done much of anything."

"How come?"

"I just really don't know where to begin. I've tried a couple of times to put pen to paper, but outside of a few meaningless sentences and doodles nothing comes out. And with each passing day, the pressure and expectations of completing it just builds up, and it's as if any little bit I can do seems so inconsequential. And then I begin to think about why I'm even trying to do this at all, why the boss of the company assigned it to me, and what will happen if I actually do it or not. This has been a strange week for me. A great week in some ways, but one that's really upended what I thought was going on in my life. On the one hand, I feel empty, like I've been running on fumes for years and only learned about it a few days ago, but on the other, I feel kind of alive, like I got everything I need right in front of me. Like I said, it's been a strange week."

"My dear Julian, what a whirlwind you're going through. I had no idea."

"What's to know? You do what you have to do. I'm sure you feel the same, at whatever your job is."

"Yes, whatever my job is."

"Why won't you tell me?"

"Why do you keep asking?"

"Look I know you said you didn't think it was interesting to talk about. But it's something I'd like to know about you, if you wouldn't mind indulging me."

"And it's not like I would dare want to disappoint you."

"Well what am I supposed to think if you refuse to tell me?"

Lydia paused. "Nothing, Jules, nothing at all. I'm a freelance graphic designer. I pick up jobs from crowdsourcing websites on a case-by-case basis and get paid a fixed amount per design. It's not a job, per se. I have no employer, I am self-employed technically, and have no job title or portfolio of work. I work mostly at home, on my laptop, and when the designs are done I send them over and get paid via online transfer. I don't work normal hours either, or any hours really, nor do I have a salary. I work when I have to, or want to, or both, picking up jobs as I need them and as they come along. I don't make much, but the money's enough to get by and to never go without."

"That's not so bad. Why did you want to hide that?"

"Not so bad, huh? That's why - it's such an unorthodox profession, that I always get weird looks or inquisitive remarks when people ask."

"It is a bit weird, I mean it must be hard living with that kind of instability."

"Hard? See this is what I'm talking about. It's actually not hard at all. I work when I want, where I want, how I want, and don't have to answer to anybody. It's liberating, and I do just fine. I think it's hard doing what you do, a nine-to-five job, week in and week out, with no purpose outside of the corporation you work for."

"Sure, there's some control you have to give up to them, but in return you get a steady income, and prospects for the future, which I have to think takes away a lot of risk."

"Risk of what?"

"I don't know, risk of not having enough money to support yourself, take care of yourself."

"But who's to say that it's truly less risky?"

"What do you mean?"

"Does your company assure you that you'll have your job, no matter what?"

"No, I guess not."

"Are you certain that whatever you do for them now will continue to be a valuable, lucrative occupation for the rest of your career?"

Julian did not respond.

"So I don't think the ordinary route is safe at all. Who knows when you might be laid off, or the economy changes in a way where your services are no longer required. What I do isn't predictable, per se, but I don't find it to be any riskier than what you do."

"I get what you are saying. Still, it can't be easy. Working freelance doesn't have a brand to it, or a prestige to build on. I mean, let's say you want to make a change, and go work for someone. What will you write on your resume? Who will write letters of reference for you? It's gotta be tough to validate yourself when compared to everyone else."

"Ah, so you're saying something's not worth doing unless everyone else agrees it's something worthwhile and valued, is that it?"

"In a way, yes."

"Hm, well all I can say is I think conforming to the status quo is overrated. I'm just not that into it."

"Why?"

"Why? How about why not? What makes conformity so compelling? It sounds awfully boring to me."

"Could be, but at least you're accepted by your peers, by your community, and that matters too."

"If someone needs me to conform to their way of thinking to be accepted, perhaps that's someone whose opinion I don't need to care about."

"You know, your unshackled approach to work and careers and all that is admirable, but I don't understand why you're so hell bent on shitting on everything normal. People go to school, they get regular jobs in regular industries, they get a house, get married, have kids, the whole thing. It may not be that sexy, but it certainly isn't terrible."

"*That*, is certainly a matter of opinion."

"Oh whatever, Lydia. You talk a big game but you sound a little full of yourself."

Lydia's eyes welled up with tears. "You know, Julian, you're being a dick. I know you're very smart and witty, but you don't need to berate other people just because they don't think you're right all the time."

"Berate you? I'm just trying to get a straight answer and you're talking in circles."

"Fine! I'll give you a straight answer. I didn't have much of a family growing up. It was just my mom and me, but we made it work, and it wasn't that bad. I certainly remember us having happy times. My mom had a decent job as a sales manager for an office supplies company. Then when I was 12, my mother was let go, as part of several rounds of layoffs from the recession at the time. The company told her they were modernizing and didn't have a place for her anymore. She collected unemployment for a while, but couldn't find any opportunities for a middle-aged woman without any graduate degrees or special training. She was just left behind. She used all her savings, then ran up credit cards just to keep food on the table for me and her. We ended up defaulting on the mortgage and were kicked out of the home where I grew up.

We then had to live out of my mother's van. I couldn't even go to school because they required a home address. We would have to find a new place to park every day, to avoid getting hassled. My mother, she was very strong, but even she would break down sometimes from the misery of it all. I remember one time I was sitting in the front seat with her, eating potato chips and a banana because that's all we could afford from the gas station. It was one of the first few days we didn't have a home, and I didn't really understand what was going on. Like an idiot, I asked my mom if I could have an ice cream popsicle for dessert. She just started bawling. I didn't understand at the time why she was so upset, but I know now it was because we had no more money, and she was so ashamed of herself for not being able to provide ice cream for her only daughter.

We lived in that van for four months, surviving on what little welfare and food assistance we could get. My mom eventually found a job in a retail warehouse, working twelve-hour shifts picking merchandise and preparing them for shipping. It gave her just enough money to afford a studio apartment, where we had to share a mattress lying on the floor. The work was grueling. I could see it wearing my mom down. She lost that smile, that exuberance she had when I was younger, often falling asleep right as she got home, only to get up to return back to work, but she never complained. She was just content knowing that I had a roof over my head and was back in school, could make friends and live somewhat of a normal life.

I remember one weekend she got a Saturday off, and I decided to make those chocolate banana pancakes I was telling you about. I was seventeen, just a few months from graduating high school. I woke up early to grab the ingredients, and prepared the pancakes just the way she had. When she woke up, we sat together on the floor and ate them, and for a brief few hours I felt like I had my mom back. We ate, we talked, we laughed, and though she was still quite tired, I knew she enjoyed it. I was just happy that this time around it was me making her feel better rather than the other way around.

After our brunch, she said she wanted to go back to bed to rest a bit more, and I decided to go out for a few errands. When I got back, she was lying peacefully on the mattress, unresponsive and cold. She died in her sleep while

I was out. They said her heart had been very weak, and that it had given out. I hadn't known about her health problems, just the way she preferred it of course. After a small funeral and a few months of living by myself as a minor, I turned eighteen, graduated high school, and have been on my own ever since.

So no, I don't mean to disparage you, Jules, or anyone else. I recognize most people grow up in much better conditions. They don't worry about where their next meal will come from, or whether they'll be kicked out of their home. And they have lots of good reasons for following the paths that are already prepared for them, because for them, why fix what's not broken? I get it, I do. Please just understand that for me, *everything* was broken, and the only thing that helped me survive was never trusting anything that was supposedly a sure thing. So I take care of myself, I don't take anything for granted, and I don't get caught up in pipe dreams about successes which don't always pan out. And if it means I'm not on track to check all the boxes that are supposedly the difference between a good life and a bad one, so be it. I'll be happy enough making sure I'm not going to get my ass kicked one day because I put my faith in something or someone that turned out to be a total sham."

Lydia had tears rolling down her flushed cheeks, and her bottom lip was quivering. She stood up, wiped the tears from under her eyes, and walked away from Julian towards the ocean. When she arrived at the water, gently crashing waves ebbed and flowed atop the wet sand. She removed her sandals, and let her feet submerge underwater. She then fell backwards and sat down, letting the waves wash over her legs and shorts, and stared out into the water with her hands clasped over her knees.

Julian spent a few minutes on the picnic blanket in silence. He did not immediately know how to respond to Lydia, nor what to do once she walked away. He felt confused at first, and then, ashamed. He saw an ant travel along the blanket, and walk up the side of the plastic cup holding the scraps of his lemon curd yogurt. The ant careened over the rim of the cup, and sped down the inside to the bottom, where remaining bits of the yogurt stuck. As the ant sampled the yogurt, its legs got caught in the sticky surface of the inside of the cup, forcing the ant to collapse in the middle of yogurt pile it was trying to eat. The ant writhed around for a few seconds attempting to escape, then succumbed to its fate, lying motionlessly in the pool of yogurt around it.

Julian rose up and walked over to Lydia, and took a seat next to her in the sand. His shoes, pants, and underwear began to soak with water as the waves washed around him, but he kept his seat next to her, mimicking her pose with his hands clasped around his knees. He sat next to her in silence, while the waves continued to crash onto his body as he sank slowly into the sand.

"I'm sorry," he began. "I don't know what I was saying. I didn't mean to upset you."

"I'm sorry too. I didn't intend to get emotional like that."

"You have nothing to apologize for. I was the one who antagonized you, and for what? I don't really have a clue what I'm doing with or what I want in my life. That's not your fault, and truth is, I'm just envious, because I see you and how happy you are and how much you seem to enjoy and be at peace with yourself, and it makes me feel like I'm just missing something. I know we only met last weekend, Lydia, but knowing you has been one of the best things to happen to me in a long time."

"That's sweet, Jules, but don't fool yourself into thinking I have it all figured out, because I don't. I just try to make the best of every day, and do what I can to prepare for a better tomorrow. It may not be the most figured-out thing to do, but it works for me, and most of the time, I'm happy with it. And I'm happy with you too. I've felt a peace being around you ever since we met. And even though I just stormed off in a tizzy, I am glad we are here today, together. "

"Well, maybe not right *here*," Julian suggested, eyeing the water beneath them. "Both of us look like we peed our pants and then some."

Lydia chuckled. "I guess it will be our thing. Do you mind if we stay here just a bit longer? I'm enjoying the view."

"Let's take all the time you want."

Julian and Lydia sat together on the beach, waves flowing at and around them, sinking lower and lower into the wet sand. They sat in silence, letting the sounds of the waves crashing and the seagulls crying fill the small space between them. The daughter and father surfing tandem were finishing their lesson, the daughter no more skilled at surfing than when they began, but much more entertained at the ability to splash and delight her father. They both paddled towards the shore on the surfboards, rode into the beach on a final wave, got on their feet, and hugged each other.

"We're totally soaked, what do you say we dry off and head back?"

"That sounds nice, Jules."

Julian got up first and extended his hand to help Lydia get up as well. They walked back to their picnic area, cleaned up the dirty plates, cups, and utensils, packed up the remaining food and the blanket, and journeyed back to their car. By the time they arrived, Julian's khakis had mostly dried, but Lydia, in white, cropped shorts, was still wet from the ocean water.

"Oh my! You can see my underwear through my shorts! When were you planning on telling me this, Jules?"

"Why ruin a good thing?"

"Aren't you the cheeky one."

"Could say the same thing to you, given the current circumstances."

"Jules!"

"I brought some swim trunks in case we ended up going into the water. Would have been useful to have back there, but you can change into them now if you want."

"Thanks, though I don't see a restroom anywhere near."

"You can use the backseat. I promise I won't look."

"Oh, that makes me feel so much better."

He raised his right hand. "Scout's honor."

Lydia changed into Julian's trunks, and rolled up her wet clothes into the used picnic blanket. They packed the car, and started the drive back to the city, with the convertible top up, and the radio turned down to a low volume, just enough to create soothing background noise for the two of them. The river road was less congested on the return trip, with plenty of open road in front of and behind them during the drive. Julian slouched back in his chair, driving predominantly with his left hand, and relaxing his right on the console in between the two front seats. As he left his hand there, Lydia extended her left hand over and placed it on top of his. She curled her fingers gently and repeatedly, sliding them over the top of Julian's hand in a slow and considered motion.

By the late afternoon, they had returned to their apartment complex. Julian pulled up in front, and let Lydia exit.

"Where are you going, Jules?"

"I have to return the car before the end of the day. The place is right around the corner. I won't be long."

"Okay, do you want me to take some of the stuff? You shouldn't have to carry it back all by yourself."

"Sure, how about you grab the food and your clothes, and bring them up to my place? I'll give you the key. I insist you let me dry the clothes that got wet on the beach."

"Oh, so you can go feeling around my underwear? How gentlemanly of you."

"I didn't mean it like that. I'd just like to hang out with you awhile longer."

"Me too. I'm just teasing. See you soon."

Julian returned the rental car, and walked back to his apartment complex. He took the elevator up to his apartment, and knocked on the door, to no answer. He rang the doorbell, then knocked once again, with still no answer. He then tried door knob, finding it unlocked, and opened the door to his place. To his surprise, he did not find Lydia, but did find Franny, chomping away at some food in her bowl in the kitchen, and barely noticing that he had arrived. The leftover food from the picnic had already been placed in his fridge, and the cooler had been washed and was sitting on his kitchen counter air-drying. He still did not see Lydia and called out her name, to no response. He walked into the bedroom to find his closet open, his bathroom door closed, and the sound of the shower water running.

He changed his clothes, from the khakis and polo he had worn all day to a pair of gym shorts and a sleeveless tank, and then left his bedroom, closing the door behind him. After Franny was finished eating, she walked up directly to him, rolled onto her back, and exposed her belly. He bent down to pet her stomach, her neck, and behind her ears, when he heard his bedroom door open. Lydia walked out with wet hair, wearing a pair of his pajama pants and a hooded sweatshirt from his college alma mater. When she saw Julian, she smiled, walked over to him, and kissed him on his lips. He kissed her back, resting his hands on her hips and pulling her closer to his body.

"I was wondering when you would return."

"I was gone barely fifteen minutes, but by all means, make yourself at home."

"Don't mind if I do. This sweatshirt is so comfortable, I just had to give it a try."

"It's my favorite one, so you're welcome. Are you all cleaned up?"

"I am, and I feel wonderful. Where are your clothes? I can put them in the washer along with mine."

"I left them in the bedroom, but don't worry I can get them."

"Not at all, please allow me. It's the least I can do for borrowing your clothes."

"That, and feeding my cat."

"Oh yes I'm sorry, I don't know if I was supposed to feed her or if that was the right amount, but she was crying so desperately I didn't know what to do."

"Yes, this is her normal feeding time, and you were close enough on the quantity. Most importantly, she is going to be your best friend from now on, now that she knows you will give her food."

"Aha! My secret plan has worked. I'll be just a moment."

Lydia returned to Julian's bedroom to grab his clothes and start a load of laundry. Julian poured himself a glass of water and sat down at the kitchen table. When Lydia returned, she also poured herself a glass of water and sat next to him at the table, looking out the window.

"I'm obsessed with this view, Jules. It's so picturesque."

"Yeah, it's something else. I'm surprised I don't spend more time looking at it. I really should."

"Well it's not much of an activity by itself, but perhaps with the right someone, it can be kind of fun. For example, see that bus coming up and stopping on the street?"

"Yeah, what about it?"

"Tell me, who's driving the bus?"

"I have no clue."

"Come on, Jules. That's no fun."

"What would be fun then?"

"What would be fun is if the bus driver's name is Gil, and he's four minutes late. Probably because he got into a fight with Brent, another bus driver who's always butting heads with him. Those two just can't get along, and everyone knows it. They both drive the same line, in alternating shifts, so the competition is always there, creating tension between them."

"Ah I see, you're just going to make up stories about the strangers who pass by, unbeknownst to them."

"They are not strangers, they are characters. Characters who come and go in and out of this world in front of you. It's not just Gil and Brent, Terry is supposed to be coming the opposite way in about six minutes. She's usually early, because she speeds too much, even with passengers aboard. Then she has to wait at the next stop even after all the passengers have come on, because there's a camera system installed at the stop which would flag her if she left too early. Terry doesn't appreciate how the transit authority has adopted Big Brother tactics to monitor her and her fellow colleagues. They should trust her to do a good job, and worry about improving the working conditions for the drivers."

"My goodness, you have quite the imagination."

"But admit it, you are now keenly interested in who's driving that bus, are you not?"

"I actually met a bus driver yesterday."

"Shut up!"

"Swear I did. She was a lady, chatted with her about 30 minutes."

"Do tell."

"She's middle-aged, divorced from her wife, her parents live with her so she can take care of her mom. Her ex has custody of her kids but she gets to see them often."

"How sad for her."

"It's what I thought too. But after speaking with her, she had this great outlook on her life. Like, even though things weren't ideal, she didn't have any regrets, nor did she feel like there was anything holding her back. She was pretty remarkable, actually."

"I agree. What was her name?"

"Her name?"

"Yes."

"Come to think of it, I don't believe we ever exchanged names."

"Jules! How did you talk to her for half an hour and not get her name?"

"I don't know. We just started to talk very casually when I was on the bus, and then just rolled right into our conversation. I never thought to ask her."

"Shame, now you won't know who she is."

"But I'm okay with that. I mean it would have been nice to catch her name, but that doesn't diminish the interaction we had, and what it meant, at least for me. I'm glad I ran into her yesterday, I don't think I'll be forgetting it anytime soon."

"Why were you on the bus yesterday? I don't know anyone who rides the bus."

"Me neither, until yesterday."

"You didn't answer my question."

"I know. It's a bit...well, embarrassing."

"Oh, now you have to tell me!"

"I was kicked out of Bo's Diner. I don't think I can ever go in there again."

"What?! How can you get kicked out of Bo's? He's like the nicest man ever."

"I'm sure he is. It wasn't his fault, it was mine. I'm not proud of it."

"I have a hard time believing you could do anything to get kicked out of and banned from a restaurant."

"It wasn't a good moment for me."

Lydia smiled and shook her head. "Oh dear, Jules, you are becoming more adorable by the minute."

Julian leaned over to Lydia to kiss her, and she reciprocated by leaning in too. They got up and retired to the den, onto the Murphy bed. Julian laid down first, propping himself up with a few pillows behind his back. Lydia followed, curling up next to him, sliding her feet in between his legs and placing her head on his arm. Last of all was Franny, who jumped up, attempted to lay down in between Julian's legs, only to find her normal spot already occupied, and then decided to lay by Lydia instead.

"I think she likes you."

"I think I like her. She's a sweet cat."

"I'm just happy she's not hissing at you."

"I'm just happy."

"Would you care to watch anything?"

"You know, I almost never watch TV. This is exciting! What should we watch?"

"There's lots of options."

"What was the last thing you watched?"

"It's a show called One Way Trip. There's a lady who can only take these special one-way flights that drop her randomly into new cities until it's time for her to leave again."

"Oh, a travel show. Let's watch that!"

Julian started the next episode of One Way Trip, the one which found Shelby Connors in Sofia, Bulgaria.

"Jules, where in the world have you traveled?"

"A few places. I went on a Eurotrip with a friend right after college. We hit the normal spots, Paris, Barcelona, Rome."

"Ahem. That's not so 'normal' to all of us, sweetie."

"Ah yes, sorry."

"What did you like most about them?"

"The artifacts of deep history scattered all through each city. Churches that were centuries old. Sculptures and castles from Medieval times. It gave those cities a feeling of, what's the word, gravitas, that you just don't get to experience over here. Even the oldest American cities are only a couple hundred years old, and it's just not the same."

"Sounds fascinating. I'd love to see them one day."

"You've never been?"

"Jules, honey, I've barely been outside the state. Let's just say some of us didn't quite have the same wherewithal to take themselves on that type of adventure."

"What about now? You could go now if you want to, particularly with your freelance lifestyle."

"I could. Would you go with me?"

"As much as I'd love to, it'd be breaking a cardinal rule of getting to know somebody."

"What's that?"

"That you can only plan as far into the future for as long as you've known the person."

"Where did you hear a ridiculous rule like that?"
"Everybody knows that rule! It's just a known thing. Like how you can't date someone if they are younger than half your age plus seven."

"You are cracking me up with your obscure regulations."

"Just because you've apparently been living under a rock doesn't mean I'm wrong."

"Okay, let's say I believe you. How old are you?"

"Thirty."

"You *old* man."

"How old are you?"

"You know it's rude to ask a lady that."

"Who said you're a lady?"

She slapped his shoulder with her free hand. "Treat a lady with respect."

"If I guessed correctly, would you tell me?"

"Okay. I suppose I can agree to that."

"Twenty-eight."

"How'd you know?!"

"Simple. You mentioned you were twelve when there was a recession. The last three recessions occurred in 1990, 2001, and 2008. You don't look like old enough to be thirty-nine, and -- no offense -- you don't look young enough to be twenty-one."

"Well I suppose I can't be too offended by that. So you guessed it, I'm twenty-eight, and congratulations, I am squarely in the age range for you to date me."

"Presuming I want to."

"Oh, aren't you getting salty."

"Hey, you came into my apartment, fed my cat, used my shower, and took my clothes. I can't tell if you're girlfriend material, or just a stalker."

"Can't I be both?"

"If you're able to cat-sit Franny when I go out of town, you can be whatever you want."

"Deal."

"If you do decide to travel, I recommend a Round the World pass."

"What's that?"

"Lots of airlines have them. It's a type of all-access ticket, where you can keep travelling around the world so long as you always go in the same lateral direction. You don't have to buy any new tickets, but can keep using your pass so long as you don't back-track the way you came. Like if you headed east from here. You could visit cities in Europe, Africa, Asia, even Australia, and then fly back home, all with this one ticket, just by lining them up west to east."

"But what if I want to go back somewhere? Like if I decide I really like a city, and want to return?"

"You'd have to buy a separate ticket if you wanted to backtrack, and when you wanted to continue your journey in the right direction, you could use the Round the World pass again. Or, if you really liked that city so much, you could just not leave until you've had your fill."

"Yes, but sometimes you don't realize how much you like something until you leave it, or it leaves you. Staying longer won't let you figure it out the same way."

"Well in that case, the Round the World pass wouldn't work for you."

"I knew you'd disappoint me somehow."

"I'm truly sorry, Lydia. Whatever can I do to make it up to you?"

"Just hold me, Jules."

Julian wrapped his other arm around Lydia's side, laying his head next to hers. They fell quiet and watched the opening scenes of the show. Shelby Connors was on a walking tour of the city, taking in the major sites and speaking to the camera about the local history. She passed by historical structures like the St. George Rotunda and the Saint Sofia church. She visited and frolicked in city parks, like the Borisova Grandina, with its decorative wooden houses and waterlily lake, and the Doctor's Garden, with the Monument of the Fallen Medic. She then rode out to the Vitosha Nature Park, to gather views of the Vitosha mountain, with its snow-capped peaks surrounded by spruce and fir trees.

"So what do you think of Sofia?" Julian asked.

"It's mesmerizing. I can't get over just how different, how exotic it looks compared to where we live."

"True, but I think exotic is all relative. Perhaps for people that live in Sofia, everything on this show is plain as plain can be, but a clip of you and I drinking coffee at the Savory Pass would be one of the most elegant and sophisticated things they've witnessed."

"I highly doubt that."

"Just saying, that's the hidden beauty of traveling, for me anyways. Before you reach your destination, your imagination runs wild with how foreign the place will be. About how different you'll have to behave. Whether you'll be able to communicate properly, not get lost, not offend anyone. You think that everything you are going to experience will be truly unique and different, something you'd never get at home. And to some degree, that's true. There are natural sites and monuments which only exist in one part of the world and nowhere else, food or drink delicacies that you simply cannot obtain here. But in most cases, wherever you are traveling will begin to look and feel just like where you came from. The people there have similar conversations, albeit in a different language, about the same problems or about the same gossip with their friends, family, and neighbors. The local politics will pit the poor versus the rich, the nationalists against the immigrants, the religious versus the agnostic. People come together over births, deaths, and weddings with ceremonial food and alcohol, often with music and dancing. These themes persist no matter where you go, which over time does two things to you. One, it can make you less interested in traveling, because you start to develop the attitude of 'seen one seen them all,' but two, it gives you a more complete perspective on different cultures, to recognize just how similar people really are. So it wouldn't surprise me at all that someone from Bulgaria would be enthralled by our local food and customs, only to eventually figure out that it's the same as theirs, just with a different spin on it."

"I like that, maybe someone watching from over there would see us and Franny curled up like this, and then look at themselves and their own sweetheart, and think about how romance and affection are universal, spanning all borders and languages. I think that would be delightful."

"But wouldn't that imply that no one, no matter who they are or where they are from, is special? That seems kind of sad in a way."

"I don't think so. For me, right now, laying here next to you is extremely special, something I would not trade for any other experience in the world. And even if it's all the same for hundreds or thousands of other people around the world, who are in a similar state as we are right now, it's no less special to me, just like it wouldn't be less special to them. I guess in that way we can all have our own form of special, even if it's more or less equivalent to what others might have."

"Special sure, although I couldn't imagine anyone thinking that we were exotic, even a little bit, what with my sleeveless tee and with your baggy sweatshirt and pajama pants. Well, to be specific, *my* baggy sweatshirt and pajama pants."

"Now now, don't be an ungracious host."

"I won't, but I will insist you return those to me, and no I cannot guarantee that you will have any other clothes to wear."

"If this is your way of putting the moves on me, I can tell you right now it is equally dorky as it is ineffective."

"Let's hold off on your judgment until the results come in."

"And when might that be?"

"You'll know it when you see it."

Sunday

Julian woke up on the Murphy bed in his den, in the same clothes he had on the night before, but all alone. He rose and went to the kitchen, to find Franny lying peacefully on the kitchen table in her post-meal coma. On the top of the counter, he found a note:

> *I fed Franny again this morning, hope that's okay. Come down to 2C when you get up. XO, Lydia*

He walked back to his bedroom. His clothes from the day before folded neatly on his bed, along with the sweatshirt and pajama pants Lydia had worn the previous night. He undressed, took a quick shower, put on a pair of blue jeans, an old grey t-shirt, and sandals, walked down to 2C and knocked on the door.

"Come in, it's open," he heard from Lydia on the inside.

He opened the door, and for the first time entered her home. It was a one-bedroom, smaller than his, with a more compact layout. The kitchen was immediately to the right, a small galley with a high counter-top that looked over the living space behind it. A small couch and a papasan chair made up the sitting area, with a square breakfast table and two chairs placed by the windows which looked out onto the alley below. Lydia was seated at the breakfast table, with two coffee mugs and a French press arranged neatly on a tray.

"I made us coffee."

"Sounds fantastic."

Julian walked over to the table, gave Lydia a light kiss on her lips, and sat down next to her. Lydia poured coffee from the French press into his mug and handed it to him.

"How did you know I would be coming over?"

"I guess I just took it on faith. Plus, I only left your place an hour ago."

"I figured. Thanks for feeding Franny, again. You better be careful or else you'll have to come on full-time."

Lydia smirked and playfully batted her eyes. "I could think of worse things."

"This coffee is delicious. What is it?"

"Medium roast, from the Kauai coffee company. I got it as a gift from an old friend who had visited. I think it works well with the French press."

"Is that what this thing is, with the plunger?"

"Yes. Wait - do you not know what this is? Am I about to tell the all-knowing Julian something he doesn't know?"

"Very funny." Julian straightened his back and lifted his chest. "I don't go out seeking to be a know-it-all, it just comes naturally when you're as smart as I am. But please, tell me about this press from France."

"Well, my innocent, unlearned friend," Lydia began, "interestingly enough, the French press was actually patented in Italy, about one hundred years ago. The concept is pretty simple. The coffee beans are ground to a coarse grind. Not like the powder you get for drip coffee, but more like Kosher salt, where there are still bits and chunks in there. Then you pour boiling water into the press, the grounds brew for about four minutes, and you push the plunger down to separate the grounds from the coffee. After that, you drink it, and it's delicious."

"I agree. It has a richness to it that normal coffee doesn't have."

"I love it because it's so simple. Just hot water, crushed up beans, and a jar. The CEO of Starbucks once said that's the best way to make coffee. I always think that's so cool, when the simplest or more natural way is the best way. It just makes things so, uncomplicated. Much of the time, it seems you have to grapple between doing something easy and getting left behind, or having to do something hard and complicated just to keep up. It can feel like a lose-lose. But in this case, simple is both easy and the best."

"I'm a fan. Sometimes it's just best to go with what's natural and effortless. If that means a plunger in my coffee, sign me up."

"Plus, it's classy as *fuck*," Lydia deadpanned.

Julian expression dropped. "Wow."

She chuckled. "Hehe, didn't expect me to go there, did you?"

"No, I certainly did not."

"Me neither. I'm just feeling giggly this morning."

"It's a good look for you."

"I think you should take me out again today."

"I'm all yours."

"Let's go to Quarry Beach."

"What's that?"

"Oh my gosh, I'm like the most cultured person ever right now. And you are quite the ignoramus, I have to say. I expected much better from you. Quarry Beach is an old rock quarry that was flooded from heavy rainfall about twenty five years ago. It's a deep blue lagoon with steep rock cliffs surrounding it. You can swim in the water, rent tubes to lounge around, or just hang out on the lawn around it. We should go!"

"Sounds perfect. Where is it?"

"About an hour away. Perhaps we can just drive a normal car this time?"

"Fair enough. I have lawn chairs we can use. I suppose we need to pick up water, beer, wine?"

"Oh I know, let's go see if your friend Herb would like to join us. I bet he has all the supplies we will need."

"Yeah let's do it. I owe him a bit of an apology anyway, hopefully spending the day together will help bury the hatchet."

"Let me guess, whatever you owe him an apology for, did it happen on Friday?"

"Ugh, yes."

"Jules, you just crack me up."

"Yes yes, I'm aware. How about I go change and grab my stuff, you do the same, we meet in the lobby, pack my car, and then go get Herb?"

"You think he'll be awake and sober this time in the morning?"

"Awake, yes. Sober? *Eh*. That won't matter though."

Lydia rang Herb's doorbell, as she and Julian waited outside his house in flip flops, bathing suits, and dark sunglasses with sun block caking their noses and shoulders. Lydia wore a red strapless bikini with an orange cover-up, and a tight-fitting baseball cap hat which almost covered her eyes. Julian had on the trunks he lent her the day before and the sleeveless tee he wore the previous evening. He sipped from a water bottle filled with ice cubes which were slowly melting away.

"Are you sure he's going to be here?" Lydia asked.

"Yeah, just give him a minute."

"I hate to barge in on him like this."

"He's going to be grouchy about it, but trust me, deep down he's going to be thrilled."

They both heard bottles clinking inside the house, a quick stumble on the floor, and a few pats of the door and door lock in front of them. Herb opened the door a few inches to peak outside, obscuring his view of Lydia to reveal just Julian standing in front of him.

"What do ya want, dickface?"

"Nice to see you too, Herb. It's not just me, the dickface, but Lydia here's too. She wants to ask you out on a date."

Herb opened up the door full to see Lydia, who smiled and waved at him once he saw her. He was dressed in a camo ball cap, a flower-patterned Hawaiian shirt with his greying chest hair escaping above the top button, and loose cargo shorts. Upon seeing Lydia, he straightened his posture, wiped his eyes with the back of one hand, while he combed the scruff of his beard with the other.

"Well, you're both dickfaces for bothering me like this, as far as I'm concerned."

"Come on Herb, I'm just here to show Julian what a real gentleman looks like. Don't make me look bad."

"Anyone looks like a gentleman next to this jackass."

"Okay Herb, I get it," Julian interjected. "I'm sorry for mouthing off to you a couple days ago. I was in a bad mood and I took it out on you. I shouldn't have done it and regret it. Bygones?"

"*Ugh.* Come on inside. You too darling. I need a minute if I'm going to be nice right now."

They both walked in and sat on the couch in Herb's living room, while Herb poured water into a kettle and put it on the stove. An infomercial for buying and selling gold was playing on a radio on the kitchen table. The narrator urged the audience to round up all their gold jewelry and other collectibles, and to sell right away, because the price of gold was currently the highest it's ever been and so it was a great time to trade in for cash. When the kettle whistled, Herb poured some tea for himself. He asked Lydia if she cared for some, which she politely refused, but he did not offer Julian. Once his teabag steeped in the cup, he threw the bag away and took his cup with him over to the chair next to the couch in the living room.

"Even though I'm incredibly handsome, I am assuming you two lovebirds didn't come over to stare at my mug all day."

"There he is!" Julian exclaimed.

"Damn, he's figured us out Jules!"
"Herb, there's nothing I'd love more than to stare at your mug all day," said Julian, who then pursed his lips to imitate a kiss.

"Sorry to break your heart Julian, but I do not feel the same way. About you, anyway. Now, Lydia my dear, perhaps you and I can work out a separate arrangement."

"Julian," Lydia replied dramatically. "Looks like you got some competition."

"Competition implies I have a chance of winning, but who really stands a chance against charm like that?"

"Okay assholes, enough with the smartass remarks. What are you doing here?"

"We'd like to invite you to Quarry Beach," Lydia began. "For an afternoon of swimming, relaxation, and good company. And if you're still pissed at Julian, then *I'm* inviting you, and with only the two of us, the good company becomes great company."

"What beach is this?"

"Am I the only one who keeps track of the local attractions around here? Herb, it's an old rock quarry that flooded a while back and is now a huge natural pool."

"You see, Herb," Julian chimed in. "People go there to do this crazy thing called *have fun*."

"Well, why would I ever want to do that?" Herb questioned.

"True. It really puts a cramp on your whole pissed-off loner style." Julian fired back.

"Yeah Lydia, I have an image to protect you know."

"You two are ridiculous! Are you going to insist on acting like toddlers all day?"

"I don't insist," Julian rebutted, then grinned. "It just comes naturally."

"I'm still trying to figure out what the fuck is going on right now," said Herb.

"Okay then, I am just going to sit here until you two get with the program." Lydia folded her arms at her chest and turned away from the two of them.

"This is all your fault, Julian."

"Yes, my fault for having the audacity to come over here and invite you out for the day. How terrible of me. I'm just the worst."

"Well it's good to hear you agree to it out loud."

"Get over yourself, Herb, we're going with or without you."

"Geez man you really know how to woo someone. First, you mouth off to me on your way to work then get all pushy with your invitations."

"Dude I already said I was sorry, what more do you want?"

"Just to rub it in your face a few more times."

"Can you at least do it on the way to the quarry? At this rate we'll spend the rest of the day arguing nonsense with you on the couch."

"And would that be so bad?"

"Quit acting like you aren't going to come with us. We're going to go and it's going to be a good time, and I don't want any more Debbie-downer shit from you."

"Yes, your majesty."

Julian rolled his eyes. "Is that a yes?"

"I suppose these pasty legs of mine could use some sun. Plus, I would hate to disappoint Lydia over there. After all, whenever she dumps you I'd like to be on her good side when she starts thinking about her options."

Lydia turned back around, and winked at Herb. "I know just where I'm going if that happens."

"Are we all done sassing each other now?" Julian asked. "I'd like to get moving if you don't mind."

"Ready when you are, Jules."

"Jules!" Herb cried out, while grabbing his crotch and gyrating his hips. "How fitting that's your new name now. I got a pair of jewels for you."

Lydia shook her head. "I'm going to wait in the car."

The Van Rohr Store was a convenience outlet, a chain of which spread across the city to offer consumer staples and other quick-trip purchase items. Each store features dry goods, fresh-made sandwiches and other to-go food items, soft and hard beverages kept chilled in refrigerated cases, and cashier-less checkout, where a machine takes an image of the customer's cart, automatically tabulates the bill, and allows the customer to pay with an electronic key fob which pairs a customer to their online account, inclusive of billing information. The original store was launched five years ago, a prototype of a retail space without the need for any full-time employees. Customers can only enter by scanning in with their account credentials, cameras would monitor for theft, and a supply team would re-stock items a few times a day. After a rocky start, having to overcome wary customers and a regulatory battle with the city, the stores began to grow in both locations and popularity.

"What should we get?" asked Julian.

"I think," Lydia replied, "because I did such a marvelous job putting together the menu yesterday, that today, it's your turn to take care of me."

"If we're doing a complete swap, does this mean you'll do the driving?"

"Absolutely not -- where is your chivalry? Herb, can you believe what has happened to the men of my generation? Wait, where'd he go?"

Though Lydia and Julian were standing together towards the front of the store by the checkout stations, Herb had disappeared into the inner aisles and was now out of view.

"I guess he's on a mission."

"You know, you were really giving him a hard time back at his house."

"Are you kidding? That guy is only happy when he's mouthing off to someone. If it wasn't me, it'd just be his radio or some hapless passerby outside his house."

"It's funny to see how much you two care about each other. Like an old couple that bickers all the time."

"Then what does that make you? The mistress, the home-wrecker?"

"Oh I'm just along for the ride. Hasn't disappointed so far."

"I'm super glad this is entertaining for you. Okay, let me grab a few things for our day at the beach, since you have deemed yourself too privileged to contribute. How about some crackers and cheese cubes? Maybe grapes, too. Also, some trail mix and nuts would be good, and some bottled water. Oh, and cookies too, do you like Milanos?"

"Okay, I take it back. I will help. Apparently you don't shop much, and when you do, you behave like a five year old in a candy store."

"What are you talking about? We don't want to go hungry."

"Just today, or over the next month?"

"Fine, you pick the food then, and I'll go find the water. I'd say we should pick up the rest of the drinks, but something tells me Herb is taking care of it."

"What tells you that?"

"Look."

Herb came out from one of the aisles with a fifth of vodka in one hand and a case of beer in the other.

"I'm more of a hoppy beer kind of guy, but I figure this summer ale should be good for the three of us," he said.

"Wow Herb, do you think we'll have enough?"

"You're right, better get another case just to be sure."

"How about a bottle or two of rosé?" Lydia asked. "I know it's a cliche, but I prefer the sweet, pink stuff."

"Could've fooled me. I thought you were asking for Miss Jewels over there."

"Glad you decided to come with us Herb. Before this week, I was worried about how infrequently I was getting plastered during the day. Now, thanks to you, that's no longer a concern."

"Happy to be of use."

"You both might be being sarcastic right now," said Lydia, "but I'm terribly excited. This is going to be fun!"

"Me too. And let's not jump to conclusions, Mr. Julian. I am well aware that drinking is not, healthy per se, but I have found that many irritations and conflicts in life can be solved just by going out and getting good and drunk. Not in a mean, nasty way, only to take a brief opportunity to drop your inhibitions and enjoy yourself without the worry and angst of everything that was getting you down in the first place."

"Well said, Herb," Lydia responded. "I can certainly drink to that."

"Me too," Julian agreed, "let's get on our way."

"Ahem, after we grab the rosé, of course."

"*Of course*," said Herb, as he bowed down low in a sweeping, exaggerated motion.

The three of them brought their supplies to the checkout station. Julian stacked them on the screening area, in front of a tiny camera affixed to a small electronic display. After a few moments, they heard a *click* sound, and the screen populated the entire bill of goods, no item left off nor incorrectly included. The display prompted Julian to touch his fob key card to the sensor to complete the transaction.

Herb was dismayed. "Are you fucking kidding me? How did it do that?"

"Computer vision," explained Julian. "It takes a picture, then that picture is analyzed to determine which items are in it. Then they are rung up to give you the bill."

"I'll be damned. That's pretty neat."

"You can do it too. Just have to sign up online then get this small chip."

"Eh, fuck that."

"Herb, you need to put sunscreen on."

Julian and Lydia were re-applying sunscreen to each other, taking turns rubbing each other's shoulders. They were standing around their home base for the afternoon, a large tarp covered in beach towels, held down by lawn chairs and a cooler holding ice and the beverages they picked up at the store. They were among many groups who had staked out their ground on the lawns around the lagoon. Some groups were comprised of children, carrying with them toys, snacks, and other comforts, while other groups consisted of guys and girls in their teens, who possessed little more than their swimwear and clear alcohols smuggled in via refilled plastic bottles. Herb was sitting in one of the lawn chairs, sipping on the first beer he cracked open from the cooler.

He was wearing all-terrain shoes, waterproof hiking shorts, an old green t-shirt, and a plain royal blue ball cap.

"I'll be fine, dear," he responded to Lydia.

"Absolutely not. Put it on your knees, your shoulders, nose and cheeks. And don't forget the tops of your ears. Did you know that's the number one place where people get skin cancer? It's because they always forget to cover them."

"Yeah," Julian jeered, "and given how pasty you are, you shouldn't be taking any chances."

"I'll do it, if it will make you both stop talking."

Lydia handed over the sunscreen, and Herb took off his shirt, revealing a thick coat of greying chest hair, from the top of his chest, almost touching his beard, down to the bottom of his belly.

"You know," said Lydia, looking bemused, "I don't think you have to worry about covering up your front side."

"Hey Herb, you know you're supposed to put your sweater on *over* your t-shirt, not under."

Herb tilted the bottom up on his beer can and drank the rest of its contents. After letting out a small burp, he smiled and mockingly flexed his arms in muscular poses.

"Jesus dude, ever thought of shaving?" Julian asked.

"Why? This is what a man looks like. You young dudes don't even have a hair on you except on your head. I bet if I pulled your drawers down I wouldn't even find a pube. Being all smooth everywhere, that's what a woman looks like, and trust me, Lydia's doing a much better job of it than you are."

"Well thank you Herb," Lydia replied. "I think. Here, let me put some sunscreen on your neck too, which looks like it's already getting red."

"Ha!" cried Julian. "A redneck!"

"Ha!" replied Herb, as he pointed at Julian. "A piece of shit!"

"Hush you two. There Herb, you're all set. Now, aren't you going to offer me a drink?"

"Coming right up. A glass of rose, right?"

"Sounds delicious."

"I'll take some too, Herb," said Julian.

"What am I, your butler?" Herb retorted. "Get it yourself."

"Whatever, just toss me one of those beers."

Lydia looked out to the water. "You know, I heard that at the bottom of this lagoon, you can still find old construction equipment. Tractors, forklifts, even old pickaxes and shovels just lying on the water floor. They were left there when the quarry flooded. It rained for days, and the entire quarry filled up to create the lagoon. After the rains, the quarry was closed down, and they considered extracting the equipment, but it was too expensive to pull out for what would have been minimal salvage value. So they just left it there.

Now, there's a expedition service that allows you to scuba-dive down there and check out the old wreckage. There's some rust and barnacles built up, but apparently most of the machinery is still preserved in a similar condition as when the quarry flooded."

"Pretty cool to see how the destruction of one thing can lead to the creation of another," said Herb.

"What do you mean?" asked Julian.

"When the quarry flooded, I'm guessing most people thought 'well, this business just got destroyed.' And they could have just wrung their hands and complained about why bad things happen to them. But others, like the people who run this beach now for instance, saw an opportunity. An opportunity to recast what had happened into something useful, beautiful even. And now, we and everyone else here get to benefit from that optimism."

"I see your point," offered Julian. "But I don't see the intrigue of touring the old wreckage, though."

"What a shocker," Lydia interjected. "My dear Jules unimpressed by something us lay people find interesting."

"She's got you there, Mr. Hemingway."

"I'm just saying," Julian started to explain, "what makes it interesting other than the fact that it's there? Just because it's underwater and twenty five years old doesn't make quarry equipment any more or less interesting, does it? I'm just not a fan of treating something as a superlative when it's not."

"Perhaps you need to see it first to make that determination," suggested Lydia.

"That's a dumb reason not to be interested in something, though." offered Herb. "There are very few things that are truly superlative, so if you were only interested in that, you'd spend practically all of your life bored and uninvolved. Maybe that's you've been doing. But something can be interesting for lots of reasons. Because it's unique, because it's beautiful, because it's special in some way. And when you open up your perspective to consider those options, there's no shortage of things in life that can be interesting, and worthwhile to explore and experience."

"Okay, you got me. Should we go explore this old quarry dump, then?"

"No, silly." said Lydia. "You have to book those tours weeks in advance."

Julian looked up at the bluffs around the lagoon. They formed a horseshoe around the sides and the back, with the front edges only a few feet above the water. They steadily rose in height around the sides and crested at about sixty feet at their highest point directly in the back. From the left side, about fifty yards away from where they were located on the lawn, was a pedestrian trail which began on the lawn in front of the lagoon and continued up the bluffs and all the way around the water's edge.

"I bet we can get a quick view without scuba gear," he said.

"How do you mean?" asked Lydia.

"Let's jump from the top of those bluffs there. The momentum of the jump should push us down underwater, maybe we can see some of the wreckage."

"What?!" exclaimed Lydia, "that's insane."

"So, too scared to do it, I take it?"

"Ohh, if that's how you want to play it. Well I supposed I can't say no now. Okay Jules, let's go."

"For real, you're going to do it?"

"Oh, want to back out, now that I've called your bluff?"

"Of course not. Just want to make sure we don't get all the way up there and you change your mind. Herb, what say you?"

Herb startled from the question. "What are you saying?"

"We're going to jump off the top of that bluff on the other side of the water," explained Julian. "Then, we're going to see if we can see some of that old quarry wreckage once we're in."

"That sounds awful. I'm in."

"You sure? Don't want your saggy body to get hurt."

"This saggy body's endures more in an afternoon of hard work than yours has your whole life. Plus I'm not about to let two youngins out-adventure me while I sit here like an asshole. Let's get moving."

"Okay. Here we go."

The three of them began their walk to the proposed jump location, heading over to the left ramp and hiking up the side of the bluff over to the backside. They walked slowly, barefoot, knowing that they could leave nothing behind once they made the jump. Julian tried to make small talk, intimating how excited he was at the prospect of what they were about to do, but his enthusiasm came off halfhearted at best. Lydia played along with his tempered exuberance, simply reiterating how delighted she was to be there and no matter what they were to do, jump or not jump, it would be all the same to her. Herb brought a beer to drink for their walk, and drank it while nodding or grunting in recognition of their dialogue.

They reached the back of the lagoon, onto the portions of the bluffs which rose highest above the water. A group of younger men were already there, in the process of jumping themselves. They were college age, full of alcohol, profanity, and courage, the ones yet to jump heckling the ones about to, echoed by the hoots and screams coming from below from those who already had. By the time the last two had jumped, the men had made a brief acquaintance with Julian, Lydia, and Herb. Once they jumped themselves, they hung back by the landing area, treading water while shouting either words of encouragement or warnings not to do it. The sounds, echoing off the walls and ricocheting upwards, were hard to discern.

"Okay," Julian said. "Time to jump. You guys ready?"

"Yeah, sure," replied Lydia. "How do we do it? Do we just, go?"

"Yeah I think so. The water looks clear down there, and it's clearly deep enough. I guess you just run off and jump."

"Alright. Let's do it together, then. On three."

"Sounds good. You ready, Herb, on three?"

"Whatever, let's do it." Herb snapped back.

"Here we go." Julian started counting, "one...two..."

"FUCK YOUR MOTHER!" Herb shouted at the top of his lungs as he jumped over, tucking his neck forward and clutching his knees to his chest in mid-air.

His body, extremities pressed firmly to his torso, fell through the air, the bottoms of his toes knifing through the air beneath him. As he approached the water, the momentum from his jump pushed his bottom forward and his head and shoulders fell backward slightly. He crashed with a flat, violent smack of the water on his back.

"Ahhh here I go!" Lydia followed after Herb and jumped out of the bluff. She kept her feet down and head up, but her leap off the ground gave her clockwise momentum that spun her around her right shoulder as she plummeted. She splashed into the water upright and facing the bluffs, submerging several feet below the surface.

Julian, quickly left by himself, begrudgingly followed suit and jumped. He kept his feet down and his body still, raising his hands above him as if in a victory pose. He was set to land in the water feet first up until the last moment, when the air resistance on his body pushed his torso towards his right, forcing his right rib cage to collide with the water after his feet broke through. The water felt like a vicious and stinging slap against his entire body, and his head snapped forward from the impact. By the time he could react, he was fully submerged underwater, the piercing bright blue color on the surface giving way to a deep, opaque grey underneath. *What a stupid idea thinking we could view the quarry equipment this way*, he thought. *There is no way anyone can see anything without a flashlight.* He started to kick his legs down and use his arms to breast stroke upwards, as he looked up to see the light above him. The water's surface appeared close above him, but with each kick of his legs and gyration of his arms, he became more dismayed when he did not breach through. His lungs began to ache as his last breath grew stale within him, and the lactic acid from his exertions surged through his legs and arms. His dismay turned into panic the moment before he emerged from the water, thrusting his ahead into the air and gasping a loud, heaving breath.

He looked around to find Lydia, in a quiet state of shock, treading water near him but barely moving an unresponsive to movements around her. He also saw some of the younger men swimming over to where Herb had fallen in, concerned he may have injured himself. Yet Herb had arisen from underwater, jubilant as can be, shouting and swearing loudly and slapping his hands on the water's surface to create huge splashes around him. The three of them paddled toward each other, said goodbye to the men who had witnessed their jumps, and started swimming back to the lawn at the front of the lagoon.

"I can't believe how bad that hurt! Why the fuck did we just do that?" Lydia cried out to no one in particular.

"I genuinely thought my asshole had ripped open," replied Herb. "I only did it because I didn't want to look like a chicken in front of you two."

"Me too!" Lydia shouted.

"Ugh, me too," concurred Julian.

"We, lady and gentleman, are a bunch of idiots," concluded Herb.

They swam leisurely to the front side of the lagoon, where a makeshift stairwell made of wooden planks and tied together by bungee cords assisted them out of the water. They walked back to their tarp and towels, grabbed a refresher beverage, and sat down in the lawn chairs. They spent the next few hours sitting idly, talking and laughing with one another about topics big and small, serious and comical. Occasionally Julian would wade into the water to wet his body and cool off from the sun, then return to the group. Lydia would alternate between the sitting in the chair and lying prostrate on the towels to even her tan, sometimes removing the strap on her bikini top when she laid on her stomach. Herb stayed seated, drinking beer after beer, getting up only to relieve himself in the bathroom by the main entrance. On his latest trip back, he took a brief stumble as he walked over a divot in the lawn and fell ungracefully into his chair.

"You doing okay there, Herb?" Julian asked.

"I'm as chill as a grill, J-man."

"That doesn't make any sense."
"It's all in your *mind*. Pass me another beer, will ya?"

"You sure about that? Your belly's looking full."

"This belly?" Herb ran his hands over his stomach playfully. "This belly needs to get fed. We need to feed the beast!"

"I cannot take you seriously. You are grotesque, man."

"You ain't seen nothing yet."

Herb got up and took his shirt off, jumping up and down in a clumsy, disjoint dance. Lydia giggled in delight as Julian pretended to look away, concealing his laughter. Herb then took his shorts off, revealing boxers that were still soaking wet and had run up his thighs, looking more like briefs. His thighs were even whiter than the rest of his body, so much so that they almost reflected sunlight. He turned his back to them, squatted low, and start wiggling his rear end left and right at them in defiance. He then took off, running around, weaving through other groups as they reacted either with wonder, disgust, or glee.

"Oh my! This is amazing." Lydia shouted excitedly.

"Not quite how I would describe it."

"Come on now, you have to find him endearing, just a little bit."

"He really is something else, I'll give you that."

"But you wouldn't have him any other way, would you?"

"No, not a chance."

Herb returned to them, breathless and panting from the impromptu jog. He leaned forward with his hands on his knees, his head down to the ground and wheezing loudly. The people most immediately around him gave quizzical looks, confused by his state and wondering why he decided to run so long and vigorously given his current condition. Once he caught his breath, he stood up, put his shorts back on to cover his ultra-white thighs, and laid down on the towels, clutching his abdomen as he to tried to calm his breathing.

"Running's not really your forte, is it Herb?" Julian asked.

"What do you mean? I'm feeling like a million bucks. Don't be jelly."

"Jelly!" Lydia exclaimed in delight.

"Look at you Herb! Using cool-kid lingo. Where'd you learn about 'jelly?'" asked Julian.

"Twitter."

"Get out of here, Herb. You're on Twitter?"

"Sure, I can be on Twitter."

"That's not what I asked," said Julian. "I asked if you were actually on it, like having an account and tweeting and all that."

"I don't know what *tweeting* means, but I just use it to look at other people's messages. I follow National Geographic so I can see the images they post. I follow news updates. There's a few army buddies who like to post as well, but it's mostly just political stuff that I don't pay attention to. And yes, there are some younger celebrity types that I follow as well."

"Um, why?" Julian inquired.

"Helps me stay up to date on what's going on."

"Like which teenage pop star is dating which professional athlete?"

"Smartass. No, that's not it. I just remember being a young guy once. I know it seems like aeons to you two, but for me it wasn't that long ago. And I remember having to listen to older people, like my parents, teachers, drill masters, whoever. And they were just so, *distant*. Like, everything they were saying had nothing to do with what me and my friends were talking about, or thinking, or feeling. And it wasn't just about them trying to discipline me or tell me what to do, they had no clue about what was on our mind, what we cared about or paid attention to at that time, even the language we use to relate to each other. We just couldn't communicate at all with them, which was sad in a way, because I knew that generation was our age once, and probably had a lot of wisdom to impart, but were just too far gone from that time in their lives to get through to us.

I don't plan on being a pop culture expert. I don't give a shit about most of it, and I don't think that will change anytime soon. But a little bit of knowledge on the words and thoughts and ideas of the generation behind me, I don't know, just makes me feel like I won't be thought of as that distant has-been who doesn't matter anymore."

"Herb, you are too sweet," replied Lydia, her eyes welling up slightly. "I know I'm a little tipsy, but that was incredibly touching, and, I just want to give you a hug right now."

"Stop! You're falling for the trap!" joked Julian.

"Julian, hush. And Herb, get up so I can hug you."

Herb sat up while Lydia crawled over to him from her chair. She wrapped her arms around his neck and rested her head on his shoulder.

"Thank you, sweetheart," said Herb, returning the hug. "You're very kind."

"You are welcome."

"Unlike this jackass."

"There it is, there's the Herb I know." Julian chimed in.

"He has a point Julian," Lydia lamented. "You barely show any affection, acting like such a tough guy all the time who is never fazed by anything."

Julian shrugged. "I'm just sauve like that I guess."

"See there it is," Lydia snapped back. "Acting like you got it all figured out. Tell me, how's that book coming along?"

"Oh yeah," Herb jumped in. "What is going on with that book, Mr. Hemingway?"

"Honestly," Julian replied. "I've written three sentences."

"That's it? And you get paid for that? Jesus, where can I apply for your job?"

"I'm not sure how much longer I'll get paid for it," Julian explained. "I'm supposed to have twenty thousand words of it done by tomorrow."

"And I'm guessing your three sentences aren't *that* long," Lydia suggested whimsically.

"Nope, not even close."

"So what are you going to do?" Herb asked.

"I'm not sure. It's not like I can cram and write it all tonight. I have no idea how they'll react when I disappoint them tomorrow, mostly because I have no idea why they asked me to do this in the first place. It's not because I'm some fabulous writer, this week has shown me that. And it's definitely not because this has anything even remotely to do with the business itself. If I had to guess, I think it's all just a game. Some big-shot executive trying to show off for a bunch of other big-shot executives, because it's all just pieces on a chessboard to them, and even that's being generous, because it assumes the game they're playing is as sophisticated as chess, and that they know how to play it. They are all so far removed from any of the actual work being done that their big ideas on vision and strategy and purpose and all that other MBA-jargon just turns to mush. Like empty calories of words which mean almost nothing to the actual workers. I'm not about to claim that I am some vital piece of the puzzle at Chimera, cause I'm not. I'm just a regular guy trying to do something successful with my life, and until about a week ago, I thought I was doing a pretty decent job. But now, I am not so sure what kind of a job I am doing, or if that's even what I want anymore.

I mean, let's say by some magical stroke of fortune I were able to write this book, and it's wonderfully successful, and I'm lauded by my bosses and peers alike and get promoted and shoot up the corporate ladder. Without thinking about it, it definitely sounds like something worth having, but is it? What would be so great about that? Sure I'd get paid more, but for what? Working even harder, longer, and with more responsibility for a company which only exists to advise other companies on how to make more money? For a company that uses an entire floor of a commercial building solely to separate the haves and have-nots? I don't have any grand expectations for my career or what kind of impact it'll have, but I'm fairly convinced that I don't want my efforts to culminate in helping a company like that.

So I have no idea what I'll do for tomorrow. But I think what I've learned this week is that whatever happens, I don't care, or let me put it another way, I'm okay with not caring. I'm okay with not knowing what I should be doing and how it is all going to work out, so long as I'm not blindly following a path which isn't going to make me happy, or lead to any kind of fulfilment in the future."

"Sounds like you're just going to do nothing, then?" Herb asked.

"Sometimes nothing isn't bad. It's not as good as doing something great, but a lot better than doing something terrible."

"It's not a bad philosophy. I mean, not one I could follow, not when I was in the army anyway. You had to do something, couldn't do nothing. But at least the choice part of it isn't up to you, so that lets you off the hook in a way, I guess."

"Well I certainly don't want anything bad to happen with you at your job, Jules," Lydia interjected, "and I thought it was pretty cool that you were going to be a writer, but if it's not what you want, maybe it's better if you just tell them so and move on."

"Move on to what?" Julian asked.

"Who knows? Just not that, I guess. Unless you have a crystal ball that tells you everything you need to know, removing the bad things from your life is about the best anyone can do."

"That," said Herb, "and getting wasted with friends on a Sunday."

Lydia looked over and raised her glass. "Cheers to that, Herb!"

"You two are the only ones wasted," explained Julian. "I've been sipping water for the last two hours."

"Wuss!" shouted Herb.

"This wuss is your only ride home, so you're welcome."

"I could always ride with Lydia."

"Yeah, but I'm riding with Jules."

"Oh, right," Herb thought out loud. "Fine, thank you for sobering up. One more beer before we pack up and go?"

"You better not pee or throw up in my car on the way back," Julian warned.

"Only if you ask me really nicely."

Herb fetched one more can of beer. He took out his keys, jammed one of them into the side of the can, and pressed it to his mouth. He then lifted his head back, and opened the can from the top, allowing the beer to flow smoothly and powerfully down his throat. When he was done, he ripped his head forward, crushed the can in his hand, wiped his mouth with the other, let out a loud burp and flashed a toothy grin.

"I don't know about you two, but I am ready to retire for the evening," he said.

"I can't think of a better way to conclude the day," Lydia agreed. "What do you say Jules?"

The sun was setting on their drive home. Herb was in the back of the car, lying along the seat with his feet pressed against one door and his head resting on the window of the other. He had the hiccups, and was nodding off every few seconds, each nod waking him up again. Lydia was in the front seat, uploading pictures from the afternoon and posting to Instagram and Facebook. Julian was driving, his left hand fixed on the top of the wheel, and his right hand resting on Lydia's thigh.

"You think Herb's going to make it through the rest of the drive?" Julian asked.

"I think you tuckered him out."

"He's not a toddler, you know."

"I know, but I just find him so adorable."

"You'll be feeling differently if we have to carry him home."

"He'll be fine. And let's just enjoy the moment. It's been such a lovely day."

"Is that your way of politely asking me to stop talking?"

Lydia leaned over to kiss Julian on the cheek. "Thanks, boo."

The sun had set by the time they pulled up to Herb's house. Julian parked on the street, turned around to view the back seat, and found Herb asleep.

"Okay, now what do we do?" Julian asked Lydia.

"Let's wake him up. Herb, you okay, honey? We're home, it's time to get up and head into the house."

Herb slowly began to stir, and picked his body up. "Let's do it, sweetheart," he said, with his eyes still closed. Julian got out of the car, opened the back door, and helped lift Herb from off the seat. He draped Herb's arm over his shoulder, buttressing him as he stumbled onto the sidewalk and the front lawn.

"Herb, where's your keys?" Julian asked, "I need to open your door."

"Don't worry about that. Let me sit here real quick," as he pointed to the lawn chairs already opened and sitting on the grass. Julian helped Herb over to one of the chairs and slid him off his shoulder and into the seat.

"Water," Herb said, and Lydia grabbed a bottle from the trunk of Julian's car. She brought it over to Herb, who opened it and took a long gulp, swallowing about one-third of the bottle.

"You know, I got to say something to you two," he began. "I never married you know. I got close once, a girl I knew in my army days, but never quite pulled the trigger. I don't regret it, I don't think I would have made a good husband, and I'm sure wherever she is now, she's happy and doing just fine without me. But that doesn't mean I don't wake up some days and wish there was someone there with me, to have coffee with and argue with over the remote control. Simple shit, I know, but that's the only stuff I think about when I imagine what it'd be like if I had gone down that road. But I made my choice, and this is how things turned out. It is what it is.

But one thing's for damn sure is that with no lady, no wife, there were no kids. When I was a younger man, that's the last thing I wanted, staying up all night with a crying baby and changing their shitty diapers. That was last thing I wanted to do. What I didn't know then was that ten years down the road, I probably wouldn't have minded having a ten-year old son or daughter, and that twenty years down the road, I wouldn't have minded having a fully-grown child, someone who I raised and who was out making their own way in life and, God willing, making me proud. But that's the crazy thing about life, it only goes in one direction, and there's no reset button to go back in time and re-do something you realized in the future would be important.

I know I'm rambling, but I just wanted to say, you two are great. I know I haven't known you all that long, and maybe I won't know you that much longer. I mean, I'd like to, but you never really know who will and won't stay in your life in the long-term. But from what I've seen from you guys, you're fantastic. Young, smart, kind. Even you, Julian, I know we rag on each other a bunch but you're a good kid, a stand-up guy. And you two go well together. I'm not any kind of expert on love or romance, but I can tell you care about one another, and my two cents is that that's all you really need to make it work. And you two kids are great, and if I had had kids, I'd want them to be like you. If I had a son, I'd want him to be like you, Julian. And if I had a daughter, I'd want her to be just like you, Lydia. So, wherever life takes you guys, just remember, believe in yourself and be confident in who you are. Don't let anyone or anything steer you towards anything different."

Julian took a few moments to respond. "I don't know what to say, Herb," he eventually replied, "that's very kind of you. Thank you."

"Thank you so much," added Lydia.

"Okay, now get out of here. The lawn and the street are spinning around and I'm about to get shitty and don't need you to be around for it."

"Ha, okay. You sure you're good?"

"I'm fine, promise. I'm just going to spend a little while out here, gather my thoughts a little bit before I head inside. And if I don't, you'll just find me passed out on this chair tomorrow. It'll be alright either way. Thanks for getting me home."

"Sure thing. Good night"

"Yeah, good night."

"Good night."

Monday

Julian looked up at the thirtieth floor of the Odyssey Tower from its base, stretching his neck as far back as it would go to try to see the top. He had dressed up for the day, swapping his casual footwear for wingtips, khakis for darker slacks, and polos for a button down, creating an outfit more formal than normal work apparel but not so dressy as to appear conspicuous. He had groomed himself in other ways as well, shaving with a razor instead of using the electric trimmer that leaves a thin layer of stubble, combing his hair back and applying a small amount of gel rather than leaving it matted and wild above his head. He even applied a spray of cologne, from a bottle he received a year ago as a gift and had never opened until the morning. The sky was cloud-covered, but the sun shone through them bright enough that when Julian looked up, he had to cover the top of his eyes with his hand to protect his vision.

He rode the elevator up to the twenty-ninth floor, then walked down to the twenty-eighth to sit at his desk. It was shortly after nine, and Anita was already at her desk. They smiled and greeted one another. Julian sat down, connected his laptop to his docking station, and leaned back in his chair as he scrolled through his email.

"Hey Julian, how are you doing?" asked Anita.

"I'm doing great Anita."

"As great as you can be for a Monday, right?"

"Haha, exactly. How was your weekend?"

"It was a lot of fun, actually. I took a last-minute trip back to my old college town, to visit some friends who are still there. It was so nice to see them. After moving here for this job, I've been feeling a little, I don't know, alone I guess. After work, on weekends, it's the first time -- I think ever -- where I've just been by myself with no one around. It was fun to spend the last two days being around people whom I'm so close to. It made me feel a little more sure of myself, if you know what I mean. We'll see how long it lasts. Geez, I don't know why I'm going on and on like this. My weekend was great! How was yours?"

"You know, I have to say it might have been the best weekend of my life."

"Really, didn't you have to work on that secret project of yours?"

"A little. Whatever happens with that project will happen. I'm not too worried about it."

"You seem kind of nonchalant about it."

"How should I seem?"

"I don't know. Worried, maybe. Or more busy or preoccupied."

"I suppose I could, but that won't help me finish the project, would it?"

"No, but, aren't people going to be mad if you come off looking so inactive?"

"Perhaps, perhaps not. I don't really know, and it's not really in my control. Nor does what anyone else thinks really matter. All I can do is focus on the things which I think matter the most, trust my judgment and ability, and hope for success."

"You think that's going to work?"

"I have no idea. But I think I'd choose this route over running around in circles trying to please everyone over everything."

"Well, I'll be rooting for you."

"Thanks. Now I think I have to go make a few copies."

Julian removed a thumb drive from his bag, and walked over to the copy area. He walked back a few minutes later with a stack of papers to find Janine waiting at his desk.

"You need to make twenty-five copies of your report for the meeting at ten. They need to be black and white, double-sided, and stapled. And you have to procure them yourself, me and the other admins won't be able to do it for you."

"I've already made the copies. They are right here." Julian pointed to the stack of paper in his hand.

"That's it?"

"That's it."

"Okay. Well make sure you find me at my desk at five before ten. I will walk you into the meeting."

"I know where it is. It's the conference room by Kendra's office, right? I can get there myself. Thanks for the offer to walk me though."

"I need to walk you there. That's how the meetings always go."

"I get it, but I'm telling you there's no need. I don't want to hold you from the other work you have to do. The meeting is at ten, right? I'll be in the room right on time, I promise."

Janine didn't reply, but turned around and walked away. Julian returned to his desk.

"I think you pissed her off," offered Anita.

"No way," said Julian sarcastically, "Janine and I go way back. We have an understanding, you see."

"Is the meeting at ten about your secret project?"

"It is. The board wants an update."

"Sounds serious, are you ready?"

"As ready as I can be I suppose."

"That must be exciting, meeting with the CEO and the board. You are really going places."

"Going somewhere, for sure."

Julian spent the next few minutes loafing on his computer, checking news websites, social media, and turning around to look out the window to the view beyond. At five to ten, he walked up the two flights of stairs to the thirtieth floor. As he walked down the long hall which enclosed the central bullpen area, the normal din -- of administrative staff jostling papers and the click-clack of shoes on the stained concrete floor -- was noticeably absent. Julian gazed into the private offices on the perimeter of the floor. Within each office, he found the executive occupying it seated behind their desk, with their back straightened up and eyes focused intensely at their monitor.

He made his way to Kendra's office in the northwest corner of the floor. Next to her office was a long narrow conference room, with a projector screen on one end and a whiteboard on the other. One long edge of the room was a full-length window, and the other a frosted pane with a clear horizontal stripe in the middle. On the other side of that stripe Julian could see that the room was full, based on the shoes and legs falling out of the chairs placed around the conference table. Julian opened the door and walked in.

The room was filled with grim, suited individuals he did not recognize, occupying every chair around the table, save one. As Julian opened the door, he heard soft chatter and other fidgeting from the group, which immediately ceased as he entered, replaced with blank, indifferent stares. As he scanned the room, he found two faces he recognized: Kendra, standing on the opposite end of the table in a dark brown pantsuit, and Mort Browning, sitting at the table about half way down on the right hand side. Unlike the other individuals, he did not stare at Julian, rather, he was writing notes on a legal pad in front of him.

"Julian, thanks so for much for joining us today," said Kendra, speaking in the general direction of the group and not particularly at Julian. "We're all very excited to read what you've prepared for us. Please have a seat." She pointed to an empty chair at the head of the table nearest him. Julian walked to the chair and took his seat, while Kendra remained standing.

"Thank you to everyone for coming in today. I know you all have busy schedules so I very much appreciate your taking your board member responsibilities so seriously. I certainly wouldn't have asked you to attend this meeting today if I didn't think it were absolutely critical for Chimera's long-term success. I realize that's setting quite high expectations, but I don't think I'm overselling it in any manner.

Among my many responsibilities as CEO, I think the most important one is to protect the shareholder value of this great company. Shareholder value can take decades to build up, and can be lost in an instant. It's constantly under attack, from competitors, from regulations, from changing customer bases to plain old-fashioned complacency. We must always be on the look-out for threats and risks, and I can think of no better way to protect that value than by thinking long-term, so we can prepare and align this company with an uncertain but promising future.

The pace of innovation in this economy is so great, so rapid, that the second we rest on our laurels for a job well done is the second we fall behind. With that in mind, we must always push the boundaries of what we do, to stay sharp, to stay competitive, to stay relevant, and I'm just so thrilled to give you all a sneak-peak into what we are doing in this effort. Mort."

Mort looked up from his legal pad, caught off-guard by his name being called. He pushed his glasses up to the top of his nose, and stood up behind his chair.

"Uh, yes, thanks Kendra. As part of Creative Intelligence, it is our goal to develop creative properties which can be utilized by Chimera in the short-run and long-run, either as strategic levers or monetizable assets. Unlike our traditional verticals, Creative Intelligence is a function that works largely outside the chain of command, giving us the freedom and flexibility to pioneer alternative, high-upside initiatives which have the potential to disrupt and diversify Chimera's revenue streams. Simply put, it is our job to outflank the future.

Today, we will be reviewing the initial chapters of what will be a complete literary work that, for the first time in modern publishing history, will be authored by a corporate entity, in this case, Chimera. Our plan is to publish this work as a novel, to generate demand via mass media campaigns on TV and radio, to make it onto the New York Times bestseller lists alongside other authors, and then, to submit to and receive a nomination for the Man Booker Prize.

Several of our most recent market research reports demonstrate that the public want corporations to show care and concern for their customers, and for society at large. That is, they want companies like ours to be more *human*. The current perception of us is that we have an empathy gap, and in Creative Intelligence we have taken that as a call-to-arms. Our goal is to open a humanization channel in all of Chimera's branding and imaging initiatives -- the novel will be just the first step. With every mention of Chimera in the press, in industry reports, or in competitors' board rooms, we want our brand to be differentiated through its humanized look and feel, which we believe will offer us separation and advantageous market positioning, particularly in image-based or social-justice markets.

And I just want to personally say that..."

"Thank you so much, Mort," Kendra interrupted. "Like I was saying earlier, there are just so many bright and driven people in this organization, who are doing just such great work and really are the driving force behind all of our success. As a leader of this company, I like to reward this type of effort as much as I possibly can, because I consider this type of passion our secret weapon. When we are battling head to head for a new contract, or working at the 11th hour to meet a big deadline, whether we succeed or fail doesn't come down to headcount, or skill, or resources. No, it comes down to passion. Passion to create something new, something truly great, something to look back on with pride and satisfaction. And the opportunity to be a part of that, in some small way, is what gets me into the office and fired up every morning.

Without further adieu, I'd like you all to meet Julian, who has graciously accepted my invitation to join us. Julian is a promising young talent at Chimera and has been leading the effort Mort just told you about, to create a truly human image for this organization. Julian, please hand out the copies you made, so we can all read and learn about the great work you are doing."

Julian got up to distribute the copies he had printed off earlier. He gave them to each person individually, with most of the recipients responding with a smile or nod. When he handed a copy to Kendra, she looked away towards the window, deliberately avoiding eye contact with him. When he handed a copy to Mort, he looked directly into Julian's eyes, with the same intensity that he had exhibited one week earlier in Kendra's office.

After he had passed around all the copies, Julian returned to his seat. "I don't have much to say by way of prelude," he said. "How about we just read?"

Julian reached for the document and began to read to himself.

Last week I saw a sparrow outside a restaurant, looking for scraps of food in the parking lot. Sparrows are surprisingly social creatures, often choosing to fly in colonies and co-locate with other sparrows, even when not breeding. They interact with humans frequently as well. They commonly live in farming areas and other agricultural terrain, feeding on insects or seeds. They are often kept as pets as well. They are difficult to raise, requiring lots of food and attention, but there are several success stories of humans raising and supporting baby and even orphaned sparrows.

It is strange that sparrows frequently and voluntarily mingle with humans, more so than many other birds and animals. When I first saw the particular sparrow that I saw -- a few days earlier it was sitting on a chair inside the restaurant -- I had assumed its co-habitation was due to pride. I had assumed that this sparrow felt entitled to something, that upon observing the food and drink available for humans, it made a determination that it too deserved those things as well, or maybe, that its life would somehow be worse if unable to have them. I felt bad for that sparrow, in its predicament to want something it couldn't have and to be less satisfied because of it. It's a hedonistic ladder we all strive to avoid, but even avoiding it is an admission of its profound and unmistakable influence on everything we do.

The second time I saw the sparrow, in the parking lot, I realized it was not about pride. It wasn't about any conspiring effort or external motivation at all. All that was happening was that the sparrow found a source of food, and friendly enough people who provided it, and instinctively reacted by coming back for more. It kept coming back because it was trying to make its life better, in some incremental way, and the decision to return to the parking lot of that restaurant is just one of many it will make in its life towards that aim. And then I felt jealous of the sparrow, for having such a simple axiom to live by. The sparrow doesn't have the time or awareness to consider whether it's station in life is good or bad or anything at all. Because of that, it does not feel the pang of desire or regret that we humans do when we consider all the things we don't have, or all the paths we might have taken but didn't.

The sparrow likewise has many paths not taken, but either doesn't know or care about them, and thus has no obligation to worry about their relative merits compared to the one it's on. Its myopia bestows upon it a liberty to act without regret or a fear of inadequacy; whatever path it takes is the right one because there aren't any others to consider. Whatever other sparrows have matters not, and whatever we humans have matters even less so. That's a blessing and a curse, a license to exist without any obligation but without any purpose either.

I can't decide if I am a sparrow, or if I should be. Whether a life without the constant comparison of scenarios unrealized would be happier than one spent in hypercharged awareness and longing. Maybe that's not something I have to decide at all. I don't know for sure, and maybe I'll never know. There is no end to that rabbit hole of doubt. I am here now and at some point I will die; that's all I know for sure. The rest will manifest in its own way, and all I can do is make the best of what little part I can control. I don't know what that makes me, a sparrow or not, and to some degree it doesn't really matter. It doesn't matter because from here on out I refuse to let the flimsy facades of false certainty that we painstakingly construct distort the crushing, beautiful reality we all must inescapably face.

As Julian finished reading, he looked up at the rest of the room. Most of the group had also finished reading. Some were flipping the pages back and forth as if they had missed something, some began checking emails on their phone, while others looked inquisitively around the room wondering what was going to happen next. Mort was back to writing notes on his legal pad, and appeared to have shrunk down further in his chair, immersing himself deeper in the panel of suits. Kendra was still staring out the window. It was unclear if she had read anything at all. After a couple of minutes, the last person with their eyes fixed to the paper looked up.

"Any questions?" Julian asked.

The board members said nothing, sitting in silence, each waiting for someone else to speak up. After a few moments, Kendra spoke again.

"I think what we've read here just now was quite powerful, quite stunning really. Even this brief sample demonstrates what kind of potential we have here..."

"Wasn't this supposed to be longer? Like, a lot longer?" a voice asked from the anonymous group of suits.

"That was my impression as well," added another.

"I think what we have here is just the beginning, isn't that right Julian? Would it be possible for us to read more? Since the board is here through the afternoon, there's plenty of time to go make more copies. I just know we'd all be thrilled to see the rest."

"Sorry Kendra, that's not going to happen."

"What do you mean it's not going to happen?"

"Because there isn't any more. What I have here is all that I wrote, not one more word nor one word less. And that's all there is going to be, because I am not going to be writing anymore, at least not for this purpose."

"Julian I don't think this is the type of behavior you want to be demonstrating. We really expect you to be a leader, and leading means..."

"Sorry Kendra, but you might have to dumb this down for me, because sometimes, I have no idea what the fuck you are talking about. One week ago, you brought me into your office and told me, a business analyst, to write a book. I've listened to you talk a big game about working with passion and giving it your all, but I think it's all bullshit, bullshit that you spew to eke out a few more dollars from your company, so you can convince everyone in this room to up your stock grants next year.

I'm not saying this because I'm mad. I'm saying good for you, if that's what you want for yourself. I'm just not going to be a part of it. And I'm okay with folks like you telling me I'm falling behind in my career or losing out on some nebulous illusion of success. Because I don't really know what I want, but I'm pretty sure that I'm not going to find it here, blindly taking orders from you. There might be someone else around here who will do it, or maybe they're just too confused or scared to do anything different, but it's not going to be me."

"Julian, I think we have a gross misunderstanding here. You see, this is not about some ruse anyone is playing. No one is trying to get one over on you, nor are we here just to prop ourselves up. This is a serious situation. We are a serious organization and expect everyone who is a part of it to take it seriously as well. And part of being serious is understanding and responding to the situation that you..."

"I'm going to leave now."

Julian rose from his chair, and left the room. Outside of the conference room, Janine was standing in the hallway, and came towards him once she saw that he had exited.

"The meeting isn't over yet. Why are you out here now? I knew your report wasn't long enough."

"The length was great, the meeting just finished earlier than expected. There might be some folks who need water or coffee or something though, if you want to check."
"Refreshments aren't scheduled until eleven."

"Okay then. I'm going to go now."

"Where are you off to? You were supposed to be in this meeting at least through lunch."

"Well I'm not, so that's that, isn't it? I think I'm done."

"Done. Wait, are you quitting?"

"I'm not quitting, but I don't plan on staying either."

"You can't do that!"

"You know Janine, you seem to be really hung up on telling everyone what they can and can't do."

"It's not me, it's the rules, Julian. Everyone has to follow them."

"Well I don't know about that, because I'm not going to. So go ahead and do whatever it is your rulebook says you have to do. I'm sure Kendra will want to have a say too."

Janine held a blank stare at Julian, but didn't respond.

"Right," Julian continued. "I'm going to head out. If I don't see you again, take care."

Julian walked down the stairs to the twenty-ninth floor, into the elevator and out of the Odyssey Tower. He took off on foot, back to his apartment, and stepped into the Savory Pass. At around eleven on a Monday, the place was surprisingly busy, with a smattering of students working on laptops, semi-businessmen and women taking calls on Bluetooth headsets, and a pair of elderly men engaged in a heated debate in another language over expressos. Behind the counter, Julian found both Lawrence and Nelson at work, perhaps both being called in to support the larger than normal crowd.

"Julian, right?" Nelson called out.

"Hey, didn't expect to see you both here," Julian called back from across the room as he made his way over to the counter.

"Wasn't supposed to be," Nelson replied, "but having too many customers is a good problem to have, if you ask me, so I'm not complaining."

"Definitely. What do you think it is?"

"Not sure, I haven't been here long enough to really understand the trends. Any idea, Lawrence?"

"What?" Lawrence responded.

"I said do you know why today is so busy?"

"No, not really. Must be a lot of people who want coffee."

"Yeah, that must be it," Julian said snarkily.

"If you don't mind me asking," Nelson rejoined, "what do you do? I've seen you in here quite a lot during the day, just curious what kind of job you have that gives you such flexibility in your schedule."

"It wasn't a normal thing, just got put on a special assignment where I could work from anywhere."

"Sounds pretty nice."

"It was, in a way, but I don't think I'll be doing it anymore."

"That's too bad. What are you going to do now?"

"To be honest, I don't really know. But I'm sure I'll find something."

"Amen to that. Can I get you anything?"

"Actually, no. If it's alright with you, you mind if I just hang out at a table for awhile?"

"Be my guest. Let me know if you need anything."

"Thanks."

Julian found an open high-chair at the bar by the window, and took a seat. To his left was a man younger than him, with a beanie and a beard, cut-off jeans and a tank top, typing on his laptop. To his right was a woman, in her late forties, reading a paperback and sipping on an iced tea.

He removed his phone from his wallet and began to make a call. On the other line, Barb answered the phone.

"Hello?"

"Hey Barb, it's Julian."

"Oh hi Julian. Um, is everything okay?"

"Yeah, everything's great. How are you?"

"Not too bad. I didn't sleep very well last night. I think it's because my doctor switched the pills I'd been taking, for my blood pressure, and it just kinda wired me up. I laid in bed almost all night, but didn't really sleep for more than an hour. Finally I just got out of bed and laid on the couch with the TV on, but that didn't work either. But that's okay, I'll be alright. Just the way things goes sometimes, you know?"

"Yeah, I hear you. Listen Barb, I wanted to apologize for what I said when we last talked a few days ago. I said some really hurtful things, and I'm sorry. I'm not proud of it. I was frustrated with some other stuff going on with my life, and I took it out on you, and that wasn't right. Again, just wanted to say sorry for that."

"Oh yeah, well thanks. It's no problem really. Is everything better now?"

"Everything's a lot better. But wait, are you seriously not upset?"

"Not really, to tell you the truth. When we were talking last time, I could tell you were angry about something, probably just blowing off steam. It happens to all of us, so I didn't take it too personally. These things happen you know."

"I see. Well, thanks. Looking back on what I said I feel terrible."

"You weren't completely wrong, Julian. I know it's very odd that I call you , and I know I can complain too much sometimes. I just get frustrated, about a lot of things in my life, and it's not your fault nor something you can do anything about, but you know, when I call you and get it off my chest, I always feel a little bit better. But I can see how that would be a burden to you, and it's not a burden you should have. So I would understand if you didn't want to talk to me."

"No Barb, that's not it at all. Looking back on it, I was glad you called me, because the truth is you are the only person who ever bothered to do so on a regular basis. I'll admit that before, I didn't think much or have much to say about what was going on in your life, but I think I would have felt quite a bit lonelier had you not bothered to call. It's a bit embarrassing to say, but I don't have that many friends, nor am I particularly involved with my family. There are just not that many people I've been close to, and though it's odd and completely random, chatting with you over these last few years has been a source of comfort, if for nothing else than just having someone to speak to."

"Well, that's what friends are for, aren't they? I mean, maybe it's too much to say we are friends, but that's what I think of you as. And yeah, I wish I could say my life was so busy and wonderful that there was no room to call someone I have barely met and barely knew, but that's not the way it is for me, and instead of wringing our hands over what could or ought to be, I figure we should make the most of what we have, don't you think?"

"I do."

"So, the reason everything's better, is that because of work and the book you had to write?"

"For the most part, yes. I wasn't able to write hardly anything. But I just went into the office today and told my CEO I wasn't going to work on it anymore, so we will see what happens with that."

"It did seem a bit weird that that's what they had you working on at your job."

Julian laughed, "yeah, that would be an understatement."

"Well it's good you won't have to worry about that anymore. Anytime you can take something stressful and remove it from your life, that's a good thing I figure. You know the older I get, the more I realize that you just have to have good people and good energy in your life, and sometimes that means making tough decisions to make it that way. To be honest, I wish I could do it more often for myself."

"You go through a lot, Barb, and no one has the magic formula on how to deal with it all. I will say that it sounds like you have decent-enough people in your life, and even if they annoy you and grind your gears a little every now and then, you should embrace them, because hey, you never know when they won't be there someday."

"Tell that to my daughter."

"Hehe. You know, I don't suppose I ever told you that your daughter and I had a little thing once?"

"What do you mean?"

"Back when we first met in college, there was some flirting between the two of us. Nothing serious at the time, but there was one instance in particular, where she really made her intentions known. I was surprised at first, didn't know what to do, but I felt the same way and let her know, at least in the same way she was letting me know. The timing could not have been worse, though. She started dating my roommate -- you remember him from that time you visited and we all went out to brunch? -- almost immediately after that.

Nothing ever happened between us, just so you know. Once, after she and her boyfriend had broken up, she came by my place, to hang out, to talk, to just be with someone, who knows. Something might have happened then, under another set of circumstances perhaps, but it didn't, even though she stayed late into the evening. When I woke up the next day, she was gone, and that was the last time I saw her.

I never told you or anyone about this before. Whether because of guilt or regret, I can't tell, I just didn't want to bring it up. I don't know why I'm bringing it up now, I just thought I should tell you about it, rather than keep it from you."

"Oh Julian, I already knew about that."

"You did?"

"Sure, dear, I knew. And don't worry it's no big deal."

"How did you know? Did she tell you?"

"No, but they never have to when you're their mom. That's something you can't possibly know unless you have children, but when it's your child, you just develop a sense for these things. When she had finished college, about the time we started talking on the phone, I remember talking to her and mentioning you. Not in any serious manner, just as an 'oh by the way' while chit-chatting over little things. And I remember her reaction, a bit stiff, a bit edgy, even though she was trying to appear indifferent, and quickly trying to change the subject. She acted the same way when I mentioned you again a few weeks later. I knew then that something had happened between the two of you, something she wasn't telling me. It's nice to finally hear what that was."

"You never mentioned any of that before."

"I guess I didn't. Same as you, Julian, it just felt awkward to bring it up. You hadn't seen each other in so long, what would it matter?"

"I understand, and you're right, it doesn't matter much anymore. You know, if you want me to call her, I can. I think I still have her number tucked away somewhere. I can reach out and subtly suggest she call you and do a better job of staying in touch."

"Thanks Julian, that's nice of you to offer, but you don't have to do that. Whatever is right and wrong between my daughter and I, it's between us, and I think I should keep it that way."

"I get it."

"So what are you going to do now that that book writing thing is done with?"

"I don't really know. But I can tell you the thing I'm most looking forward to is spending more time with this girl I met."

"Oh my! Do tell."

"We just met the week before last. She lives in my building, and we just spent last weekend on a couple of day trips. I really like her. Can't stop thinking about her."

"Isn't that just lovely. She sounds delightful. I'm happy for you Julian. I remember when I first met my husband. Gosh, this must be close to forty years ago now, my how time can fly. We were both right out of college, and he was a friend of one of my sorority sisters back in school. We met at a party. I remember he must have already been to two or three spots before that, coming in very confident, and very, very drunk. But once he saw me, man that was it. He wanted to talk to me all night, and wouldn't let me leave unless I gave him my phone number, which of course I did. He was cute, and despite his bravado, I could tell he was sweet too.

I remember I was seeing someone else at the time. A nice guy, someone I had met back in school, who became neighbors with me when he moved here for a job. We had been on a couple dates, just enough to where it'd be more natural to describe myself as 'with' him rather than not with him. I didn't want to upset him, he had done nothing wrong, but I had really just grown smitten with the guy who is now my husband, and he was all I was thinking about. Ultimately I decided to break it off with the first guy, and so I met him at a bar one night to tell him in person. He was disappointed but understanding, and we were able to leave as friends. Truth is it was one of the better break-ups that can be had. But when I got home, I found my husband, absolutely wasted and disheveled outside my door. I had no idea what was going on, and when I tried to ask him, all I got were frustrated slurred responses that were impossible to understand. I was worried to see him like that, but even more worried that something had happened which would end whatever relationship we had.

I brought him in for coffee, and when he perked up I finally got out of him that he had seen me with my-ex that evening, and had assumed that I was going out with someone else. So he proceeded to drink heavily with his friends who were egging him on the whole time to forget about me. A dozen shots or so later, he was completely plastered, but all he wanted to do was see me, despite his inebriated and saddened state. And so he came over, and he waited for me. It was a disaster of an evening, but it was the first time I looked at him as someone I could really love, and that's really what led us to eventually get married."

"But it sounds like you guys barely talk anymore. What happened?"

"I know it sounds cliché, but sometimes thing start out great and just don't work out. Each day with its tribulations has the potential to grind away whatever intimacy you may have, little by little, until one day you wake up and wonder who this stranger is lying next to you. Not that you are definitely going to marry this girl, Julian, but if you start to get serious that's my only advice, do whatever you can to keep everything fresh, fun, exciting, so you always feel about her the same way you felt that first time you guys hit it off."

"That's very sweet, Barb. I'll remember that."

"You're welcome. Sorry to cut it short, Julian, but I have to make another call. Maybe we can talk later."

"Sure thing, my line's always open."

"Take care."

"You too."

Julian hung up the phone, quickly scrolled through his contacts, and called another number, one which had lied dormant in his directory for longer than he could recall.

"Hello? Julian, is that you?" the voice on the other line asked.

"Hey man, long time no speak." Julian replied.

"Yeah no kidding dude. How's my little brother doing?"

"Hanging in there, yourself?"

"Me? I'm doing well, you know, same old same old. Still working the same gig at my law firm, doing some traveling here and there. Shit -- sorry man, I still can't believe you are calling me right now. Everything okay?"

"Yeah, it's all good. Just thought I'd see how you were doing, maybe catch up a little bit."

"Yeah good call. I can't even remember the last time we talked. Can you hold on a minute? Let me head back to my office so I can talk a little more openly. Hold on a sec." Julian waited on the line until his brother picked it up again. "Sorry about that, it's all good now."

"I forgot they set you up in your own office. How fancy for you."

"Sure sure, yuck it up. There's nothing fancy about working 70 hour weeks though, let me tell you. It's a fucking grind out here, eat or be eaten."

"Damn, sounds rough. You get any time to actually enjoy all that money they pay you?"

"Of course, man. This is New York. I got a good group of friends from law school that live in the city with me. We go out quite a bit, and it works, because most of them are working the same crazy hours that I am. So if we want to go get lit on a Wednesday night or something no one bats an eye. Well, maybe the married ones now. They're starting to chip off a bit and start the domesticated life. Good for them I say, you know, if that's what they want to do. Doesn't change the fact that they get super boring though, even they would agree with that."

"Haha, good to hear you still have that cutting sense of humor."

"What's going on with you?"

"I think I might have quit my job today, or maybe I was fired, I can't really tell."

"Jesus, Julian. What did you do?"

"Well, I kind of walked out on the CEO when she was talking to me about doing some work for her."

"Look at the balls on you, kid."

"Man I didn't even try to make it a big scene or some kind of statement or anything like that. I was just kind of done, and so I left. I have no idea what they'll do about it, but right now it feels pretty good."

"Well you're lucky you got a job where you can bounce around anywhere. Gives you that "fuck you" power, you know? The power to just say 'fuck this' and go work somewhere else. That power is not easy to come by in my line of work. The law scene is so incestuous if I sneeze on one partner, all their buddies in the other firms are gonna catch a cold, you feel me? Makes the ability to just walk out on somebody a little less, shall we say, manageable."

"I don't really think it's something anybody ought to be doing, at least not regularly, but what the hell, what's done is done. Anyway, now that I have all this newfound time on my hands, I was thinking of taking a road trip, maybe going up to Vermont to see the folks. What do you think?"

"Sounds like a good idea. You know, the two of them never shut up about you. Julian this, Julian that, Jesus Christ you'd think I was chopped liver or some shit. I think it's cause they don't see you as much, they just think you must be great at everything."

"Weird, I never get that sense when I talk to them."

"Trust me dude, it's there. All it takes is for them to meet someone new, especially with kids, and they become a bragging machine the rest of the night. That's all they want to do."

"If I make it up to Vermont, would you be able to come by as well? It'd be great to see you."

"It'd have to be the weekend. Work's too crazy to take any time off, but I can make the drive up on a Friday night or something."

"Okay, I'll try to make that timing work. I'll let you know."

"What the hell you want to go visit mom and dad for?"

"Just figured I was overdue for a visit. You know, now that we are all adults, I feel like I need to be real with them a bit more. I think they're stuck trying to still treat me like a child, maybe cause I'm the youngest, I don't know. If I go visit them now, I'm thinking maybe we can just wipe the slate clean a little bit."

"They're going to shit themselves if you tell them you lost your job."

"Oh yeah, there's that too I guess. Maybe you can convince them this means I'm doing really awesome."

"Fat chance, kid."

"Worth a shot. Okay let me text you tomorrow with the details of my trip. See you in Vermont?"

"Sure, Julian. Hey, thanks for calling. Good to hear your voice."

"Yours too. Later."

"Later."

Tuesday

Julian woke up to the pangs of cat claws digging into his bare chest. He opened his eyes to find Franny sitting directly on top of him, eyes closed in a peaceful joy, pushing down with her front paws, alternating left and right in rhythmic fashion. With each press, her claws released slightly, creating minor and mostly painless lacerations and welts on his skin. At first, he let her be, as she purred louder with each passing second. When it became clear that she would continue indefinitely unless prompted to stop, he lifted her off of his chest and onto the pillow next to him, then got up and rose out of bed. It was nine-thirty. He had not set an alarm and was pleasantly surprised to see that he was able to sleep through the interval in which he normally woke. He was able to sleep just long enough to feel more rested than normal, but not so long as to leave him feeling drowsy and lethargic.

Franny, upon seeing him on his feet, immediately jumped off the bed and ran towards the kitchen, suddenly remembering that she was long overdue for her morning meal. Julian followed her in, grabbed her food from the cabinet, and scooped it into her bowl. She ate her food methodically and contentedly as he rinsed out her water bowl and filled it with fresh water. He then poured himself a glass, and as he drank from it, opened his front door to pick up a package. He had left it there when he had come home previous day, opting to leave it unopened and unattended until the following morning. Now, he brought it back to the kitchen, and used a knife to cut through the tape holding the top flaps together. From within, he lifted out a French press, sealed in bubbled plastic packaging. He had ordered it on Sunday, after drinking coffee made from Lydia's, and via expedited delivery, it had arrived at his apartment the previous afternoon.

Julian opened the French press and assembled the pitcher and the plunger. He then opened a bag of coarsely ground coffee beans, purchased from the Savory Pass special courtesy of Nelson, and put a kettle on his stovetop. As he waited for the water to boil, he walked around his apartment, observing the view from his kitchen overlooking the park, and the view from his den looking over to the office building across. He saw his balding friend, the individual who worked in the office directly over from his window, who spent the day browsing LinkedIn and other news articles while feigning diligence around his colleagues. This time, the man was standing up, writing on a white board fixed to the office wall. He wrote agitatedly but intermittently, in between long spells of deep thought, with one hand holding the butt of the marker to his lips, and the other hand wrapped over his abdomen, clutching his side. At one point, the man left the board, opting to walk in small circles around his office, muttering to himself and gesticulating wildly with his arms. Julian stood in his den and watched as the man went back and forth, writing and thinking, eventually covering the board with annotations inside drawn circles and connected by lines with arrows on them. Just when the whiteboard looked completely filled, Julian heard the kettle whistle. As he turned to return to the kitchen, Julian saw the man throw the marker on his desk, raise his hands in bewilderment, grab the whiteboard marker, and furiously erase all the notes he had compiled.

Julian poured the boiling water into the French press and added the coarse ground coffee beans. He set the timer on his oven for four minutes. As he waited, Franny finished her breakfast, and started prancing around the apartment, alternatively looking for toys or other items to play with, or plausible locations for napping the rest of the day. When the timer counted down to zero, Julian stirred the coffee beans around in the press, attached the plunger to the top, and slowly pressed it down through the liquid, accumulating the coarse beans underneath on their way to being crushed and pinned down at the bottom. Once the plunger made its way through, Julian poured a cup for himself in a coffee mug. It was a gift he had received from his brother the last time he had visited, a black mug with the Manhattan skyline painted around the outside in blues and whites, adorned with yellow twinkles for stars.

He took a sip, the first sip of coffee from his own French press. It tasted rich, smooth, but not quite as tasty as the coffee he had had at Lydia's. He was inspecting the bag of grounds he had bought from Nelson when he heard his doorbell ring. He walked over to the front door to answer it, to find Zane standing on the other side.

"Good morning, Julian," he said.

"Morning. Come on in. You want any coffee?"

"Yeah, sure, what do you got?"

"Just made some using a French press I bought. Come check it out."

"Sounds good."

They walked back to the kitchen. Julian poured Zane a cup, and they remained standing while taking sips from your mug.

"I brought your stuff back," said Zane, as he removed a bag from his shoulders and dropped it on the kitchen counter, "including the bag you left by your desk."

"Oh yeah, thanks. Geez, I kind of forgot about that."

"Did you really quit?"

"I didn't quit. I didn't do anything. I just left. I'm not sure what else anyone told you, but that's the truth."

"No one told me anything. I just saw that your meeting with Kendra and the board ended early, and then you were gone."

"I guess you've been pretty close to Kendra this week. Seemed to know more about what was going on than I did."

"Yeah, sorry about that. I was being interviewed for a new director position, in sales and business development. A couple of VPs were involved. They told me most of what was going on with you. I should have told you, but everything was being kept under the radar because it was a new position."

"It's okay. Well congratulations, the new position sounds like a promotion, is that why you were on the thirtieth floor last Thursday?"

"You knew about that?"

"Haha, yeah. I had to meet Kendra at the same time, saw you in one of the offices."

"Shit, man. So I guess you knew. Well, sorry I had to keep things from you, I didn't really like it. But yeah that's what it was for."

"When do you start?"

"I don't know man. I don't even know if the job is still going to go through, based on everything that happened."

"How come?"

"Have you not heard? Oh right, you probably haven't checked your email at all."

"What is it?"

"Kendra's out, dude. She resigned late last night. Something about the need to consolidate our core business lines, and to apply a steady hand to a wavering ship. Very poetic, you know how she talks. But yeah, her resignation is effective immediately. Crazy."

"Who's taking her place?"

"You're never going to believe it."

"Let me guess -- Mort Browning."

"How'd you know?!"

Julian smirked. "Wild guess."

"What happened in that meeting with the board yesterday?"

"I presented the work I had done on the book. It wasn't much. When Kendra asked if they could see more, I said no, and that I wasn't going to work on it anymore. Then I left, and here we are."

"You serious?"

"Yeah, man. That's what happened."

"I wonder if whatever happened in there is the reason she is resigning."

"I don't know, but you know what, who cares? Life will go on at Chimera, life will go on for Kendra, for me, and for you too man. I don't know anything about this new job of yours, but Mort seemed like a stand-up guy, I'm sure it will all work out."

"Thanks, I hope it does. But even if they still offer me the job, I don't know if I should take it."

"What?! What are you talking about. It's a director position, and you're younger than me! You have to take it."

"Yeah but how do I know that's the job I should take? I mean, I could just get dead-ended there, particularly if Mort or whoever in the new leadership decides they want to pick their own guy."

"You're being too paranoid. Take the promotion for it's worth, an advancement in pay and stature and the opportunity to get involved in bigger and better things."

"I don't know man."

"Jesus, what is your deal? Isn't this the type of opportunity you've been gunning for all along?"

"I don't know, I'm just...afraid. Like what if this doesn't work out and I'm stuck? You know, lots of people end up as corporate ladder-climbers for most of their careers. All it takes is one change in the winds and they could be on their ass, too old to start over anywhere and too young to have it all squared away for retirement. I don't want that to be me."

"It probably won't be. Not if you make sure of it. But you can't let fear of the unknown cripple you, particularly if it stops you from doing something that's obviously going to make you better off."

"Yeah, but..."

"But nothing! At some point, you got to back yourself, and trust you got what it takes to get the job done. I think you got what it takes, all that's missing is that you think that way too."

"Well, thanks. I'll think about it some more."

"You should."

"So, you didn't quit, are you planning on coming back?"

"I'm not sure yet. I'm taking a couple of weeks off. Going to drive to Vermont and visit my parents. It's been awhile since I've seen them, and even longer since we spent quality time together. It's been overdue."

"So you're just going to leave for a couple of weeks, and come back...maybe?"

"Yeah think so."

"But like, are you going to report time off? Are you still going to get paid? Are they going to keep you in the same role?"

"Who knows? But the cool thing is I'll probably be fine whichever way it shakes out, right?"

"I guess..."

"Trust me, man. It's all good."

"When are you taking off?"

"Today."

"Oh wow, okay. Well I guess I should say goodbye then. I have to head back to the office to meet with those VPs anyway."

"Sounds good man, good luck."

"Thanks, and I'll guess I'll be seeing you later, maybe?"

"Yeah, maybe."

Zane shook his head. "Alright then." He shook Julian's hand, and walked out of the kitchen and towards the exit. Before he got there, he turned around.

"Hey Julian, you mind sharing with me what you wrote for that meeting yesterday?"

"Tell you what, if I come back to Chimera, I'll send it over and we can read it together."

"Sounds like a plan. See ya."

"Bye Zane."

Julian finished his coffee, rinsed out the grounds left in the French press, and left it out to dry. He grabbed his keys, and left his apartment to head downstairs, out of the building, and over to Herb's house.

To Julian's surprise, the front lawn of the house was relatively picked up. No beer cans lying around, nor lawn chairs splayed out or open coolers collecting dust. The garage door was closed, concealing the large and diverse collection of broken appliances behind it. Julian walked up to the front door and rang the doorbell. After a few seconds, Herb appeared and opened it. He had shaved his face, all the way down to the skin and with a razor, evidenced by a couple of cuts on his chin on which he had applied antibiotic ointment. He also had combed his hair, slicked back and slightly over to the right. His button-down shirt was unwrinkled, and properly tucked into neatly-pressed khakis atop worn but presentable brown loafers.

"Herb. What's going on? You look...*good*."

"Well thanks Julian, but you're really not my type, and if we went and had sex now I've have to get all dressed up again."

"That's just terrific Herb. Where are you going?"

"There's a VFW luncheon every month, on the other side of town. The venue is shit and the food is terrible, but I like to go whenever I can, see some old buddies from the service, get to know others too."

"That sounds nice. It's a good thing you go."

"Well it beats doing nothing. Besides, for some of the other guys and gals, it's one of the brighter spots in their life, so I try to make the effort even if it means someone else can enjoy it. What are you doing here?"

"I'm leaving town for a couple of weeks."

"Are you and that lover boy of yours from work going to run off together?"

"Smart-ass. No, but Lydia is going to join me."

"That's great, kid. You know, you two look like you're really onto something. She's a keeper. Don't do anything to fuck it up."

Julian laughed, "I won't Herb."

"I'm fucking serious. If you do, you can bet your ass there's no running back to her for you. She'll already be with a real man by then." Herb pointed to himself with his two thumbs and flashed a smile.

"Oh I have no doubt."

"Where are you going?"

"To Vermont. My parents live there, and I'm going to visit them."

"Jesus, man. First you ask Lydia out to a day-long picnic on your first date, now you're taking her to your parents? What the fuck is the matter with you?"

"I don't know man. I just got no game, I guess."

"Yeah, I can tell. Well, have fun with it, assuming you don't get dumped along the way. Vermont is nice. Did you know that Vermont is one of only four U.S. states that were previously sovereign states?"

"I didn't. Is that true?"

"Yep. For a few years before the Revolutionary War. Did you know it was the first state to enter the Union after the original colonies?"

"I didn't know that either."

"Christ, Mr. Hemingway. Too busy writing books, maybe you ought to read one for a change."

"Maybe I will. And I'm not doing that writing thing anymore."

"Why not?"

"Told the CEO I was done with it."

"Well good for you. That company of yours sounded like a real prick. But if you were any good at the actual writing, you should keep it up. You never know where it might lead you."

"I'm not sure I was any good, but I appreciate the encouragement."

"So when are you heading out?"

"Today, actually."

"Well gee, thanks for the heads-up, asshole."

"I'm sorry, it was a spur of the moment type thing. But, I have a favor to ask you."

"What is it?"

"Can you watch my cat?"

"You have a fucking cat?"

"Haha, yes, I do. Her name is Franny. She's a bit aloof to strangers but after she knows you she's pretty docile and easy to get along with. Just needs to be fed twice a day."

"How long are you going to be gone?"

"A couple of weeks."

"And you just think I have nothing else to do but to hang out here and check on your cat for all that time?"

"Well, do you?"

"No, but that's not the point."

"I know it's a big favor, and you don't have to do it if you don't want to. I just thought you might. Who knows, maybe you and Franny might even become friends."

"You know, I seem to recall my life from about a week ago. There was no you, and there was definitely no playing house with a damn cat."

"Is that a yes?"

"How am I going to do it? I don't even know where you fucking live."

"I'll take you over, right now. Show you where everything is, and give you the key."

"Well shit man, we better hurry up. I have to be at my luncheon by noon."

"Let's go."

"So this is where the food is. The scoop is in the bag, you just take one big one out and put it in the bowl when it's time for her to eat. Once a day, rinse the water bowl and replace it with fresh water. The litter box should be fine. It's automatic, and cleans itself, though there was this one time it broke on me, and Franny really had to take a shit. But anyway, that's probably not going to happen to you. Herb, you listening?"

Herb was looking down at this shoes, where Franny had circled by his legs numerous times, purring at every instance, and had now decided to lay down directly on his feet.

"Your cat is a real animal. Look what's she doing. How am I supposed to move now?"

"You're loving this."

"I am not. This cat seems nice and all, but this is kind of ridiculous." He looked directly at Franny. "Hey, I'm talking to you, you're going to have to behave if we are going to get along." Franny looked back up at him and rolled on her back, stretching her fore and hind legs in opposite directions.

"I'm sure you're going to handle her just fine. You're welcome to come by whenever you want as well. You can stay, watch TV, hang out with her if you like. She'd like it."

"Thanks, but I think just getting the feeding right will be plenty."

"You got it. Is there anything else you need to know?"

"I'm good. You gave me your number, right?"

"Better yet, I followed you on Twitter."

"Ass. Okay then, I have to get going to my thing. Take care of yourself, Julian."

"Same to you, Herb. And thanks again, I'll see you when I get back."

Julian extended his hand to shake Herb's, but Herb had already turned around and walked out, much to Franny's chagrin. Julian returned to his room, went into his closet, and pulled out an empty suitcase. The moment Franny saw the suitcase out, she let out a darting hiss and ran out of the room. Julian hoisted it on top of his bed, and unzipped it to open it up. He went to his dresser and grabbed several articles of underwear, socks, shorts, and t-shirts. He went into his closet and picked out jeans, slacks, polos, button-down shirts, and shoes. He then started packing, starting with his shoes assembled on the bottom of the suitcase. Then, he layered two pairs of pants over the shoes, forming a smooth and padded bottom.

Once the clothing cushion had been established, Franny returned to the bedroom and jumped into the suitcase, lying down on the packed pants and stretching her front paws over the edge of the container. This was a game Franny was fond of playing, subverting Julian's attempts to leave while gaining his undivided attention. He began by attempting to stuff socks and underwear in the pockets of the suitcase formed around her; she was happy to swat them away. He tried to place a shirt on top of her, bluffing as if she would be packed along with his clothes; she quickly squirmed her way out and back on top. He then tried to pick her up, only to be playfully clawed and scratched until he stopped. The game would have continued as long as Franny and Julian desired it to, but Julian had a schedule to keep. He picked up the suitcase from one side, and tipped it over, steeper and steeper until Franny jumped out. He continued his packing while she laid on the bed near him, bathing and grooming herself.

Julian recalled a time from a few years back, when Franny was younger, fully grown but with a mind and personality of a kitten. He lived in a different place then, a townhouse inside a complex of other townhomes outside the city. The complex had lots of trees and grass, and Julian would leave his front door open to allow the nature-scented air to waft in, and to let Franny lay on the front step to watch the birds flying by and fluttering about. One day, when the front door was open, a neighbor's cat walked into the townhouse. Whether the cat was lost or just visiting, Julian wasn't sure, but he walked in like it was his home and sought out Julian for attention and adulation. Franny, who had been sleeping on the living room couch, sprang onto her feet once she sensed the other cat entering. She then crouched down into an attack position, jumping down onto the floor and advancing slowly and methodically toward the intruder, keeping low to the floor and delicately and silently lifting her paws on and off the ground.

When she got within a few feet of the other cat, she pounced. The other cat shrieked in surprise and darted away, running up the stairs two or three at a time with Franny on his heels. The second floor of the townhouse was sturdy but hollow, making each leap and jump from the two of them sound like a cacophony of stomps and thuds from above. Left and right across the upstairs hallway he heard them, along with the shrill cries of both cats in the role of either the hunter or hunted. Julian made a move towards the stairs and was on his way up to try to separate the two, when the neighbor's cat bolted down the stairs, followed shortly by Franny. At the bottom of the stairs was a small divide, separating the stairwell from the living room on the other side. It was tall enough to reach Julian's shoulder when standing on the ground floor, and wide enough to serve as a bookshelf on one side. When the chased cat was halfway down the stairs, instead of continuing the rest of the way down, he leapt high and far, clearing the divide and landing on the couch in the living room all the way on the other side. Franny made a similar leap, but she landed on the divide itself, standing tall and fierce like a lion defending her turf. The neighbor's cat, seeing such a display of dominance, quickly ran back out the front door. Franny remained tall and proud on the divide, eyeing the other cat until he was gone. Then, she returned back to the couch, made a quick circle then laid back down, nuzzling her head against her paws.

Julian recalled this story and felt happy at the realization that his precious animal could transform herself into a stalwart protector. Prior to that tussle, she had known only human comfort and acted so, eating her food from a bowl and receiving rubs on her ears and belly almost every night. But the moment another creature trespassed on her property, all her survival instincts came to the surface to exercise their might. In that moment, he realized that cats, like all beings really, need not be just one thing, and can have many aspects of themselves wrapped and warped around one another at the same time. That he need not and should not be surprised when different sides of himself and others are unearthed when presented with varied circumstances. No matter how long or how consistently he may adhere to one style, one path, even one identity, he may have within him endless new versions of himself waiting for the opportunity to emerge.

He finished packing his clothes, and closed the suitcase. He surveyed the rest of his apartment, checking for lights which might still be on, chargers which might still be plugged in, thermostats set to the right temperature. Franny, upon seeing the suitcase closed and on the move, resigned herself to the situation and jumped on the bed in the den to lie down. Julian went in there and gave her a kiss on the head. "Goodbye Franny, I'll see you when I get back. Be good to Herb," he told her, then walked out of his apartment.

He walked down the stairs to Lydia's place, and knocked on the door. After a few seconds with no answer, he knocked again, this time a little louder. Lydia opened the door in an exasperated state.

"Is it time to go already?!" she asked.

"I'm afraid so. Running late?"

"Late? I've barely started. Are you ready to go?"

"Sure am. But it's ok, let's catch you up. Need some help packing?"

"No, I got it. Just come inside, and I'll finish up real quick."

Julian followed her in, and continued on into her bedroom. He found piles of clothes on the floor, on her bed, and on her dresser, far from any appearance of logical organization. He looked at her, and she looked back with a grimace of frustration, which slowly transformed into a half-smile of embarrassment.

"I'm sorry," she said, "I can't figure out what to bring."

"It's just a few days in Vermont. Surely you don't need all these clothes?"

"I know, I know. But should I be bringing casual clothes, nice clothes? What about the weather, do I need to bring anything heavy? And, I know this sounds random, but like, are we going to be doing laundry at your parent's house? Are they going to be handling my pajamas, bras, underwear?"

"Wow, okay. I see why you've been struggling..."

"I'm not struggling Jules, I'm just running behind."

"...you are nervous to meet my parents."

"I am not! I just need to put a few things together."

"Okay, sounds great. Let's start with weather -- it's the same as it here, so just wear your normal stuff, and you'll look great."

"Thanks Jules, but shouldn't I bring something nice, at least for the first day when we all meet?"

"See, I told you you were nervous!"

"Okay fine! Yes I'd like to make a good impression, alright?"

"It's sweet, but trust me, my parents are laid back and they are going to love you. You just have to be yourself. And you don't have to bring anything too fancy. We might go out to dinner one night, but even then, the restaurants are casual. The rest of the time we'll be hanging out at home, so whatever's normal and comfortable will be fine."

"If you say so, I just don't want them thinking I'm risqué or anything."

"Well, maybe don't bring *these*." He found a pair of thong underwear in one of the piles on the floor and lifted them on his finger.

"Don't be a creep, it's not a good look for you."

"I mean, maybe you should wear them, and then throw them in the hamper with my clothes, and then let my mom come find them in the bedroom."

"...you think they'll let us stay in the same room?"

"You know, now that I brought it up, I don't know."

"Well I'm not going to be the one to bring it up. Jules, you have to find out!"

"Easy, easy. Now that I think about it, my brother brought a girlfriend home once. It was Thanksgiving, I believe. Probably a poor choice to introduce his girlfriend to the family during the holidays. He had assumed she would stay in his room with him, but when it was time for bed, my mom and dad started taking linens from the closet and making a bed on the couch. It was super awkward, and no one knew what to do. Finally, my brother said 'Dad, it's not very hospitable to make our guest sleep on the couch.' And you know what my Dad said? God love him, he said, 'I know, that's why it will be you!'"

"Jules, I don't know if you are trying to help but none of this is making me feel any better."

"Look, everything's going to be great. They are going to love you, and it won't matter what clothes you wear. But we do have to get going sooner or later, so, can I help you pack?"

"Fine, yes come on."

They spent the next few minutes assembling Lydia's clothes for the trip, and packing her bag. Julian organized her suitcase, while she put the remaining clothes in the closets and drawers from where they came. When he finished packing, he closed the suitcase, and turned to find Lydia admiring herself in the mirror. She was wearing an obnoxiously floppy hat, the kind one might wear to the Kentucky derby, drooping down onto her shoulders and completely covering her eyes. She turned around to look at him, and smiled.

"How do I look?"

"Now where did you get that?"

"I bought it one time, when I had a gift card to a store I had never been to. I went to shop there one day, and had no idea how high-end it was. It turned out this hat was the only thing the gift card would cover. So I bought it. Don't you like it?"

"I like it if you like it."

"That's not really an answer."

"And that's not really a hat, more like a blanket on your head."

"Ha! Well if that's how you feel, then I'm definitely wearing it. It's a nice sunny day out, maybe I'll need it for the ride. How long is the drive anyway?"

"It's a while, so you better get comfortable."

"Well in that case, I'm going to have to reconsider everything. My shoes, my pants, my top. I want to make sure I'm prepared. And what about drinks and snacks for the car? We probably should stop at a convenience store so we don't get hungry or thirsty."

"Fine with me, so long as we actually get going."

"Don't be pushy mister, you can't rush beauty like this."

"Clearly."

They were eighty cars deep in standstill traffic on the main highway out of town. Cars had piled in behind and around them, leaving them locked in a sea of automobiles with no avenues of escape. They could not see far enough ahead to determine the cause of the jam, though the sight of drivers immediately in front of them turning off their engines and leaving their vehicles to stretch suggested the delay may not be temporary.

"Just our luck, huh? Why would there be so much traffic on a Tuesday?" Julian asked aloud.

"Who knows, but it's kind of fun, no? There's literally nowhere to go, so you don't have to worry about navigating us. We can just be."

"Hard to see how sitting here could be considered enjoyable."

"Well when you're with *me*, how could it not?"

"Aren't you charming?. You know, just a few cars ahead of us is an exit and the service road looks pretty clear. If only we could move up a bit closer."

"If only this, if only that. How about we just chill out and the traffic will move when it moves, hm?"

"And when do you think that will be?"

"I don't know but, oh! Is that next exit Exit 21?"

"Looks like it."

"Julian, we have to get off there. I know the best place for us to go."

"You mean other than my parent's house, you know, our destination?"

"There will be plenty of time for that. We have to make a quick detour."

"Ah, so now you really want those cars ahead of us to move."

As Julian said it, drivers returned to their vehicles and the cars ahead of them started to inch forward slightly, and he inched along with them. Within moments, they had moved far enough for Julian to take the exit.

"Some of us just have the magic touch," Lydia claimed cheekily.

"It was just a coincidence. Where are we going?"

"You'll see, take a right ahead and drive about two miles. It will be on the right."

Julian followed Lydia's directions. As he approached the intersection where he had to make the turn, he rubbernecked over to the highway to see the source of the traffic. A man and his dog were on the shoulder of the highway. By the look of it, the dog had darted out into oncoming traffic and the man ran out to save him, forcing the vehicles in every lane to suddenly break to a full stop. Given they were stopped long enough for their drivers to consider leaving their cars, the dog must have remained loose and about the highway for some time, but now that the man had moved to the shoulder, the cars were moving again, but only gradually as they slowed considerably to gaze at the man with disapproving looks as they drove by.

"Unbelievable," Julian said in frustration.

"Don't worry, this is going to work out for us, better than you could have imagined."

He continued on the directed path until they reached a large gas station on their right, one with several pumping stations immediately off the road, a separate parking lot, and a deep and broad one-story brick building behind them both.

"That's it!" shouted Lydia. "We're here!"

"I still don't know what *here* is."

"Check out the sign."

Barry's General Store: World's Largest Soda Collection. Samples Inside!

"No way."

"Come on, we have to try out all the sodas."

"How did you find this place?"

"Amazing what you can find off the beaten path sometimes."

They entered the building to find two dozen circular soda fountains, each containing some fifteen different flavors. They were arranged first by geography -- Africa, Asia, Europe -- and then by color and type for the North American ones. A small line formed at the front, where an attendant collected fees for a stamp on one's hand, which secured admission to obtain samples. When Julian and Lydia entered, they first headed in different directions, Lydia going towards the geography fountains and Julian going towards the section specializing in root beer.

"Why are you going over there?" he asked.

"When else will I get a chance to try soda from all over the world?"

"But they look gross. What's the point of trying them if they'll be bad?"

"Bad compared to what? I've never had them before. I'll only know after I try. Which ones are you going to have?"

"The root beer."

"Won't they all taste the same?"

"Of course not, some are sweeter, others more spicy. Some are made with real sarsaparilla, others not. Each one will have its own flavor profile to differentiate itself."

"Seems like overkill."

"I don't mind. Each one was made with its own inspiration, no need to judge any one of them for being too similar to another."

They split up to try their preferred flavors. The room was mostly filled with younger children and their parents, making Julian and Lydia appear conspicuous as they jousted and grappled for access to various soda dispensers. For Lydia, her involvement brought extra delight to those surrounding her, as she laughed and joked aloud about the exotic, fruity soda flavors she sipped from around the world. For Julian, he mostly got in the way of others, those miffed at having to wait in line behind a grown man delicately and studiously sampling root beer as if it were fine wine. Upon having their fill, they met again near the fountain dedicated to historical flavors -- those developed before 1950 and preserved ever since.

"I'm going to be so sick after we're done here, but I don't care. It's going to be so worth it!" said Lydia, holding her stomach.

"Sick or not, we're going to keep up the pace on our drive either way."

Back in the car, Julian pressed harder on the accelerator as they sped through open road ahead of them. The road was recently paved with asphalt, offering a smoother and quieter ride, one Julian took advantage of by turning on cruise control and loosening his grip on the steering wheel. Lydia opened the passenger window, extending her arm outside to feel the wind blow playfully through her fingers.

"Hey Jules, I know I was a bit nervous this morning, but I wanted to say thanks for inviting me on this trip with you. I'm excited to meet your parents and brother, and I'm having a lot of fun."

"You're welcome. I wouldn't have asked if I didn't care a great deal about you Lydia. I'm just happy you're coming along for the ride with me."

"We have quite a ways to go. Do you think we'll make it there okay?"

"I'm not sure," he said, pausing briefly. "Let me tell you when we get a bit further down the road."

Made in the USA
Middletown, DE
22 July 2018